Learn THE PLAY

NEW YORK TIMES BESTSELLING AUTHOR

KAYLEE RYAN

Guy Cover Design: Lori Jackson Design
Cover Photography: Michelle Lancaster
Special Edition Cover: Mary, Books N Moods
Editing: Hot Tree Editing
Proofreading: Deaton Author Services, Jaime Ryter, Jo Thompson, & Jess Hodge
Paperback Formatting: Champaign Book Design

Learn
THE
PLAY

CHAPTER 1

Reid

THE SUN SETS OVER THE OCEAN AS I WATCH ONE OF MY BEST friends from college marry the love of his life. This has been a recurring thing for me lately. Two of my best friends back home have also fallen victim to the love bug.

Landon's smile is so big that I fear his face might crack, and his bride, Tessa, is gorgeous, with only eyes for her new husband. When Landon called me to tell me he was getting married, I wasn't too surprised. He's just like the rest of us: Once we're all in, that's it. I knew she was it for him. What surprised me, though, was the phone call a few weeks later, telling me he was going to be a dad.

"You gonna be next?" I ask Case, my other best friend from college. Case, Landon, and I were roommates, and we've been close ever since. Sure, they get to play together, while I was picked up by the Rampage, but I've found my place there—my teammates, my Rampage family. I miss Case and Landon, but that's all a part of life, right? Things are constantly changing, and we learn to adapt to the outcome. I've gotta admit, mine is pretty damn good. I love my life, and our careers allow us to afford traveling to see each other, giving us the entire off-season to catch up.

"No prospects, but damn if their smiles don't make you wonder what you're missing out on." He laughs. "You?"

"Same. I've got it at home, too. Beckett and Reynolds have both been drinking the water."

Case tips his head back in laughter. "So that leaves you, Sinclair, and Vaughn?"

"Yeah, but Daddy Sin has his hands full at the moment, being a single dad. Well, mostly single. Shared parenting. He gets his son one week, and his baby momma gets him the next."

"That sucks. No chance of working it out?" he asks.

I grimace. "No. She was already back with her ex when she found out she was pregnant. They're still together."

"Fuck, that's awkward as hell," he mutters.

"You have no idea. Sinclair is handling it like a pro. All he cares about is his kid."

"I get that," Case says.

"The Rampage ladies are rallying around him to help out when he needs it. Hell, even I watched the little guy a few weeks ago."

"Really? You? And who are these Rampage ladies? Why don't we have Cougar ladies?" he jokes.

"That's Knox's and Landry's ladies, as well as their best friend. They dubbed themselves that, and it's just kind of stuck." I shrug. "And yeah, I've watched him. It's not so bad. Baby Camden pissed on me, but it could've been worse. Landry and Rowan had him, and he shit all up his back. Luckily, Rowan was there to bail Landry out." I shudder at the thought.

A baby cries, and we all turn to look at Landon holding his infant son in one arm, while the other is wrapped around his wife. They're both smiling down at baby Lance with so much love in their eyes.

"You can't even tell she just had a baby three weeks ago," Case says, nodding toward the happy couple.

"Should you be able to?" I ask him. I don't know shit about this stuff.

"Fuck if I know. I just assumed you'd be able to tell, and what kind of wedding night are they going to have? She can't—you know." He wags his eyebrows. "Right?" he asks.

"Dude, why are we talking about this?" I ask him. "I don't know these answers."

"I'm just saying." He shrugs and tips his beer to his lips.

Landon guides his new bride to sit and gently hands her their son. Immediately, her best friend, Autumn, Tessa's mom, and Landon's mom swarm her to fuss over the baby. I watch as my best friend smiles at them, before lifting his gaze and searching the room. When he sees us, he comes walking over, and I swear, there's pride in his strut.

"Great day," he says, taking the seat across from us. "It's not the tropical wedding we first talked about, but our son is here, and that's everything." He turns to look over his shoulder at his wife and son.

"Married life looks good on you," I tell him.

"You should try it." He pulls his gaze from his wife and son. "Both of you."

"And disappoint the ladies?" Case asks, chuckling.

"He's not wrong," I joke. "I mean, with you all dropping like flies, someone has to take one for the team and help the single ladies have some fun."

"I'm telling you. You have no idea what you're missing," he says, turning his attention back to his family.

"How's the team doing after all that shit with Brown went down?" Case asks.

"Solid." I nod. "Why didn't you assholes warn me?"

"He was a solid guy, or so we thought. He said he wanted the trade to follow his girl," Landon tells me, his eyes darting back to his wife. "We had no idea he was… Yeah, I'm not even sure what to call him. I'm just glad Landry's girl is okay, and he's getting what he deserves."

"Definitely," Case agrees.

Landon glances back over at his wife and newborn son. He's smiling wider than I've ever seen him. He's completely enamored with his family, as he should be. He'd fit right in with Knox and Landry. I've never met a woman who had the power to change me so completely.

"Go on," I tell him, nodding toward where Tessa is now standing, swaying back and forth with their three-week-old son in her arms. "That's where you need to be."

He grins. "Thanks for coming, both of you. I'll be there when it's your turn." With that, he taps the table with both hands, stands, and moves back to his wife and son. He wraps Tessa in his arms and smiles down at their baby. Not gonna lie, I'm hit with a little bit of envy.

"He makes it hard not to want that, watching them together."

"Yeah," I agree.

We sit in silence for a while, just watching the guests of the small, intimate wedding. The hotel is massive and right on the beach. The wedding was at sunset, the perfect backdrop. I'm happy for my friend, but I'm ready to slip away and get a drink away from the love fest. Not that I begrudge him his happiness. I don't. But damn, it can sometimes be a hard pill to swallow when everyone around you is loved up and you're the lone single guy. Well, Case is single, too, but the way he's eyeing the blonde bartender, he's got plans to keep his bed warm tonight. I, on the other hand, need a stiff drink.

"I'm gonna go grab a drink," Case says, his eyes locked on the bartender. "You want anything?" he asks, standing.

"Nah, I'm all set. I might go take a walk, get some fresh air."

"Yeah," he says, slapping a hand down on my shoulder and walking away.

I meet Landon's eye and nod toward the door, mouthing that I'll be right back. He nods, and I make my escape. The sun has long since set, and the breeze from the ocean feels nice compared to the stuffy reception room. I don't know where I'm going, but I'm enjoying the sound of the waves crashing against the shore. It's not something I get at home in Nashville, and when we're traveling for games, it's all work and no play.

When I reach the beachside bar, I settle on a stool in the corner away from the crowd and order a beer. I consider something harder, but the last thing I need is to get shit-faced and have someone recognize me and take photos to sell to the tabloids. My team is coming off a two-year league championship-winning streak, and we don't want that kind of bad publicity.

"Thanks," I mumble to the bartender, keeping my head low as he delivers my beer and rushes off to help the next customer. I'm just about to take my first sip when someone plops down in the seat next to mine.

Glancing at the newcomer out of the corner of my eye, I see her shoulders slump as she exhales a heavy breath. "That bad?" I ask, unable to stop myself.

"You have no idea," she grumbles. She rests her arms on the bar and slumps forward, resting her forehead against her forearm.

"What can I get ya?" the bartender asks.

"Something fruity where I can't taste the alcohol," she says, lifting her head and blowing her hair out of her eyes.

I take a minute to look her over. She's got long brown hair that drapes across her back in soft curls. From my view, it seems as though she's got a banging body, but it's not until she turns to glance at me that her true beauty hits me full force. So much so, that my breath literally stalls in my lungs, causing me to cough and act a fool, drawing attention our way.

Her big brown eyes sparkle. I shit you not, they sparkle as if they have diamonds in the center, as she takes me in. Reaching over, she pats me on the back. "You okay there…?" Her voice trails off.

"Reid," I say, tapping at my chest, trying to force air back into my lungs. "I'm good," I tell her as I wait for some sort of recognition to flash in those stunning eyes of hers, but nothing happens.

"Bellamy," she says, offering me her hand to shake.

I take her small hand in mine, and fuck me, her skin is soft. "Nice to meet you," I say, my voice husky. I don't understand what's happening to me right now. I've met dozens of beautiful women in my life and interacted with them as if it were just another day. Never once in my life has a woman made me feel so off balance.

"You, too." She nods at the bartender in recognition of the fruity drink he just placed in front of her, as she brings the glass to her lips and drains half of it. "Much better," she says, under her breath.

"Bad day?" I can't help but ask. When I sat down, I intended to enjoy a beer and keep to myself, but this beauty just changed that. She's immediately captured my attention in her coral flowing dress, big brown eyes, and dark brown hair that looks smooth like silk.

"If you count having to attend the wedding from hell a bad day, then yeah. The worst," she says, taking another hefty pull of her drink. She smacks her lips before licking a small drop of her fruity drink that lingers on her bottom lip.

I catch the bartender's attention and point toward her drink, lifting my beer to let him know to bring us both another. "Want to talk about it?" I ask. Why? I have no fucking idea. I'm not Landry—I don't thrive on the gossip—but this gorgeous girl seems like she needs to get something off her chest, and I'm here for whatever passes those full, luscious lips.

"Depends, do you need a nap?"

"What?" I ask, furrowing my brow.

"I'm sure you have better things to do, looking all snazzy tonight, than listen to me whine and put you to sleep."

I chuckle. "Try me."

The bartender delivers our fresh drinks. She downs the remainder of her first and pulls the second one close.

"One of my college sorority sisters got married today. There were twelve bridesmaids. Twelve!" She shakes her head and takes another drink. "Anyway, we're not close. We never really were. She's one of those mean-girl controlling types, and everything has to be her way or the highway."

"Bridezilla," I mutter.

"Yes!" She points a manicured finger at me. "Exactly that. Wear your hair like this, not too much makeup, that's not enough makeup, you dance to this song, but leave enough space on the dance floor so that we're the focal point," she rattles off in a high-pitched tone. "I'm a terrible friend, because I snuck out, and to be honest, I don't want to go back."

"Well, look at it this way. Now you know how not to be when you get married," I say, my eyes glancing down at her bare ring finger.

She scoffs. "You have to be dating to even consider marriage, and I'm single as a Pringle," she says, taking another long pull of her drink. "What about you? Wife? Kids?"

"Nope. Also single as a Pringle," I say, lifting my beer to my lips to hide my smile.

"Is there a reason?" she asks.

"That I'm single?"

"Yeah."

I shrug. "I guess I just haven't found the person I want to spend forever with. I won't settle. She'd have to be my dream girl."

"Oh, tell me more." She turns to face me. In this little private corner of the bar, the move feels intimate.

I ignore her request for more and toss her words back at her. "What about you? Is there a reason?"

"Mostly because all men are jerks."

"Hey now." I place my hand over my heart as if she's offended me.

"Fine, present company excluded, but the jury is still out." She gives me a look that says she's not convinced that I'll prove her otherwise.

"Sounds like you've had your heart broken."

"Sure, if you count your dad loving his job more than you, and walking out on me and my mom, then yeah, you could say that."

"Damn," I mutter. "I hate that for you."

"Yeah, I hate it for me, too. Other than that, there have been a few relationships. Nothing that ever lasted. What about you?"

"No serious relationships. I date here and there," I admit.

"So, no dream girl. Tell me what the requirements are."

I take a long pull of my beer and think about her question instead of avoiding it this time. "She's someone who's not afraid to stand up to me and for what she believes in. She's independent, yet still needs and wants me around. She understands that my career sometimes requires me to travel, so she'd have to trust me, and I her. Her idea of a good time is spending time with friends, and just being—real."

"Real as in what? Boobs? Hair? Lips?" she asks, her lips quirking in a smile.

"All of it. But mostly, I want her to be real with me. I want someone who's going to order a steak and devour it at dinner if that's what she wants. If she wants dessert, I want her to eat that, too, and enjoy it. Life is too short to pretend or worry about social standards. I want her to be with me for me. Not for my career, or who I know, or what either of those things might bring her. Just me. Just Reid."

"Wow. Yeah, I wasn't expecting that." Her eyes sparkle with something I can't name.

"What about you?"

Just as I did, she takes a drink and gives her answer careful thought. "I want to be the center of his world. I know careers are important, but I watched my father ruin my parents' marriage. He was never willing to put her first. I want to be real, too. I never want to have to question where I stand, and I want to eat the damn steak, and the dessert." She smiles, and those big brown eyes light up the room. "I want to find my someone. I want to know that if my day was good, we're going to celebrate it together, and if it's bad, I want to know that I can count on him to lend me his ear and his shoulder to pick me up when I'm feeling down, and I'll do the same for him. I want someone who will call me on my shit, and someone who will hold me in their arms every night." She takes another quick sip of her drink. "Is that too much to ask for, Reid? Tell me, I can take it."

"No. It's not too much at all. What you've just told me is that you're my dream girl," I say, not an ounce of humor in my tone as my eyes hold hers.

She laughs. It's a light, airy sound that wraps around me like an embrace. "You think so?"

"Only time will tell."

"How much time are we talking?"

"Well, you don't want to go back to your event, and I don't want to go back to mine. How about we grab fresh drinks and take a walk on the beach?"

"That's—not what I thought you were going to say."

"What? You thought I was going to suggest that we go back to my room?"

"Or mine." She smirks.

"How am I going to know if you're really my dream girl if we don't get to know one another?"

"Did Tabby put you up to this?" She narrows her eyes at me.

"Who's Tabby?"

"The bride."

I can't help it. I toss my head back in laughter. "I don't know Tabby, but I want to know you." For the first time in my life, a woman has captured my attention, and I'm asking for more of her time.

CHAPTER 2

Bellamy

REID INSISTS ON PAYING FOR OUR DRINKS AND MOTIONS FOR me to lead the way toward the beach. The oceanside bar of the hotel makes the journey more convenient, and there's a long stretch of private beach that we get to use for this little late-night stroll of ours.

"So, what brings you to this hotel? Looking for your dream girl?" I ask. His stride matches mine. I try not to think about how sexy his forearms are covered in all those tattoos, or his messy hair that he manages to make look sexy—nope, not thinking about that at all.

He chuckles, and I don't hate the sound. "A wedding. One of my best friends from college just married his best friend."

"Did she have twelve bridesmaids?" I ask.

"Just one, her matron of honor."

"See?" I nod. "She's got it right. Just close friends and family. Why must so many feel the need to make a spectacle out of everything? I mean, they're in love, we know that, or they wouldn't be getting married. Think of what they could have done with all of that money that was wasted on one evening. It should be about the love and the moment, not what it looks like on social media and how many people you can invite." I huff out a breath as Reid's soft laughter greets my ears.

"Feel better?" he asks, grinning.

"Marginally." I stick my tongue out at him, unable to hide my grin.

"I happen to agree with you. More and more, it seems like weddings are for those in attendance, not the couple getting married."

"This!" I say, turning to face him. "It shouldn't be about color schemes, cake flavors, and seating charts. It should be about love. Two people sharing their love for one another."

"I like the way you think, Bellamy." He leans his shoulder into mine, and my body heats at the contact.

"So, are you from around here?"

"Nah, flew in from out of town. You?"

"Same. I love the ocean, but if I had to choose, I'd choose the mountains any day."

"The beach is a nice place to visit, but I happen to agree with you. I'll take the solitude and the cool, fresh air of the mountains."

"Ocean air can be cool," I tease.

"Yeah, but come on. There's nothing like driving up the mountain with your windows down, the shade of the trees, and that cool breeze."

There's familiarity in the way he speaks about the mountains. He either visits frequently or he lives close to them. "Hmm, maybe you should write greeting cards for a living," I joke.

"Nah, I'd be shit at it," he says, laughing softly.

"Siblings?" I ask. Something about this man compels me to know more about him. It's not just that. I'm not ready for this night to end, so keeping him talking seems like the best way to make this stroll on the beach last longer.

"Nope. Just me, myself, and I. I always wanted a little brother or sister, but it never happened. I guess my parents figured they got it perfect the first time, so why try again?" He smirks. "What about you?"

"One and only. My parents weren't around each other enough to have another one. My dad worked all the time, and when he wasn't away for work, he was working at home. They divorced when I was ten."

"That's tough. I'm sorry to hear that."

"Not your fault." It's my dad's fault. He put his career before our family. He's the one who should be saying he's sorry. I was young when my parents split, but I don't remember a time when he apologized.

"I know, but I'm still sorry for you. I know how lucky I was to have both of my parents in my household growing up. It's something that I want for my future kids, hence the reason I'm still unattached."

"Are you looking for her? Your dream girl?"

"No. I mean, not actively. But if I find her, I'll be sure to hold on tight," he says, bumping his shoulder into mine.

"You want kids, then?" I ask.

"I do. At least two if my dream girl and I are lucky enough to have them."

"And if you're not?"

He stops walking to turn to face me. "What do you mean?" His brow furrows as he tries to understand the meaning behind my question.

"What if you meet your dream girl and she can't have kids? Then what? Is she still your dream girl?" I don't know why, but I have this urgent need to hear his answer.

"Of course, she would be. It's not her ability to give us a family that makes her my dream girl. It's her. There are other ways to start a family, such as adoption. There are kids out there desperate for their forever families. One of my best friends back home, his wife grew up in foster care. There are kids like her who need love, too."

My heart pounds in my chest. It's the look in his eyes—the intensity of his gaze beneath the moonlight and the sincerity of his tone. Reid, whatever his last name is, just might be one of the good ones.

"You travel a lot for your job. What happens when your dream girl, or your kids, need you? Then what?" I don't know why I'm pushing this. It's not like this is a date, or that I'll ever see him again once we part ways tonight, but I still want to know his answer.

"What are we talking about here? Having a nightmare and needing Daddy, my wife needing my arms around her, or are we talking illness or something?" he asks, giving my question serious thought.

I move to sit on the sand, not thinking about the mess it's going to make of my dress. I hated it anyway, and the wedding is over, so who cares? Reid follows my lead and sits down next to me. He's close, so close his body is aligned with mine, and I surprise myself when I don't want to move away, widening the space between us. Instead, I stay where I am, soaking up his warmth and the zing of heat that seems to light my body on fire from his touch.

"All of it, I guess." Tilting my head back, I close my eyes and soak up the warm ocean breeze. "My dad was never there, and when he was, he wasn't. You said you travel for work, and I don't know, I guess I just wanted to see what other men would have done in his shoes."

Reid is quiet. I keep my eyes closed, not wanting to face him. I feel too raw, too exposed, and to a stranger, no less. It's not until I feel his fingers lace through mine that I lift my head and open my eyes.

"No details," I blurt. I don't know why, but this man, this moment, feels far too intimate, something I steer clear of, but it's not enough to make me run from him.

Reid nods, and even in the moonlight, I can see him swallow hard. "My job is important to me, but not more so than those I love. Your question is a hard one to answer. If my kid is sad, and I'm not there to put them to bed, I'll video call them and read them a story. Even if I have to pack their books with me while I travel to make that happen. My wife, that's a little harder, but I'd do everything in my power to make sure she understands that I might not be there, but she's still in my heart and on my mind. I do get breaks in travel, and while I still have a job to do, I'd give every spare minute I have to them. When I find my dream girl, a day won't go by—whether I'm there or traveling for work—that she and our children won't know that they're my everything."

My heart rages in my chest at the sincerity of his words. Even if I wasn't looking at him, I'd hear it in his voice. I can't help but feel jealous of his future family. They'll have something with Reid I never got as a kid.

"If it's worse, if they're sick—" He shakes his head. "It's impossible to think about, but I'd be there. Whatever it took, even if I had to give up my career, I'd be there every fucking step of the way." He squeezes my hand gently. "I'm sorry you didn't have that, Bellamy."

There is a lump in the back of my throat. Emotions threaten to choke me. I focus on pulling in even breaths and slowly exhaling. "Your future dream girl and children will be lucky to have you, Reid." I don't know what this feeling is inside my chest. It's a squeezing, overwhelming feeling I've never felt before. I don't understand it, but I know it's the man next to me, his words, his touch, and the sincerity beneath his words that caused it.

"I don't know about that, but I'm gonna work my ass off every day to make them think so." He nods, as if he's agreeing with his declaration. "What about you? You want kids? Your dream man?" he says, lightening the mood.

"I've always said no. I never want to go through what my mom went through, or what I went through, but it's hard to give that same answer after hearing yours."

"Don't change for me. I want your real."

"My real is that if I could find a man who thought like you did, as long as he doesn't have a career similar to my dad's, then yeah, I'd like to give the happily ever after with kids a shot." My stomach rolls at the thought of finding the forever kind of love Reid speaks of.

"That's enough of the heavy. How about another drink?" he asks.

"I don't know. I kind of like this midnight stroll thing we got going on."

"Babe, we're sitting in the sand; we're not doing much strolling," he says, and I can hear the smile in his voice. Seeing it even in the moonlight has my belly tightening for reasons that have nothing to do with fear, but desire. It's been a long damn time since I've had this kind of connection with a man. Hell, I'm not sure that I ever have. Figures I'd meet him while thousands of miles from home. That's my luck.

"We'd better get to strolling, then." I stand without dropping his hand, and once I'm on my feet, I tug, and he grumbles but gets to his feet.

"Where are you taking me, woman?" he asks, pulling gently on my hand, and suddenly I'm in his arms, and my head is pressed against his hard chest.

Damn, he's hiding some muscles under that dress shirt. I could tell he was fit, but this… I want to stand here all night and feel him up. I don't know what's going on with me, but I'm acting so out of character. Maybe it's the wedding. Perhaps it's the fact that we're both here, in a neutral location away from the reality of our real lives. Whatever it is, I'm here for it, at least for tonight.

"I'm good here," I tell him. His deep, husky laugh wraps around me as his body shakes with laughter. "Fine," I concede, pulling away. "I'd like to walk the beach a little more. Join me?"

He nods toward the wide-open beach. "Lead the way," he says, never letting go of my hand.

I should pull away. I shouldn't let myself pretend for a single second that this man could be different from the others. Different from my father. Whether it's the alcohol or the atmosphere, I'm throwing caution to the wind for one night. When the sun rises, I'll never see this man again. Besides, it's just a little walk on the beach; what can it hurt?

"Favorite color?" he asks, swinging our joined hands between us.

It's an innocent gesture, but my body still heats from the contact of his calloused hands.

"Green. Not just any green, emerald."

"That's very specific," he teases.

"Can't blame a girl for knowing what she likes. What about you?"

"I don't know. Blue."

"What shade of blue? Royal? Baby blue? I need particulars here, mister." He releases another laugh that washes over me. It's almost as comforting as the hug he just wrapped me up in.

"Navy blue."

I nod. "Navy blue it is. Okay, music?"

"All of it. I can't pick a favorite. What about you?"

"Same. Why choose when there are so many good options out there?"

"You'd fit in just fine with my friends back home. We play Name That Tune a lot when we're just hanging out, sitting by the fire."

"Is that what you do for fun?"

"Mostly. I have four best friends back home. Two of whom just recently got married. Another who just became a dad, a single dad. Well, kind of. They're not together. It's a long story, but they're co-parenting and making it work."

"He sounds like one of the good ones."

"Yeah, our job schedule is hectic, but he does what it takes to make it happen."

His words just confirm what I already knew. My dad didn't want to do what it took to make it happen. He was selfish and chasing his career, and he forgot that he had a family at home who missed him.

"You two work together?"

"We do. All five of us work together. They're my family."

He says it with such conviction that there's no room to guess if he's telling the truth. His five best friends are his family. "They must be good people."

"The best. What about you?"

"I work a lot. I have a best friend named Amanda. We met in junior high and have been thick as thieves ever since. Then there's my mom. She's been my best friend my entire life."

"Lucky girls," he says, his voice husky.

I stop walking and peer up at him. There's a part of me, a very large part, that wants to rise on my tiptoes and press my lips to his. It's the smaller part, the rational part, that keeps me from acting on that particular impulse. "I think I'm ready for that drink." My voice doesn't sound like my own.

He bends down, his lips barely an inch from me. "Drink it is," he says huskily. Without releasing my hand, we turn and head back to the oceanside bar of the hotel to grab another drink.

We take our same seats in the corner. It's intimate, something I try not to think about. Our conversation never ebbs, and the drinks keep flowing. I'm once again reminded that I've never had this kind of instant chemistry with a man.

"Last call!" the bartender hollers.

No. No. Time went too fast. I'm not ready to leave him. Perhaps I should ask him to come up to my room. I've never had a one-night stand. I've always been someone who needs to be in a relationship, or at least dating, for a while before I fall into bed, but apparently, Reid is my exception.

"You want another?" Reid asks.

"No, thank you."

He nods. "Can I walk you to your room?"

He knows I'm staying here; we both are. That's something we've already discussed tonight. "Yes, please."

When we get to my room, I'll invite him in. I'm not ready to say goodbye. I know we're both not from here, and once he walks away, I'll never see him again. I need something more than just our conversation to remember this night. To remember him. I want to know what it feels like to have his lips on mine. I want to know how far those tattoos go up his arms. Are they anywhere else on his body? I need to know everything before we say our final goodbyes.

I can hear Amanda's voice in my head telling me to live a little. She's married to her college sweetheart, Ethan, and she claims to live vicariously through me. Much to her dismay, it's not a very vibrant life—more work, and not much play.

Reaching for my purse to pay for my drinks, Reid stops me, placing his hand over mine. "Drinks are on me." He gives me a look that dares me to argue with him, so I nod.

"Thank you, Reid."

"I should be the one thanking you. I got to spend the evening with a beautiful woman."

"Flattery."

He leans in and presses his lips to my temple. I freeze as he whispers, "Truth." He pulls away, signs his receipt, shoves his wallet back into his pants, and offers me his hand. "Shall we?"

I nod, not trusting myself not to beg him to spend the night with me. Instead, I take his hand, and together, we make our way to the elevators. Once the doors close us inside, he wraps his arms around me from behind. It's a simple gesture, but my body heats up having him this close.

The doors slide open, and we step out, hand in hand. When we reach my room, I turn to face him. He steps in close, which has me moving until my back hits the door. His hands rest above my head, caging me in.

"I don't want to say goodbye to you."

Yes! "Then don't," I breathe.

"I need you to lay this out for me, Bellamy. I need your words. There are no expectations here."

"Pity." I smile up at him. "I was expecting an orgasm."

A slow, sexy smile pulls at his lips. "Just one? You can do better than that."

"Can you?"

"Is that what you want? You want me to follow you into your room and show you how many orgasms I can pull from your sexy body?"

"That." I nod.

He chuckles. "You sure this is what you want?"

"Yes." I don't hesitate with my answer.

His lips press to the corner of my mouth before he drops his hands. "Unlock the door, Bellamy." His voice is gritty with desire, and my panties are ruined.

I do as he says and turn, giving him my back. My hands tremble as I swipe the keycard and push open the door. I'm not scared. I'm turned on.

Once we're in the room, the door closes behind us with an audible click. Reid turns the lock. I face him and find him leaning with his back against the door. "What's wrong? Change your mind?" I tease.

He reaches down and grips his hard cock through his pants. "Never," he assures me. "Just trying to take this slow."

"Why?"

"I don't want tonight to end," he confesses.

There is so much sincerity in his words that it has me swallowing back a lump of emotion. This man is not afraid to speak his mind or ask for what he wants. I barely know him, but I feel it in my bones that if he says it, he means it.

"We have all night," I assure him, kicking off my shoes. Reaching up, I start pulling pins out of my partial updo.

"Bellamy?"

"Yeah?" My eyes collide with his.

"Strip."

CHAPTER 3

Reid

BLOOD RUSHES IN MY EARS, LOUD AS THUNDER, DROWNING out everything except the heat of her gaze. The room is suddenly hot, too hot. Everything is still—the beauty before me and the breath in my lungs.

This wasn't how I saw our night ending. I was just being a nice guy, enjoying the company of this gorgeous woman, but with each hour that passed, the thought of leaving her stretched my control like a rubber band, ready to snap.

Bellamy sucks in a heavy breath, her chest rising rapidly with the action, and a slow, sexy smile tugs at her lips. "If I'm getting naked, so are you." She raises her brow, as if she's daring me to challenge her.

That's not going to happen. The woman before me is the most beautiful woman I've ever laid eyes on. It's more than that. She's fun, open, and honest, and that's something I don't see much of with the women who try to capture my attention. My gut tells me it's not because she doesn't know who I am, but that's who she is. Good to her core.

My hands are steady as I start to loosen the buttons of my shirt. Part of me wants just to rip them off and say fuck it, but the way Bellamy's eyes heat as each button releases has me digging deep for my patience and undoing one button at a time.

With each button that is freed, I step toward her. By the time we're standing just a few inches apart, my shirt is hanging open, my chest and tattoos on full display. Bellamy and those sparkling brown eyes of hers devour every inch, making my skin burn from her gaze.

Tentatively, she reaches out and presses her palm against my abs. Her breath shudders as she leans in close. My hands move to rest lightly at her hips, holding her steady. In a way, I'm using her as a crutch to keep me steady, as well. For the first time in my life, the nearness of a beautiful woman has my knees weak.

"You must spend hours every day in the gym," she says, letting her fingers explore.

My cock aches as it presses against the zipper of these damn dress pants. "Something like that," I admit. I'm not ready to tell her what I do for a living. In this moment, I'm just Reid. I'm not my job or my bank account, and it's a heady feeling.

My grip on her hips tightens. "You're wearing too many clothes. This coral color looks beautiful on you, but I'm certain it will look better on the floor." I wink.

"It's not my fault your washboard abs and all these sexy tattoos distracted me," she says, tracing her index finger over a tattoo on my chest.

It takes Herculean effort to step back, out of her reach. I make quick work of discarding my shirt, tossing it to the chair in the corner. I don't stop there. I work at my belt and unfasten my pants, letting them fall. I kick them out of the way, and finally, my fingers slip beneath the waistband of my boxer briefs, and I slide them over my hips, down my thighs, and they, too, get kicked, to be found later. Holding my hands out at my sides, I present myself to her. "You can trace them all if you want, but not until you're naked," I tell her, as her eyes run over my ink, taking her time as if she's cataloging each piece. It's as if she's staring into my soul.

"Bellamy." Her eyes snap to mine. "I need to see you." My voice is husky and filled with need for this woman.

The beauty before me tilts her head to the side. "I didn't expect you. I didn't expect this," she says, gesturing between the two of us.

"Say the word, and I leave. No pressure."

"What? No." She shakes her head. "I don't want you to leave. I just— I've never done this before. I've never slept with a man I've just met."

"You're in control," I tell her. "We do as little or as much as you want. If you want to lie naked on the bed and watch TV, I'm your guy." I wink at her again, which causes laughter to bubble up in her chest. I love the sound. I don't think I've ever thought those words before. I know I haven't. That's the effect this woman has on me. I enjoy every single piece of her.

"What about this?" she asks, her small, soft hand gripping my cock.

"Yours if you want it," I tell her, my voice gritty with my desire for her.

She holds my gaze as she gently strokes me, driving me insane with lust and need, all for her. "I want it." She rises onto her toes, placing her lips a breath away from mine. "I want you," she says, before pecking my lips with a kiss.

It's not enough.

I don't know that any amount of time with this incredible woman will ever be enough.

I don't know where she's from or where she's going from here. I don't know where she works or her last name, but I know that if I don't get inside her, my life might be over. She's more than I ever could have hoped for—more than I expected when she sat down next to me.

My hand slides behind her neck, angling her mouth just right, as I lean in close, holding her gaze. "My dream girl," I whisper as my lips crash with hers. Her body molds with mine as I devour her mouth. She meets me stroke for stroke, and I can't help but think she's my perfect match.

I kiss her until we both need to come up for air. When I pull back, her lips are red and swollen, and her eyes are glazed over with lust. "Tell me what's next?" My words deliver as a demand, harsher than I intended, but my tone doesn't seem to faze her.

I work to pull air back into my lungs and keep my hands to my sides. I need her to tell me what she wants. Her answer is a silent one in the form of her pulling her dress over her head and dropping it to the floor.

My eyes are glued to her as I watch her reach behind her back and unclasp her bra. There's no seduction tactic. She simply slides the straps over her shoulders and lets her bra fall from her fingers. The entire time, her eyes never leave mine.

I want to take in every inch of her, but I can't seem to tear my gaze from those big brown eyes with diamonds in the center. I'm mesmerized by this beautiful woman before me. She leans forward, breaking our eye contact, and that's when I allow myself to take her in.

She slides her barely there panties over her thighs before stepping out of them. When she stands back to her full height, I take my time. I start at the tips of her toes. They're painted a pale pink to match her short, manicured nails.

My gaze travels up her toned, tanned legs, over her thighs, and to her bare pussy. My cock weeps to feel her warmth, and my fingers ache to trace her folds, to see how wet she is for me. I can see from here that she is.

Stepping forward, because I need to be closer, I reach out and trace my index finger over her belly. She quivers at my touch. I swallow hard as I continue my journey. When I reach her full, round breasts, I test their weight in the palm of my hand, tracing one nipple, and the next with the pad of my thumb.

"Reid." She moans my name. Her eyes flutter closed as she tilts her head back, enjoying my touch.

I want to demand she open her eyes and see that it's me who's making her feel this way, but I'm a selfish bastard and want this time to study her. Her long, slender neck is begging for my mouth. Those full, kissable lips are swollen from my kisses. It's not until I reach her eyes that I step forward again, my naked body aligning with hers.

"Open for me." Her eyes pop open, and every ounce of desire I feel for this woman is staring back at me. It's not enough. I need her words. I know they say actions speak louder, but I need her permission to consume her. "Tell me."

"I want you. I need you. I want to experience this night with you, and everything you have to offer."

"Everything?"

She nods. "I don't know you, but I feel like I do. You're a stranger to me, but my gut tells me that I can trust you."

"What else is your gut telling you, sweet Bellamy?" I ask, leaning forward to trail kisses down her neck.

"Th-That tonight will be one I'll never forget. A moment in time that I'll cherish forever."

Fuck me. Her words affect me more than they should. I shouldn't want her this badly. My lips trail back up her neck, across her cheek, and to her lips. She nips at my bottom lip before stroking her tongue against mine.

Bending, I place my hands on the backs of her thighs and lift her. On instinct, she wraps her legs around my waist, never breaking our kiss. My cock is right where it needs to be. It wouldn't take much for me to align myself at her entrance and push inside, but that's not how this night is going to go.

If this is all I get with her, then I'm going to make it count. Instead of pushing her back up against the wall and losing myself inside her, I carry her to the bed and lay her down gently. She shuffles to settle her head on the pillow.

"Beautiful," I whisper, my voice raspy. I grip my cock, willing myself to savor this night with her. The woman before me is pure perfection, and rushing my time with her would be a dishonor to her beauty.

"You need some help with that?" She nods to where I'm gripping my cock.

"Yes, but not yet," I tell her, as I climb onto the bed after her. She spreads her legs, and my mouth waters at the sight of her. Moving to my belly, I settle between her thighs. Placing my hands beneath her ass, I cup her cheeks and lift her to my mouth.

"Oh, fuck," she moans, as I trace her clit softly with my tongue. I take my time, teasing her, tasting her, loving that it's making her squirm. I feel her body move, and I look up to find her resting her weight on her elbows as she watches me.

"What's up, dream girl?" I ask. The smile she graces me with is bright and beautiful, just like her.

"From one-night stand to dream girl, huh?" she teases.

I nod, then blow a soft puff of air against her pussy, and she moans. "If the shoe fits," I say, loving her reaction to me.

I don't give her a chance to reply before I dive back in for more. I allow myself to get lost in her taste and make her feel what my body can do to hers. I want her screaming my name and coming all over my face. Then, and only then, will I allow myself to feel her warm, wet heat around my cock.

When she buries her hands in my hair and tugs as she lifts her hips, searching for me, I know she's close. I don't stop, just like she demands that I don't, until the tidal wave of bliss washes over her. Only when her body falls to the bed do I lift my head, wiping my mouth with the back of my hand, and take her in.

Her body is flushed from her orgasm, her breathing is labored, and her eyes are closed. I spend several heartbeats just staring at her and memorizing this moment. It's one I'm certain, no matter where life takes me, that I'll never forget.

I could never forget her.

My cock throbs to the point of pain. Moving up her body, I settle between her thighs, my cock brushing her wet pussy. I hold my weight on my hands, which are placed on either side of her head, and I grin down at her. She must feel my stare because her eyes flutter open, and she offers me a lazy smile.

"Hey," she says, and my grin grows wider.

"How ya feeling?" I smirk.

"Meh," she says, and I shift my weight to one hand so I can tickle her side. "Mercy!" she cries out, and I stop immediately.

My hand traces up her side, while I bend my head to kiss her. She doesn't shy away from my kiss, even though I'm certain she can taste herself on my tongue. How can it be that I've never been inside her, but I already feel as though I'm addicted? Or at least I could be. I push the fact that this is a onetime thing to the back of my mind and focus on the present.

"I'm good, but I could be better," she says when I lift out of our kiss.

"Oh, yeah? What would make you feel better?"

She loops her arms around my neck and smiles up at me. "You inside me."

Fuck. Yes.

I kiss her again, this time, a hard peck against her lips. "Hold that thought," I say, as I scramble off the bed and toward my pants. I dig for my wallet and pull out the single condom that I have in there. One and done, that's all I'm going to get with her. You can bet your ass I'm going to make it count.

Jumping back onto the bed, she bounces and giggles as she does. I move between her thighs and tear the condom open with my teeth. In a matter of seconds, I'm wrapped up and ready to enter paradise.

Leaning over her, I brace my palms on either side of her head. She stares at the space between us, where our bodies are about to be intimately connected. She takes me in her hand and guides me toward where she needs me.

Inside her.

I push forward, not stopping until I'm all the way in. We both moan at the contact. Her hands slip under my arms, and her nails dig into my back. I remain still, closing my eyes, relishing the feel of her warmth wrapped around me, giving her time to adjust to my size. It's not just that. I need a minute to talk myself down. I'm so damn close to losing control, but I don't want that. Not tonight. Not with her.

"Reid?"

Slowly, I peel open my eyes and stare down at her.

"I need you."

Something moves inside my chest at her plea. It's strong and powerful and causes a swarm of emotions to swell inside me. Want, need, desire, lust… I feel it all. At the edge of all of that, though, there's something else that lingers. Something I've never felt before, and something I'm too scared to try and name, so I push it down and focus on her.

On us.

On this moment.

"I'm right here," I tell her, and then I start to move.

I set a steady pace, rocking my hips. Her nails bite at the skin of my back, and it fuels me. I want her mark on me. I know that I'll look at them in the mirror every day until they fade and remember this moment. If I could live here, in this room, inside her for the rest of my days, I'd be a happy man.

She feels like so much more than a stranger to me. It's as if we've known each other forever, and I already know I want to see her again. How can I walk away from this connection we have? It's intense and explosive and like nothing I've ever felt before.

Is this how Landon, Knox, and Landry felt when they fell? I'm not saying I'm in love with her, but fuck me, I'm in something with this incredible woman lying beneath me.

Bellamy brings her legs up, locking them around my waist and pulling me nearer. My cock twitches inside her, knowing she needs me closer. Dropping down to my elbows, still trying to keep the majority of my weight off her petite frame, I take her lips with mine. My hips still as I get lost in our kiss, as I get lost in her.

"My dream girl," I whisper against her lips, before breaking out of the kiss and thrusting my hips. I'm close. I can feel the burning starting at the base of my spine. It's as if I'm resting at the edge of a cliff, just waiting to jump and soar through the sky.

"Reid!" Bellamy calls out my name as her pussy locks around my cock with a crushing pleasure unlike anything I've ever felt before.

"Bell!" I call out as I lose the battle against my control. My lips find hers, and I kiss her, trying to show her that this is more than just a hot night of sex. It has to be, right? Nothing that feels this good, this right, should ever be a onetime thing.

CHAPTER 4

Bellamy

REID'S FOREHEAD RESTS AGAINST MINE AS WE TRY TO CATCH our breath. When I sat down next to him at the bar, I never would have guessed that this night would end with the best sex of my life. Is it because being with him is forbidden? Okay, maybe not forbidden, but as my first one-night stand, I feel like I'm breaking the rules I've set for myself.

However, I don't regret it. Not a moment spent with him will ever be a regret, but a memory I'm sure I'll look back on often. To be honest, he might have ruined me for all men in my future. Just my luck, my first one-night stand would set the bar for great sex.

"Let's get you cleaned up." He eases back and climbs off the bed, offering me his hand. I take it, allowing him to help me to my feet.

"Reid!" I yelp when he bends and tosses me over his shoulder and carries me to the bathroom. I wince when he places my naked ass on the cold bathroom counter. "Cold," I mutter.

Reid steps close, and I open my legs for him. His lips connect with mine. His kiss is potent, making me dizzy with need. All too soon, he steps back, breaking our connection. My eyes are fixed on his every move as he disposes of the condom, before reaching in and turning on the shower.

I keep my eyes fixed on his toned ass cheeks, which he catches me doing when he spins around. "Like what you see?" he teases.

"Meh." I shrug when we both know you could bounce a quarter off his ass. The heat of my blush gives me away for sure.

"Riiight." He chuckles, drawing out the word with a smirk on his lips, as he grips my hips, lifts me from the counter, and places me on my feet. "Let's get you cleaned up," he says, smacking me lightly on the ass.

"Hey." I turn to look at him over my shoulder.

He grins. "You got to stare at mine, so I get to spank yours."

I open my mouth to give him a sarcastic reply, but nothing comes. We both know it's because I like his hands on me. Doesn't matter if he's smacking my ass or letting those large, calloused hands of his explore every inch of my skin. In just a matter of hours, I've come to crave his touch, and that's not good.

This is why I've never had a one-night stand. I can't keep feelings and sex in two separate boxes. They're the same to me, and Reid's not helping. He's sweet and patient, and damn him for making me want him. He's already rocked my world more than once tonight. I should be satisfied and ready to walk away, right? Isn't that how this is supposed to work?

Shaking out of my thoughts, I step under the hot spray. Reid does, as well, closing the shower door behind him. He turns us so that the water is beating down on his back. His arms hold tightly around my waist as he pushes my hair to one shoulder and kisses my neck.

"How are you feeling, dream girl?" he asks softly.

"Come on now, you've already had me. You don't need to keep showering me with sweet words. I was a sure thing," I tease. My words betray my body's reaction to him referring to me as his dream girl. He's still looking for her. He can't expect me to believe that suddenly, I'm that girl for him. I can't let his monster cock or his wicked tongue pull me into a false sense of security.

Gently, he turns me to face him. One hand wraps around my waist, settling at the base of my spine and holding me close to him. The other cradles my cheek, and he tilts my head so that we're eye to eye. "I'm not that guy, Bellamy. I won't lie to you and give you pretty words to manipulate you. That's not what this is. With each minute that passes, the more I learn about you, the harder I fall."

"You're not supposed to fall," I whisper.

He leans down, his lips a breath from mine. "You can't stop me." Dropping his hand from my cheek, he grabs one of my hands and places it over his heart. His blue eyes hold me captive. A tremor of emotion that I refuse to name shakes my chest. I want to close my eyes, to break the intensity of his stare, but his gaze ignites something in me I can't name—something I *refuse* to name.

Finally, he breaks the spell, drops my hand, and reaches for the shampoo. I stand still, letting him lather my hair. I've never had a man wash my hair for me. I know I should tell him to stop, that I can handle this on my own, because I can, but I also know that when the sun rises in a few short hours, our time together will be over. So, instead, I stand still and allow him to take care of me, while trying to ignore the fact that he's the first man ever to want to do so.

"Switch with me."

Doing as he says, we swap places. My back is to the spray, so I dip my head, letting it rinse out the shampoo. My eyes are closed, so I don't see him coming, but I feel him suck a nipple into his mouth. He does this thing with his tongue and his teeth. A nip, and then a soothing caress; it has my knees going weak and my pussy throbbing for more of him.

I grip his forearms to keep from falling. His wicked tongue is going to be the root cause of me crashing to this shower floor.

"I've got you," he assures me.

The next thing I know, I'm being lifted in the air. Automatically, I lock my naked, wet body around his and hold on tightly. Reid turns us and pushes my back up against the shower wall. "I can't get enough of you," he growls.

I've read about men and their growly voices, but hot damn, the real thing has nothing on fiction. I want to tell him that I feel the same, but I choose to keep my mouth clamped shut. There's no point in pretending this can be more than what it is.

His lips trail down my neck, and his hard cock grinds against me.

"Please," I moan, because damn if I don't crave feeling him inside me again.

"Bad news, beautiful," he says, nipping at my ear.

"What's that?" My body stiffens, waiting for his rejection.

"Only had one condom."

"What? You don't carry more than one?" I ask.

He thinks this is the funniest thing in the world because he tosses his head back in laughter. "No, Bellamy, I don't carry more than one. I know that we don't know each other very well, but I don't do this sort of thing often."

"You don't have to lie to me," I tell him, looking over his shoulder.

"I won't lie to you. Ever. It's been almost a year since I've been with anyone, and she was—" he starts, but I raise my hand and place it over his mouth.

"Stop. I don't want to hear about *her*," I say, hearing the jealousy in my tone.

"There is no her. There's only you."

"You and that silver tongue." I shake my head.

"Hey, you like my tongue, and I happen to know my tongue really likes you." He wags his eyebrows, and now, we're both grinning. "But truly, I'll never lie to you. That's not who I am. The last woman I was with was someone I've known for years and dated casually for events and such."

"It's been longer for me," I confess, feeling as though I should give him the courtesy of the same information. I'm aware of the fact that we should have had this conversation before we fell into bed together, but I can be honest with myself and say it wouldn't have mattered. As long as he's unattached, and there is no faded mark on his ring finger, and no one has been blowing his phone up all night, wondering where he's been.

"So, yeah, as bad as I'd like to feel your pussy gripping my cock, we're going to have to take that off the table. But I've got you," he tells me. "I'm going to lift you, and I want you to wrap your legs around my neck.

"What? Your neck? No. I can't do that. I'm too heavy."

"Yeah, right." He laughs. "Trust me, Bellamy. I've got this."

All I can do is nod, and then I'm being lifted. I toss my legs over his shoulders and bury my hands in his hair to keep from falling. My back presses against the wall, helping to stabilize me.

I don't get the chance to ask him what he's doing because he dives right in, sucking my clit into his mouth. He grips my ass cheeks, and with each stroke of his tongue, I step a little closer to the edge of bliss that my body already knows he can provide.

I grip the strands of his sandy blond hair and hold on for dear life as he brings me to yet another orgasm. I feel boneless as my body slumps against the wall. Reid manages to lift me off his shoulders and moves to the shower seat, with me straddling his hips.

"You still with me?" he asks. My eyes are closed, but I can hear the smirk in his voice. He's proud of himself, as he should be. No man before him has ever learned to play my body like he has.

"I'm still here," I say, wiggling my hips, making him groan.

"None of that," he says, gripping my hips to stop me.

"I let you have your way with me," I tell him.

"I know, baby, but we don't have any more condoms." The tone of his voice tells me that it was painful for him to recite those words to me.

"Maybe just the tip," I say, drunk on lust. This isn't me, I've never taken this kind of risk, that's not who I am, but apparently, it's who I am with him. Reid makes me feel things, makes me want to risk things I never would have considered before meeting him.

"That's a dangerous game, Bellamy." His hand slides under my hair and grips my neck, pulling my forehead down to his. "I don't even know your last name," he says, his voice gritty with desire.

"Just a little," I say, lifting onto my knees to reach between us and grip his cock.

"Motherfucker," he says, as I stroke him.

"Tell me no." My voice is almost pleading. This is risky as hell. I'm on the pill, but that's not 100 percent effective.

"Are you on the pill?"

"Yes. I take it at the same time every day."

Lifting his head, his dark blue, stormy gaze seizes me. "You want this?"

"With you. Just—I need to feel you, Reid."

He nods. "Do it." He drops his hand from my neck, and suddenly his hands are no longer on me.

"What are you doing?" I ask, needing to feel those rough hands of his against my skin.

"You have complete control over this."

"Do you not want to?"

I don't know what I expected, but it's not a soft smile. "Do I want to give you something I've never given anyone else? Yeah, dream girl, I do."

"What do you mean?"

"I've never been bare inside a woman."

My mouth falls open. "Oh, we don't have to," I say, releasing my grip on his cock.

"Don't you dare," he says, moving my hand back between us. I take him in my palm and stroke him gently. "I'm all in if you are."

His eyes bore into mine, and in that instant, something shifts—an understanding, silent but absolute. We both want this despite the risks. That's all either of us needs as I slide down onto his cock.

"Fuck. Fuck. Fuck," he chants. He fists his hands at his sides, and his eyes lock onto where we're connected.

"Wow," I breathe. "I didn't know it would feel so different."

His eyes snap open. "Looks like I got to give you another one of my firsts tonight, too." He moves, sitting up straighter, both of his hands resting against my cheeks. "You're unlike anyone I've ever met before."

"I hope that's a good thing?" I say, rocking my hips, making us both moan at the friction.

"Of course, it is. That's why you're my dream girl," he says as he leans in, and the world narrows to the space between us.

When his lips finally find mine, it's not gentle—it's raw, urgent, like we've both been holding back too long. His hands are in my hair, mine gripping the bare flesh of his toned shoulders like he's the only thing keeping me upright.

The kiss deepens, heat surging between us, each movement charged with something that feels like hunger and something that feels like home. There's no hesitation, no pause—just the crash of two people who need, and finally take.

"Bellamy," he warns. "I'm close. I need to pull out."

"Yeah," I agree, because that's the right thing to do. The responsible thing to do.

"Fuck!" He cries out as he lifts me off his cock, and his hot cum hits my belly. I stare down at us, at the mess we made, and I can honestly admit that this is the hottest, sexiest moment of my life.

I made him lose control.

"Turn," he commands, and I do as he says. Scrambling off his lap to turn and face the spray. The water hits my belly, washing away his release. "Lean back," he murmurs, and I do, sitting back on his lap and resting my head on his shoulder.

His hands trail over my quivering belly to my pussy. "I hate that you didn't come before me," he whispers, his deep voice causing desire to race down my spine. "Let's fix that, shall we?" he says, before plunging two fingers deep inside me. He's relentless in his pursuit of my orgasm, which has me calling out his name as my release washes over me.

His strong arms band around me as he buries his face in my neck. I don't know how long we sit here, letting the warm water wash over us. I want to stay here forever, but I know that's not reality.

"Let's get cleaned up," he says, tapping my thigh. I stand, and so does he. He takes his time lathering my body with his hands. I take my turn to return the favor. Our hands and mouths are everywhere. I can't seem to get enough of him, and that scares me. I don't trust easily, but this man is someone who's wiggled his way past all my defenses, and in their place is a yearning for something I wasn't sure I'd ever have.

I push it down deep as he turns off the water, and we step out of the shower. Reid wraps a towel around me. He takes another and starts patting at my hair, while he stands there dripping water all over the bathroom floor.

"You're a fall hazard." I nod to the puddle he's standing in.

"Gotta take care of my girl first," he says, making my heart squeeze in my chest.

"I've got this. Handle that." I smile up at him, and he does as I ask, relinquishing the second towel he used on my hair and grabbing another for himself. Quickly, I brush out my hair and tie it up in a wet knot. I hate going to bed with damp hair, but I'm exhausted. I toss my toiletries back into my bag on the counter and step out of the bathroom with Reid on my heels as he flips off the light.

"Bed," he says softly, and I nod, climbing under the covers. Reid turns off the bedside lamp, casting the room in darkness, and slides beneath the covers next to me. "Sweet dreams, Bellamy."

"Sweet dreams," I whisper.

Closing my eyes, I will sleep to claim me, but it never comes. Instead, I watch as shadows stretch across the wall as I lie here, watching the minutes tick past on the bedside clock. Hours pass, and still sleep never arrives. Reid, on the other hand, is out cold. His breathing is deep and even, and I can't help but wonder what it would be like to fall asleep next to him every night.

No. I can't think that way. Another glance at the clock tells me it's a few minutes past six. My flight leaves at ten, so I don't need to go yet, but then again, I do. I need to slip away, leaving Reid, the incredible memories, and the orgasms he gave me in this hotel suite.

As gently as I can, I slip out of his arms and wait to see if he wakes up. He doesn't, and I heave a sigh of relief. Tiptoeing around the room, I get dressed and pack my bag as quietly as I can. I'm pretty sure I have everything, but if not, oh well, it can be replaced. I need to leave now. I'm scared to death that if he wakes up, I'll look into those blue eyes of his, the ones that seem to see into my soul, and I'll never be able to walk away, which is crazy, because I barely know him.

Reid, whoever he is, is now also my first and only one-night stand. I won't ever do this again; it would taint my memory of him. The last several hours and all the moments since I sat down next to him at the bar are forever his.

"Goodbye, silver tongue," I whisper as I slip out the door, making sure to close it softly behind me. Rushing toward the elevator, I hit the button and wait, while continually glancing over my shoulder for him. The doors slide open, and I exhale, stepping inside.

My one night of passion. The night that ruined me for all other men has come to an end, and I'm walking away, knowing that the man sleeping soundly in my hotel suite has changed me.

At the checkout counter, I let them know to call up at ten to wake him, and I give them strict instructions not to give out my name. The guy behind the counter smirks and assures me that guest privacy is of utmost importance. With a mumbled "Thank you," I roll my suitcase out front to wait for the shuttle to the airport.

CHAPTER 5

Reid

I DON'T HAVE TO OPEN MY EYES TO KNOW SHE'S GONE. THE ROOM no longer feels charged. Instead, it's cold and empty. I wish I could lie here and bask in the time we shared, but I have a flight to catch, and I need to see for myself that I'm right.

Slowly, I peel my eyes open. The spot next to me, where I fell asleep with her in my arms, is cold. The sun is shining through the windows, and if I had to guess, my dream girl is long gone. A faint trace of her perfume lingers in the air—lavender and something I can't name—but it's already fading. I stare at the ceiling for a moment longer than necessary, hoping that maybe I'll hear the soft pad of her feet returning from the bathroom. But the silence is loud.

She's not here.

That doesn't stop me from tossing off the covers, searching the bathroom, and even the small closet. It's ridiculous, but what if she was planning to get a jump scare out of me or something? I know that I'm reaching, but fuck, I met the woman of my dreams, had the most incredible night of sex of my life, only to wake up alone.

I had plans. I wanted to get her number, find out where she was from, and make arrangements to see her again. Sure, the season is gearing up, but I could make it work. For her, I would make it work. However, she took that away from me by sneaking out of this room like a thief in the night. That's when it hits me that this was her room. Surely, I can charm the front desk into giving me her details—at least her last name. I can start my search from there.

The phone rings, and my heart lurches. Could that be her? I scramble to answer. "Hello?"

"This is the front desk. We were asked to give you a wake-up call," a soft, feminine voice says. Not Bellamy's voice.

"Thanks," I mutter, and hang up without saying goodbye. It's rude, I know, but I can't help it. I guess I should be glad she thought to have them give me a wake-up call. Otherwise, I could have been sleeping the day away, which isn't something I usually do, but last night was a long, intense one, and we both needed rest. I should be happy she was thinking of me when she snuck out undetected.

I need a shower and to go back to my room. Begrudgingly, I get dressed in my clothes from yesterday and take one last look around the room. I see something sticking out from the bottom of the bed. Moving, I reach under and grab it, seeing that it's her panties. Fuck me. I can't just leave them here, right? I mean, what if some perv comes along and wants to beat his meat with them? Nope, not happening. Decision made, I slide the white lace into my pocket as I make my way to the door. I hesitate, my hand on the knob, the weight of memories settling on my shoulders like a winter coat. Twisting the knob, I rush out of the room and to the elevator to take me to my room two floors up.

Twenty minutes later, with Bellamy's thong tucked safely into my luggage, I roll up to the front desk. "Hey, man, I was hoping you could help me out." I flash a grin, not that I think it will work on him, but I'm going to try regardless.

"Sure thing, Mr. Montgomery. What can we do for you?"

Here goes nothing. "There was this girl. Room 1302, I didn't get a chance to get her number."

The attendant smiles. "There's always a girl." He chuckles. "Unfortunately, it's against privacy policies to give out that kind of information." His face is a mask of a man who is not willing to break the rules—just my luck. I mean, I get it, it's his job, and it's against the law, but damn, I need to find her.

"Right. Of course. Thank you." I knew it was a long shot, and I briefly consider trying to bribe him, but that's the last thing I need in the headlines. *Tight End for the Nashville Rampage was arrested for bribing a hotel attendant, trying to get private information on a female guest.* Yeah, no thanks. I'll pass on that.

We had a connection. I felt it, and I know she did, too. I can only hope that she comes back into my life in some way. That's fate, right? Meeting again in the most unexpected way? My dream girl had better be ready. If I ever see her again, I won't be letting her get away so easily the second time. I'll get her last name, her number, and maybe, if I'm lucky, I might be able to win her heart.

"How was the wedding?" Knox asks.

We're sitting outside on Landry's back patio. The ladies, Corie, Rowan, and Sloane, are in the pool. We were supposed to be playing poker, but none of us were feeling it. Instead, we're sitting here sipping on beers, shooting the shit.

"It was good. Landon's all smiles, and his wife, Tessa, is great. Case was his usual horndog self," I say, laughing as I think about Case hitting on the female bartender.

"Hook up with any bridesmaids?" Landry asks.

Instantly, memories of my time with Bellamy flash through my mind. It's been nothing but the Bellamy show in my head since that night. It's only been a few days, but I can't seem to stop thinking about her. "Nah, it was a small wedding. The matron of honor was there, but so was her husband. It was chill." That's not a lie—it was chill. The wedding was nice, and the night was spent with the most incredible woman I've ever met. How much more chill could it have been?

Camden leans over toward me, holding out his little arms, and I take him from his dad. "Hey, little man," I say, bouncing him on my knee. He giggles, and damn, he's the best medicine for my mopey ass.

"What gives?" Baker asks.

"What do you mean?" I keep my eyes on Camden, making funny faces at him. It's better than facing his daddy. Landon, Case, and I were tight all through college, and we still are. But these four guys, they're in my life day in and day out. My closest friends, even closer than Landon or Case, and they know me well enough to know that I'm being a mopey asshole. It's not something they're used to seeing from me. I'm the one who's laughing, smiling, and having a good time. But that's hard to do when I'm caught in my head.

"Come on now, Montgomery," Landry says. "You can't hide behind the cuteness that is our nephew."

Camden might not be our nephew by blood, but damn if we all don't love him as if he were. Family isn't always blood. "I'm not." My defense is weak at best, and I know that the guys can see right through me.

"Don't make me bring my wife over here," Knox warns, and I can't help it; I laugh.

Corie is not only Knox's wife, but Landry's little sister. She knows us all well, and it's nothing for her to bat her pretty green eyes to get us to spill. Add in Rowan, Landry's wife, and Sloane, Corie's best friend, and I wouldn't stand a chance.

"Fine, there might have been a woman," I say, making another silly face at Camden, which he rewards me with a giggle.

"And?" Foster asks.

Sloane appears beside me, holding her hands out for Camden. "Y'all have been hogging him all night. It's our turn."

I wait for her to comment about my confession, but it never comes. She's only here to steal my little buddy.

"Release the baby, Montgomery!" Corie calls out.

"No, he's mine." I hold Camden against my chest and wiggle him around. His laughter fills the air around us. Damn, I love this kid.

"Don't make us come over there!" Rowan adds.

"See." Sloane smirks, and she lifts Camden from my arms and snuggles him. He rests his head on her shoulder, and she carries him to where Corie and Rowan are now sitting in lounge chairs, waiting for their turn.

"Thief!" I call after her. Sloane just tosses her hand up in the air in a wave.

"The woman?" Baker prompts.

Huffing out a breath, I close my eyes, tilt my head back against the chair, and start to talk. I tell them about Bellamy sitting next to me at the bar, how we walked on the beach, and ended back at the bar, talking the night away, until the bartender kicked us out. I tell them how incredible she is.

I open my eyes and meet each one of theirs before saying, "She didn't recognize me. I was just Reid." Knox and Landry both hum their agreement. They know what it's like to find ladies who don't have a single fuck to give about the zeros in our bank accounts.

"Are you sure?" Baker asks. If anyone is going to be skeptical, it's going to be him. He's the one sharing his son with a one-night stand, but that's a story for another day.

"I'm positive. No hint at all, and we went back to her room. Not mine. She even tried to pay for her drinks." I don't tell them that we slept together, but I'm sure they can read between the lines.

"So, what's the issue here?" Knox asks. "Are you missing her that bad? Call her, man. We have a few weeks left before training camp starts. Go see her. Wherever she is." His eyes glance over to where his wife is now holding Camden, and a goofy smile lights up his face.

"Yeah, about that. I don't have her number."

"What?" Landry asks.

"We didn't share last names or numbers. Hell, I guess her name might not even be Bellamy, but her eyes were honest. The things we talked about. It wasn't just surface level, although there was some of that, too."

"Tell me you didn't slip out on her," Knox says.

"Nope. She got the slip on me," I confess. "I thought I had more time. I thought I'd wake up with her in my arms, just how we fell asleep, and I could tell her that I wanted to see her again, but I didn't get the chance. Guys, I'm telling you, she was unlike anyone I've ever met before. Not getting her name or her number will be the biggest regret of my life."

"What about sleeping through her sneaking out?" Foster twists the knife that's already tearing me up inside just a little more.

"Yeah, that too. We were up late, and I guess I was either dead to the world or she was quiet as a mouse as she slipped out of her room." I don't tell them about her thong or the wake-up call. Those aren't important, at least not to this conversation. Those pieces of her, of our time together, are just for me.

A wake-up call might sound lame to hold on to, but she cared enough to make sure I was up. If I were just someone she was never going to see again, someone who didn't mean anything, she wouldn't have done that, right?

"So, what are we going to do?" Baker asks me.

"What do you mean? I already tried to get the hotel to tell me who she was, but I failed. The guy wasn't breaking the rules for me. I didn't press because I don't need that headline circling the globe."

"Good choice," Foster agrees.

"There's nothing I can do." I shrug.

"You could hire a private investigator," Landry suggests. "She was attending a wedding there, as well, right? There has to be a way for someone to find out who she is."

"Yeah, but if she wanted him to know, she would have told him," Foster counters. "There was a reason she slipped out while he was sleeping."

"I hate to admit it, but Foster's right. I don't want to invade her privacy like that. Besides, maybe it's a fate kind of thing. If we ever cross paths again, I won't let her go so easily a second time."

"You think that will happen?" Foster asks, furrowing his brow. It's almost as if his mind is somewhere else, as if the question is about more than me and my dream girl.

"I don't know, but I'd like to think so. She's the only woman I've ever met who's made me want to know everything about her, to spend every minute with her, and that was all within a handful of hours."

"What happens if you meet someone?" Knox asks.

"Yeah, you never know when someone is going to enter your life that changes things," Landry agrees, glancing over his shoulder where his wife is now getting her turn with Camden.

"I won't." There is conviction in my tone. "Guys, I'm telling you... she's my dream girl. We have so much in common. The things we want out of life, weddings, kids, music, food, all of it. And we're compatible in other ways, too. As in no one in my past exists before her."

"I met a girl like that once," Knox says, his voice smug. "I married her."

"Same," Landry agrees.

"Yeah, so if I'm lucky, I'll get to see her again, and when I do, I'll make damn sure to get her name."

"And until then?" Baker asks.

"He gets through the day," Foster answers for me.

There's something there with him. He keeps dropping these subtle hints, but none of us press him. Foster is one of those people who won't open up until he's ready. He knows we're here for him when he is.

"He's right," I agree. "I just have to keep going through the motions. But if that day ever comes, I'll make sure she understands that in one night, she changed something inside me. She made me fall for her, and while I can't say that it's love I'm feeling, I know I want to get to know her better. I want more of her time and her laughter. I want it all, and I can be patient when I need to be."

"If you need help learning the play, we've got you." Landry nods.

I laugh. "Thanks, man." I'm not going to tell him I don't need his help, because honestly, I don't know. I could be dreaming, living in a fantasy land where my dream girl comes back to me. The chances of us meeting again are slim to none, but I have hope. The kind of chemistry we shared is once in a lifetime. Surely, the universe will bring that back to me, right? Back to us? It sounds out of reach even to my own ears, but I'm not giving up hope. Not yet. I told Bellamy that if I ever met my dream girl, I'd hold on tight. My grip was loose the first time around. The second, I'll be sure she knows my intentions.

I just hope I get the chance. In the meantime, maybe I should take Landry up on his offer and learn the play. I don't know much about being in a relationship, nothing really, except for the fact that I want one with her.

With my dream girl.

CHAPTER 6

Bellamy

It's been two weeks since I slipped out of my hotel room, quiet as a mouse. Two weeks, and I haven't stopped thinking about the man I left behind. His presence still lingers in my thoughts, a quiet echo that refuses to fade. No matter how hard I've tried to forget him, I can't.

It's as if my mind and my body have decided that no other man exists in the world, at least not for me. I've never had the kind of connection with anyone as I did with Reid. It's alarming and surprising, because let's face it, men are jerks. Okay, maybe not all of them, and yes, I can admit that my opinions are skewed because of my father, who put his career above his family.

I don't know what it's going to take to get this man out of my head. The memory of my time with him is distracting me. Yesterday, my boss, Grant, was standing at my office door, watching me stare off into space. I'll give you one guess as to what I was thinking about. Luckily, Grant Riggins and his brothers are laid back and easy to work for. He teased me for it, asked me his question, and then disappeared back into his office.

Something's got to give. I can't keep this up. Reid was just a man. A man who will forever hold a piece of my past, one I'll never forget, but it was my choice to sneak out, so I need to deal with the consequences and stop thinking about a stranger I'll never see again.

My phone rings, pulling me out of my thoughts, and I answer without seeing who it is.

"Bellamy? I expected your voicemail," my dad greets me. From the sound of his voice, he's happy he reached me.

Inwardly, I groan. Fucking Reid and his sexy abs. He distracted me again, because my dad's right, he would have gotten my voicemail otherwise. "Hi," I say, trying to keep the annoyance out of my tone.

"It's so good to hear your voice, sweetheart."

Good thing he can't see me rolling my eyes. "What's up?" I ask, not bothering with pleasantries. Not with him. He made his choice.

"How have you been?" he asks.

"Fine."

He sighs, and the sound is heavy even through the line. "Listen, there's this work thing—the one I mentioned to you last summer. I'd really love it if you would come. It's family day," he explains.

"I wish I could, but I'm busy."

"I didn't tell you when it was," he counters.

"Work is swamped right now, Dad."

"It's the first week of July—in two weeks. Sweetheart, I'd really love to see you," he says, and I can hear the longing in his voice, but he's about fifteen years too late.

"Sorry," I tell him, even though I'm not. I don't know if I'll ever be able to forgive him for leaving us. He put his job first, leaving Mom and me on our own.

"I'll send you the details, in case you change your mind. I really hope you do."

"We'll see," I tell him, just like my mom used to when I'd ask for something when I was little and she damn well knew I wasn't going to get it. I should feel guilty for giving him an inch of false hope, but in his gut, he knows that I won't be there. It's going to take a hell of a lot more than an invitation to a work thing, as he called it, to move our relationship forward.

Sure, he calls and texts frequently, but it's the effort he puts into coming to see me that he's always lacked motivation for. Calls and messages are fast, and he can get right back to work.

"You can bring a friend, or if you're seeing anyone…," he offers, his voice trailing off.

"Not seeing anyone," I tell him with a sigh. And the last man I did see is the only reason I answered this call, but I keep that to myself.

"I hope you've been well," he says, and the longing once again present in his tone giving me pause.

"Yeah, I'm good. I was in Los Angeles two weeks ago for a college friend's wedding," I tell him, tossing him a bone of information about me. It's not something I usually do, and something twists in my gut when his tone tells me he's glad that I did.

"That's wonderful. I hope you had a great time, and I'm sure it was nice getting to catch up with a friend from college."

"She was kind of a bridezilla," I confess, because the alternative is blurting out that I met a man, spent an incredible night with him, then ran scared at what he made me feel in just a matter of hours. Not a conversation I want to have, especially with my father.

"Oh, well, did you get to visit the ocean?"

Twist the knife, Dad. "Yeah, the ocean was nice. Took a walk on the beach my last night there. Hey, I have a few things I need to finish up today before I head home, so I need to go," I tell him, glancing at the clock. It's true, but I really just want to end this uncomfortable conversation.

"Good. Good. Well, I hope to see you in two weeks. I'll send you all the information."

"Okay."

"I love you, sweetheart."

"See you," I tell him, ending the call and tossing my phone on my desk. I have so much anger in my chest where my father is concerned. I hate being a bitch—that's not who I am at all—but I don't know how to get past this pain.

My phone vibrates, and I don't have to look to know it's my father, but I do anyway.

> Sperm Donor: Attached is the flyer with all the information.
> I hope to see you there.

Instead of looking at the flyer, I close out of the message and text my best friend, Amanda.

> Me: Drinks. My place.

> Amanda: Tough week?

> Me: Something like that.

> Amanda: I had plans to be on your couch when you got home anyway. You've been avoiding me.

> Me: Lies. I'd never avoid my bestie.

She's right. I've been avoiding her because I'm unsure how to break the news to her about Reid, and the silence feels wrong. Then, telling her the details about that night also feels bad. Selfishly, I want to keep Reid and our time together just for me.

> Amanda: Uh-huh. I'll bring dinner. Any requests?

> Me: Anything. I'll stop and grab the wine, and plan on staying.

I make a mental note to grab a couple of bottles of wine. Something tells me I'm going to need them.

Amanda: Sounds like a plan. See you soon.

Tossing my phone back on my desk, I push Reid, my dad, and even my best friend out of my mind so I can concentrate, finish my work, and start the weekend.

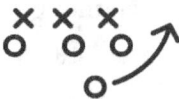

Just as she promised, Amanda is sitting on my couch when I get home. "Hey," I greet her. "Have you been here long?"

"Nope. Maybe five minutes." She points to the coffee table with two pizza boxes, two plates, a stack of napkins, and two coffee mugs. "Gave me time to get set up."

"Perfect Pies," I say with a groan. "It's been forever since I've had their pizza."

"We ate there before you left for Los Angeles for Tabby's wedding." Amanda laughs.

"Right? That was over two weeks ago." Kicking off my shoes, I drop my bag next to the recliner, place the wine bag on the coffee table next to our dinner, and join my best friend on the couch. "I need to change, but I need Perfect Pies pizza more." Tossing open a box, I slap a slice on a plate, then open the next box, add a couple of breadsticks with sauce, and hand it to Amanda before doing the same for me.

"Damn, that's good," Amanda says after finishing her first bite.

"Good choice," I tell her, taking a massive bite. "How was your week?"

"Same old."

"Booked any hot talent lately?" I ask her. Amanda is a talent coordinator, and she's always finding great new artists to bring into their bar.

"I don't pick them based on their looks." She sticks her tongue out at me.

"Oh, I know they have to sound good, too, but you get all those headshots to drool over all day, while I get to look at shipping and inventory reports." Don't get me wrong, I love my job. The Riggins family is incredible to work for, and even though they're all madly in love with their wives, they're easy on the eyes. Still, Amanda gets hundreds of demo tapes a week that almost always come with headshots, and some of them are drool-worthy. My bestie has a fun job.

"The worst part is when they have the look, but their voice just doesn't match it. It makes me feel bad to turn them down, but we only have so many days in a week for me to get talent on the stage."

"You book talent for one of the hottest bars on the strip. You're damn good at what you do. Don't feel bad about having to say no. That's just a part of it."

"I know, but you should read some of the letters. They talk about struggles, like living in their cars, and that hits me in my feels."

"I love your soft heart," I tell her.

"Enough about me." She places her now-empty plate on the coffee table and pours us both some wine into the coffee mugs.

"Why are we using coffee mugs?" I ask her.

"I don't know. I guess it felt like wineglasses were too fancy for pizza and breadsticks on the couch."

"I don't care what I'm drinking it out of, as long as I'm drinking it."

"About that, are you ready to share what's been going on with you?"

"Whatever do you mean?" I ask, taking a hefty sip of my wine.

"Bellamy." Her tone holds a warning, one that I take, because she's my best friend, and I know I can trust her with this.

"The wedding was a pain in the ass, just as I thought it would be." Might as well start with the stuff that I know she's already assuming happened.

"I told you to tell her no. Just because you were sorority sisters in college does not mean you have to fly across the country to be bossed around to be in her wedding. And, you haven't talked to her since you graduated from college." She gives me a pointed look.

"I know." I sigh. "You're right. She was just as bad as I had imagined that she would be. As soon as all my bridesmaid duties were over, I dashed and hit the hotel bar."

"Ah." Amanda turns to face me, crossing her legs. "Now, this is where the story gets interesting. Please proceed." She waves her hand in the air as if she's royal, before taking a big chug of her wine.

"If me rushing out of the wedding like my ass was on fire, only to plop down at the oceanside bar and order a drink is interesting, then yeah, I guess so."

"Girl, I see right through you. What was his name?"

I open my mouth to lie, and the truth comes out. "Reid. Don't ask me for his last name because I don't know. We didn't exchange anything but first names. Hell, Reid might not even be his real name."

"Did you give him your real name?"

"I did. He didn't give off creeper vibes, and he was—I don't know—easy to talk to, I guess."

"How much time did the two of you spend talking?"

"All night. Well, most of it. We ended up taking a walk on the beach. We sat for a while and talked, and then ended up back at the bar, in the same seats we were in before we walked on the beach, and talked until the bartender announced the last call and kicked us out."

"And?"

"And what?"

"Bellamy!" she scolds.

"Fine. He was gorgeous, Manda. He has messy, dirty-blond hair, and he's not a surfer; he wasn't from LA. He's got lots of ink, his muscles have muscles, and his eyes are ocean blue, sometimes light, sometimes dark."

"And how would you know that, hmm?" she asks.

"Well, I might have invited him back to my room after he refused to let me pay for my drinks."

"You make it sound like the drinks are what sold you, when I know it was the ink and the muscles, and those eyes of his sound like a damn good bonus." She smirks.

"It was the whole package. He was sweet and charming, and we talked about everything. Not just small talk like the weather, but it was deeper. I even told him about my dad."

"Wow, he must have been a charmer."

"He was, but he wasn't. I mean, I didn't get the vibe that he was trying to charm me, you know? He was just being him, and that was more than enough."

"So, you invited him back to your room."

"I did."

"Bella," she warns.

"We spent the night together. It was... the hottest night of my life," I confess.

"Are you going to make plans to see him again? Where's he from?"

"I don't know."

"Okay, but you got his number, right? When a man has those kinds of skills in the bedroom, you make sure you have a way to reach him."

I wince. "Unless you're me, and you have daddy issues, which relate to pushing those issues on every man, and you sneak out before the sun has barely risen, leaving him sleeping in the bed in your hotel room."

"Bellamy!"

"I even made it a point to tell the front desk attendant not to give my information out to him, but I did have them schedule a wake-up call so he wouldn't miss checkout."

"So, let me get this straight. You met a man—one who didn't annoy you and one you trusted—you had great chemistry with, in and out of the bedroom, you don't know his last name, you don't know where he's from, and you didn't get his number?"

"That about sums it up."'

"Girl, what were you thinking?"

"I don't know, okay? I panicked. I felt too much. It was too much too soon, and I had to leave."

"What if he was the one?"

"What?"'

"The one!" Her eyes widen dramatically. "The one man who was meant for you, and you left him all blissed out in a deep sleep. He's going to pine after you for the rest of his life, and you'll both be lonely and miserable because you were too afraid to pick up your big girl panties and see where things might go."

"He probably lives in Washington or something, too far for us to be able to make it work. And speaking of big girl panties, I left without mine. I got dressed, looked for my clothes in the dark room, and didn't realize until I was home that I was missing something."

"Oh, I bet he found them and took them with him. He holds them in his hands every night as he drifts off to sleep, dreaming about you."

"Stop." I push her arm, laughing at her. "That's not happening. He might have taken them, but I doubt it. I'm sure he was angry that I left. He admitted he wasn't the one-night stand type, not since college."

"Wow, you all did talk about everything."

"We did. Now, the issue is that I can't stop thinking about him. I remember every moment. It's so bad that Grant busted me daydreaming earlier this week, and today was even worse. My dad called, and I was lost in thought, so I answered before checking to see who it was," I grumble.

"How is Daddy Will?" she asks, waggling her eyebrows.

"No. Just no."

"Come on, Bella, you know your dad's hot."

"Can we not, please?" I beg her.

"Fine. What did your father want?" she asks.

"He's got this work thing again that he wants me to go to with him. He even said I could bring a friend or a date if I wanted to. I ended up telling him I wasn't dating and that I was at Tabby's wedding a couple of weeks ago. I gave him way more than I usually do."

"Oh, he invited you last year, too, right?"

"He did."

"When is it?"

Grabbing my phone, I pull up his message and hand it to her. She reads over the screen, and a slow smile tugs at her lips.

"We're going to this. I'll be your plus one."

"What? No. No, we are not going. I don't want to go and pretend to be the dutiful daughter to a man who left us."

"We'll be friendly, shake a few hands, smile, eat some good food, then post up and watch the eye candy."

"Manda," I groan.

"Please? For me? Besides, your dad's been trying the best way he knows how to connect with you. I know you're still angry with him, and I'd never tell you to forgive him, but he is your dad, and he's trying. Even your mom said that you should have gone last year."

"Ugh," I groan because I know that she's right. "Why do you want to go so badly?"

"The eye candy, of course." She grins. "And I'd love to see my bestie be able to reconnect with her father."

"I don't want to go," I whine.

"I'll be there. We say hi, shake a few hands, and then we disappear into the crowd. Come on, it'll be fun."

"Fine, we'll go."

She grins as she opens up my phone, and her fingers fly across the screen. The whooshing sound of a message being sent hits me as she hands me my phone.

Me: Amanda and I will be there.

He replies immediately.

Sperm Donor: Really? Oh, sweetheart, I'm glad. I can't wait to see you.

"Fuck my life," I mutter, before grabbing another piece of pizza. I might as well eat my feelings.

CHAPTER 7

Reid

THE SUN IS SHINING BRIGHT, AND THERE'S LAUGHTER GOING on all around me. I smile when I'm supposed to, join in on conversations when appropriate, but after four very long weeks, I'm still thinking about her.

About Bellamy.

My dream girl.

At first, I thought my need for her stemmed from her walking away, but it's more than that. Of course, I knew that all along. She made me feel, and that's not something anyone before her has ever done. I was only trying to convince myself otherwise. Side note: It didn't work.

"How'd you convince Natasha to let you have our little buddy for today?" Knox asks Baker, holding Camden's hands as he stands on wobbly legs, bouncing up and down on his knees.

Baker scoffs. "She asked me. I was going to call her and ask her if I could have him just for today, but she beat me to it. There's another shoot in Paris she just 'had to go to.' It's not even her shoot. She just wants to be there," he says, frustration in his tone. "I don't care, because it gives me more time with my son. She's missing out on time we'll never get back. I'm sadder for him than her, but thankfully, he's young enough that he won't remember. I worry that when he is, he'll start to resent her."

"You can't worry about that," Rowan, Landry's wife, tells him. "You have to do what you can. Love him, never talk ill of her to him, and whatever happens, happens. You can't make her want more time with him. Besides, he has us." She nods to where Corie and her best friend, Sloane, are sitting across from her.

"Yeah, so hand him over." Corie holds her arms out for Knox to pass Camden to her.

"We need to give Camden a baby cousin," Knox answers, not handing the baby over to his wife.

"Fine. Gimme." She motions for Camden to come to her, and he leans over, falling into her arms, knowing she'd never let him fall.

"Wait, did you just…" Knox's voice trails off, his mouth hanging open in shock.

"You keep saying we need a baby. I'm pretty sure you know how it's done, big guy. If not, I'm sure Daddy Sin can give you some tips." Corie smirks at her husband.

Knox stands from his chair. "Hand off the baby. We gotta go."

Corie's head tips back in laughter. "Sit down, Beckett. We're not going anywhere. It will happen when it happens."

"But we should start practicing," he tells her.

We're all laughing at him, but Knox is as serious as I've ever seen him. He's ready for this. He's ready for them to start a family, and from the lovesick look in Corie's eyes, she's more than on board, but she's not leaving. Not yet, anyway.

"Today is family day," she reminds him.

"Fine," Knox grumbles as he sits back in his seat.

"Who's been walking around with Coach Warner all day?" Landry asks.

He prides himself on knowing all the gossip within the Rampage facility. He's buddied up with Harry, the head of maintenance, and together, the two of them gossip like a bunch of hens. But if you need to know something, they're the two you go to. I'm certain whoever this newcomer is, it's annoying the hell out of him that he doesn't know her or how she fits into our Rampage family.

"Maybe one of them is his girl." Foster shrugs.

"Nah, too young for him."

"Age is just a number," Sloane fires back.

"He could be their dad," Landry counters.

"Maybe they have a daddy kink?" Rowan shrugs.

"Roe," Landry warns, making his wife laugh.

I love that my best friends are happily married, but it's depressing as hell. It's been four very long weeks of not being able to stop thinking about someone who's a stranger to me, outside of the one incredible night we spent together. It might have only been a handful of hours, but I feel as if I've known her for years. She's cast her spell on me, and I don't know if I'll ever break out of it.

"Whoever they are, they must be important," Landry muses. "He's going from group to group, introducing them."

"You'll find out soon enough," I tell him, making sure I'm engaging in the conversation. To be honest, I couldn't care less who Coach Warner is showing around. Unless she's my dark-haired, sparkling-brown-eyed beauty from Los Angeles, I'm not interested.

Baker whistles. "If they are the coach's ladies, he's got damn good taste."

"I mean, if he's getting double the action, maybe he'll take it easy on us in training camp." Foster laughs.

"Nah," Knox says. "He's a hard-ass when it comes to the game, and we don't want him any other way. We're looking for a three-pete, fellas."

"Hell yeah, we are." Landry bumps fists with Knox.

"Looks like we're next," Baker says.

"Ah, and here we have a few more of my starters," Coach Warner says. He goes around the table introducing everyone, and when he gets to me, I turn to be polite and freeze.

Standing next to Coach Warner is Bellamy, my dream girl. The woman I can't stop thinking about. "Bellamy?" I know it's her, but it comes out like a question because I can't believe she's here.

"R-Reid. Hi." She waves, her face flaming.

"You know my daughter?" Coach Warner asks, crossing his arms over his chest.

Fuck yes, I do. "Yeah, she's my dream girl," I tell him, pushing back from the table and standing. I can hear my friends talking all around me. They know from my words alone that this is her. Fate brought her back to me.

The woman standing next to Bellamy is smirking as she steps back, allowing me to get closer. I don't stop until I pull her into a hug. "Missed you, Bell," I say just low enough for her to hear. Her audible intake of breath tells me all I need to know—she didn't know I'd be here. Everything we shared that night was genuine. I can only hope now that she knows what I do for a living, she's still willing to stick around.

Wait. Oh, fuck!

She's the coach's daughter. My dream girl hates football.

Fuck me.

"How do you know my tight end?" Coach Warner asks Bellamy.

Sliding my arm around her waist, I answer for her, since she seems to be in shock. "We met a few weeks ago, four to be exact, at a wedding in Los Angeles. I didn't know she was from Nashville. We talked about everything but last names and where we were from." I look down at Bellamy, and she must feel my gaze because her eyes collide with mine. "I wasn't sure I'd ever see you again, but here you are. Fate brought you back to me."

"Aww," Corie says, but I don't pull my eyes from Bellamy.

"Montgomery," Coach growls.

I hate to, but I tear my gaze from Bellamy to face him. "What's up, Coach?"

"Take your hands off my daughter."

"Coach, did you miss the part where I told you she was my dream girl?"

"We should go," Bellamy says, stepping out of my hold—at least she tries to.

"Oh no, sweetheart. You slipped away once without me getting your number. I'm a man who learns from his mistakes, and I won't be making that one a second time."

"You don't want my number. I—I don't date football players." She scrunches up her nose, as if the thought alone disgusts her.

Looks like I've got my work cut out for me, but that's okay. I'm up for the challenge. I know what I felt that night. I know what we shared. And she does, too. That's why she slipped out before I was awake, and why she's trying to run now. It was intense and bold, but I'm not afraid of it. All I have to do is prove that to her.

"Bro, Coach has smoke coming out of his ears," Landry jokes.

"Sorry, Coach, but I need to talk to our girl for a minute." Not giving anyone a chance to stop me, I guide Bellamy several feet away, thankful that she comes willingly.

"What are you doing?" she asks. She's not angry, but she doesn't look thrilled to see me either.

"I didn't think you'd want to have this conversation in front of your dad."

"Sperm donor," she mutters.

"Yeah, I didn't know Coach had a daughter." Hurt flashes in her eyes, and I immediately regret my words. "I'm sorry, babe." I pull her into my arms. At first, she's tense, but then her body relaxes into mine. "I'm sorry.

That was insensitive." She lets me hold her for a few more seconds before she pulls away. "I can't believe you're here."

"Reid." She sighs. "It was one night."

"Bullshit. It was every fucking thing, at least admit that."

"Fine. It was… something, but you're a football player. Not just any football player, you play for my dad. The man who left my mom and me for his career. You remember that, right? The man who's your coach left his family."

"It was more than something, and yes, there isn't a moment of that night that I don't remember."

"One-night stand."

"See, that's what you thought. Sure, that's what we said, but that night with you changed me. I had plans to wake you up slowly, spend time holding you, and I wanted to tell you that a single night with you would never be enough. I wanted to get your number, your last name, and no matter where in the world you were, we'd make it work, because there's a spark between us, one unlike anything I've ever felt before, and I don't want to just let that pass us by. I think we owe it to ourselves to see what happens when we let the sparks ignite."

"I don't date football players."

"I'm more than just my job, Bellamy. I'm still the man you spent the evening talking to about everything. I'm still the same man you spent the night with. Football is my job. I can't change that, and I don't want to change that. I love the game, but does that mean I don't deserve to find love?"

"Football took my dad from me, Reid." Her voice cracks. "I hate the game, and after fifteen years, I'm still struggling to forgive my father and let him into my life. I didn't even want to be here today. I let my best friend, Amanda, talk me into coming. Why should I care about the sport that took my dad from me? He chose football, Reid. He chose his career, and I can't do that again. I won't." She crosses her arms over her chest, just as her father did when he was glaring at me moments ago, but I keep that similarity to myself. I'm certain that pointing it out wouldn't help my case of getting more time with her.

I need to tread lightly here. "I'm not your dad, Bellamy. I'm me. I'm a man who met his dream girl, and all I want to do is spend more time with you. I want to take you on a date. No, lots of dates. I want to spend hours talking to you, getting to know you better. I want to hold you while we sleep, and I want more of you, any fucking way I can have you."

"You don't mean that." She looks off into the distance to avoid my gaze.

"Bell?" I take her hand in mine, giving it a soft squeeze. Her eyes come back to me—my brown-eyed girl. "I do mean that. It's been four weeks since that night, and you're all I can think about. Ask my friends. I told them about you. I told them you were my dream girl, and that I hoped one day you'd come back to me."

"Right," she scoffs.

Pulling my phone out of my pocket, I call Knox. He picks up immediately. "Can you come over here?"

"On my way."

I end the call, shoving my phone back into my pocket.

"What are you doing?" she asks, panic in her tone.

"I want him to tell you who you are to me." Knox is the calmest and most serious of the five of us, next to Foster, and then Baker, who became more serious when he found out he was going to be a dad. Damn, maybe I should have called him over. He could be the perfect example of a father who can have a career.

Oh well, too late to change my mind now.

"I'm your one-night stand, Reid. That's who I am."

Fuck, she's killing me here. I can see it in her eyes. She wants to fall into me, just as badly as I want her to, but she's fighting it. She's set on football players being bad, and it's going to take a damn hard fight to change her mind.

"What's up?" Knox says, his eyes bouncing from me to Bellamy.

"This is Bellamy. Bellamy, this is my quarterback, and one of my best friends, Knox Beckett."

"Nice to meet you." Knox offers Bellamy his hand, and she takes it.

"You too," she says politely, but she's guarded.

"Knox, what do you know about Bellamy?"

He raises a brow. "What do you mean?"

"What have I told you about her?" I ask him.

Understanding passes between us. "Well, you said you met a beautiful woman named Bellamy at Landon's wedding, and you called her your dream girl. You had some drinks, walked on the beach, and closed down the bar together."

"Thanks, man." I nod.

"I hope to see you again soon, Bellamy," he says, before turning and walking away.

I watch as he leaves, and my eyes land on my coach. He's staring daggers at me, but her best friend is all smiles. That's encouraging. Turning my back to them, I block her view. I want all of her attention on me.

"Say something."

"Reid, we can't do this."

"We can. You have to let us. Give me your number. We'll start slow, but it's just you and me. No others between us while we figure this out."

"You expect me to believe that?"

"Your dad didn't cheat, Bellamy. He worked too much. Just because I'm a football player doesn't mean I don't know how to keep my dick in my pants. You can't just lump me in with your dad or every other football player you've heard bad things about. That's not fair to either of us."

"How is that not fair to me?" she asks, just as I was hoping that she would.

"You're robbing yourself of the opportunity to see what this is between us. Even if we don't end up dating." We totally will. "I'm a pretty awesome guy." This makes her crack a smile, but she quickly schools her features.

"I should get back."

"Please?" That single word stops her. Her big brown eyes, with diamonds in the center, find mine and hold. "We take this at your pace. Let's exchange numbers. We'll start there."

"Reid." She hangs her head, and on instinct, I pull her back into my chest, wrapping my arms around her. "You're making this harder than it needs to be," she says, her voice muffled against my chest, but I can still hear her.

"Because you're my dream girl. Do you remember what I told you that night?"

"You said a lot of things."

"You know what I'm asking," I say, pressing my lips to the top of her head. Fuck, I can't believe she's here in my arms.

"You said if you ever found your dream girl, you'd make sure that she and your kids knew they were your everything," she finally says.

"Give me the chance to show you. I know your father crushed your heart, but I promise you, I'm not him. I'll do whatever you need to prove that to you. I don't care how long it takes, or what kind of hoops you make me jump through, I can learn the play, Bellamy."

"If I give you my number, will you let me go?"

"Today. I'll let you go today," I correct her, because I'm not giving this woman an inch for her to take a mile. I'm also going to have to learn to sleep with one eye open if I'm ever lucky enough to get her into my bed.

"Give me your phone." I don't bother to hide my smile as I hand it to her and rattle off my code. She freezes, and I smirk. "I have nothing to hide." I shrug. She drops her head to enter her number and hands my phone back to me. Immediately, I search for her contact and hit dial. Her pocket rings, and I nod to her to answer. She rolls those beautiful brown eyes, but retrieves her phone from her pocket and answers.

"Hello?"

"I missed you," I tell her, my eyes locked on hers.

"Is it possible to miss someone you barely know?"

"You tell me. Did you miss me, Bell?"

"You have my number," she says instead. "I should get back to Amanda."

She's not worried about her dad, but about her best friend. "Okay, babe, let's go." I end the call, as does she, and lace her fingers through mine. She doesn't pull away, which surprises me, but I'm taking the win all the same.

"Coach, take care of my girl for me."

"Montgomery," he says with a growl, and I chuckle.

"Bellamy, this is my family." I take the time to introduce everyone, even though Coach already did, because these are my people, and she's my girl. I needed to be the one to tell them, and her, the importance that each of them plays in my life. "This is my dream girl, Bellamy," I finally say, after making my way through everyone.

"It's so nice to meet you." Corie, Rowan, and Sloane take turns pulling her into a hug.

"Oh, and this is her best friend, Amanda."

The girls start chatting while I watch them, pretending that my coach isn't staring daggers at me. That's fine. I can take his wrath on or off the field. He might not have thought she was worth fighting for, but I sure as fuck do.

CHAPTER 8

Bellamy

I'VE STEPPED INTO AN ALTERNATE REALITY. A DREAM WORLD, THAT has to be what this is. There's no way that Reid is here and works for my father. The hottest night of my life was with a football player— one of my dad's football players.

"We should exchange numbers," one of the women suggests. I think her name is Corie, but honestly, the last thirty minutes have been a blur. Well, not all of it. I still remember his touch and his words, but who's who is lost on me.

"Oh, um." I don't want to tell them no. They seem nice, but I'm spiraling.

"For sure," Amanda says, jumping in to save me. She rattles off each of our numbers, and our phones beep three times each. I'm guessing they've texted us their numbers.

"You'll have to join us for girls' night. The more the merrier," another says. "We're constantly outnumbered." She points at the group of guys behind them over her shoulder.

"I… I need to go to the restroom." The words are barely out of my mouth before I'm bolting away from them. I don't worry about the scene I'm causing. I just need to get away. I need to breathe. I need air that I'm not sharing with *him*. Air that's not thick with desire and memories of a night that was supposed to remain in my past.

Finally, I spot the bathroom. Slapping my hands against the door, I push inside. Thankfully, it's empty. My legs shake as I make my way to the sink, resting my hands there, and bowing my head.

"Fuck my life," I mutter, just as the door opens. I snap to attention, standing to my full height, trying to pretend like my world didn't just tilt on its axis. Looking in the mirror, I watch for the newcomer, and when I see him, my breath stalls in my lungs.

He takes a few steps but stops short of being within touching distance and holds my gaze in the mirror. "Are you okay?"

"W-What are you doing in here?"

He tilts his head to the side. "You're here."

"Reid," I groan.

"I see those people every day. I just found you again. You were as white as a ghost when you ran off, and I needed to make sure you were okay. Amanda and the girls are outside, but I made them let me come in first."

"Why?" My voice cracks at the question.

My eyes never leave his in the mirror as he steps closer. His steps are soft and slow, as if he's afraid I'll spook, and I'm not so sure that I won't. When he finally reaches me, he wraps his arms around me from behind, pulling me back into his chest. His eyes remain locked on mine.

"I needed to know you were okay," he finally answers, his voice low and soothing.

"It was one night," I remind him.

"Was it? That's not how I remember it."

"Your memory is lacking."

"Hmm," he says, burying his face in my neck and breathing me in.

"I don't think so. You smell the same. Your body feels the same wrapped in my arms, and look at us, Bell, you still fit me perfectly, just like you were made for me."

I open my mouth to argue with him, but he's right. His messy, dirty-blond hair, those vibrant blue eyes, and his inked-up arms look good next to me. I can admit that to myself, but not to him. Before I can form a response, there's a knock at the door, and then footsteps as the door opens.

"Everything okay in here?" Amanda asks, stepping into the bathroom with Corie, Rowan, and Sloane on her heels.

"I'll leave you ladies to it." I watch in the mirror as Reid presses his lips to my temple. "Take care of my girl, yeah?" he asks as he drops his arms from around my waist and steps back. He hesitates before finally walking out of the bathroom.

I exhale a heavy breath. Damn, that sexy, infuriating, intoxicating man.

"Wow," Amanda says, fanning her face with her hands. "You said wedding guy was hot, but you didn't tell me he was *that* hot," she says, making the other three laugh.

"Are you okay, Bellamy?" one of them asks. She steps next to me, placing her hand gently on my arm. "I'm Rowan, Landry's wife."

"I'm sorry," I mumble.

"What? Why on earth are you apologizing?" she asks, her brow furrowed.

"For acting like a fool and running off like that. I just needed a minute."

"Corie." One of them raises her hand. "Knox's wife," she adds helpfully. "First of all, you didn't act like a fool. Secondly, there's no crime in needing a minute to catch your breath. It's obvious that you didn't expect to see Reid here today, or at all."

"No. I didn't expect him to be here, and not at all," I agree with her.

"I know that you don't know us," Corie says. "I know we're strangers to you, but I promise you, Reid's a good man. He came home from that wedding defeated. He's always happy and smiling, but that spark has been missing over the last month."

"Until today," Rowan adds. "The moment he saw you, we had the old Reid back."

"I gotta be honest here," the third one says. "I'm Sloane, by the way, not married to any of the Rampage hotties, but besties with this one since we were kids"—she points at Corie—"and this one because we said so." She laughs as she points at Rowan. "She did marry my pseudo brother, which is her brother, after all." She nods to Corie. "Anyway, back to what I was saying. Honestly, it's hot as hell to see Reid chase after you the way he did. You should have seen that man's face when you jogged off. It was a mix of concern, fear, and determination."

"What?" I shake my head, trying to process her words.

"Concern, because he didn't understand why you ran. Fear, because you were running again, and determination because no matter how fast you tried to run, he was always going to catch you."

"That's not creepy at all," I mutter. I'm thankful they've reintroduced themselves now that I'm coherent enough to remember their names, but of course, they're going to be on his side. They're his family, after all.

"I think it's sweet," Amanda says. "You're too close to this entire situation to see what we see," my best friend says gently.

I don't ask her what she sees because I'm not sure that I want to know. It doesn't matter, because Reid, whose last name I now know is Montgomery, is a professional football player, one who works for my father, or under him, I guess—I'm not exactly sure, but they're together—mixed with the game that stole my family from me. I'll never do that to my potential future children. Never. So, what they see doesn't matter, because Reid and I can never be anything more than a night of shared passion.

"He's a football player."

"I'm guessing there's a story there," Corie muses.

"Yeah," I say, then decide I might as well tell her. "My father left my mom and me for his career. Football ruined my life. I swore I'd never date a professional athlete."

"Rules were meant to be broken, Bellamy," Amanda says gently.

"Not this one." Never this one. Football ruined my life.

"I'm sorry," Rowan says. "But you're wrong." My mouth falls open at her words. "I dated a football player, who emotionally, mentally, and physically abused me. It wasn't his career; it was the man. Now, here I am, married to a football player who would rather cut his own arm off than even consider ever harming me." She pauses, giving me time to process her words, and the bathroom is silent as I do. "I don't know what happened between your parents, but I can tell you it wasn't football that's to blame. It could have been any career. Don't hold someone else's mistakes or shortcomings against Reid."

"He's one of the good ones," Sloane speaks up. "I'm not married or dating any of them, so I feel as though I can speak about this a little better. I'm not biased."

"Your best friends are married to his teammates," I say, still fighting like hell to maintain my hate for the game.

"They are, but I'm not. I can't speak to all athletes, but I do know that those five men out there are loyal to a fault. Whatever you do, whatever reason you don't want to be with Reid, don't let it be his career."

"We're going to go," Corie says. She steps forward and wraps me in a hug. "We're planning on a girls' night once training camp starts. You two are coming," she tells me, then looks at Amanda, who's standing next to me.

"That sounds fun," Amanda replies.

"They won't be there," Rowan assures me.

I nod, because what else can I do? My head is spinning, and to top it off, I still have to go back out there and face my dad. I would just leave, but

I know Amanda would never let me. Not to mention my father will have questions, and I'd rather get that particular line of questioning over with so he's not blowing up my phone or worse, showing up on my doorstep.

"How are you?" Amanda asks once it's just the two of us remaining in the bathroom.

"I don't know."

"Bellamy," she says, in that tone that says, *I know you're lying to me.*

"He made an impression on me before we ever took things back to that hotel suite."

"I know that. You never would have offered for him to come in if he hadn't."

"It's hard for me to wrap my head around the fact that the man I can't stop thinking about is a football player," I admit, scrunching up my nose.

"They're right, you know? He's not his career."

"Everyone is their career."

"To a certain extent, I'll agree with you. But, tell me this, was he the cocky asshole you imagined him to be? Hell, your dad doesn't even fit the bill." She holds her hands up in the air. "I'm not defending him. I don't know all the details of what went on in your parents' marriage, and honestly, neither do you, but I have been there every day since the split, and he's never stopped trying, Bellamy. Not once. You've blown him off, ignored his calls and requests to see you, but he still keeps making an effort."

"He left us," I say, feeling the hot tears prick the back of my eyes.

"I know," she says, hugging me tightly. "But Reid didn't leave you, Bellamy. *You* left *him*, and he's here telling you that he's not going to let you walk away a second time."

"He doesn't get to make that call."

"You're right—he doesn't—but I saw the conviction in that man's eyes. He's going to give you a fight."

"There's nothing to fight over."

"Oh, Bella, it's you, my friend. He's going to fight you for you." She gives me another tight hug and steps back. "I'll give you a few minutes. I'll be right outside waiting for you."

I watch as Amanda leaves, and I turn back to face the mirror. My eyes are glassy with tears, but otherwise, you wouldn't be able to see the turmoil that's churning inside me. I never thought I'd see him again. I'd hoped there might be a way, but deep down, I was convinced it would never happen. Now, here he is, playing a game I hate, playing for my father, who I can't seem to forgive. How is this my life?

Blinking away my tears, I take a few deep, even breaths before pulling open the bathroom door. I expect to find my best friend. Instead, I find Reid standing with his back against the wall, arms crossed at his chest, and legs crossed at his ankles. When he sees me, he stands to his full height and takes one giant step so that he's standing toe to toe with me.

"Hi." He offers me his hand, and hesitantly, I place my palm against his, and we shake. "My name's Reid Montgomery. I'm twenty-nine years old, an only child, and I grew up in Atlanta, Georgia, but now I live here in Nashville. I play tight end for the Nashville Rampage. It's a pleasure to meet you." He gives me a soft smile.

Reid Montgomery.

"What are you doing?" I ask, my voice calm and even, not revealing that my insides are shaking. Being this close to him again, and knowing what we shared that night, being calm is no longer possible.

"What I should have done the night we met. I should have told you who I was and what I did for a living, but, Bell, it was so damn nice just to be Reid, the man. Not the football player. I knew immediately that you didn't recognize me, and I craved that. You're the first woman to see me. We talked and laughed, and by the time we closed down that bar, I knew you were going to change my life. I knew that no matter how our night ended, it wasn't going to end there. I wanted more time with you. When I woke up, you were gone. I tried to convince the hotel to give me your information, and they didn't. I even considered hiring a private investigator, but my gut told me I'd see you again. I just had to hold out. All I had to do was keep a tight grip on my memories from that night, and that one day, you'd come back to me. Now, here you are, and I'm not letting you just walk away from me again."

"You don't get to make that choice."

Lifting his hand, he rests his palm against my cheek, and I can't help but lean into his touch. "I'll never force you into anything, Bellamy. But I also can't let you go. So, no, I can't keep you from walking away from me, but I can keep following you. I can keep showing up. I'm not him, Bell. I'm not your father, and my career does not make it impossible to make you a priority in my life."

"Stop," I say, my voice cracking. I want his words to be true. I want so desperately to believe him, to fall into his arms and feel his strength. It's been a month, but I've never forgotten how it felt to be wrapped up in his warm embrace.

His thumb traces gently across the apple of my cheek. "I want more time with you."

"I don't date football players."

"Then date me. Date Reid the man, not Reid the football player. Give me a chance to show you that I'm not him."

"I don't know if I can," I confess.

"Everything okay here?" My dad's voice carries down the hall, followed by the sound of his footsteps.

"Fine," I grit out. I don't want to deal with him right now.

"Montgomery, get your hands off my daughter," my dad grinds out.

"With all due respect, Coach, you don't get to dictate my private life or hers. We're both adults, and we don't need your permission. Sure, we'd take it, but we don't need it," he says, meeting my father's stare, before he turns his eyes to me.

They soften, and a little piece of armor around my heart cracks. Not from the look alone, but for how he stood up for me. Stood up for us, even though we're not together, to my father.

"I'll give the two of you some time," he says softly and leans forward. I suck in a breath, thinking he's going to kiss me, but his lips land on my forehead. He holds them there for far longer than needed, before he pulls away and strides off down the hallway.

"Care to tell me what you're doing with one of my players?" my dad asks, arms crossed over his chest.

"Nope."

"Bellamy." His tone is warning.

"You missed the chance, Dad," I say angrily. "You left us, so you don't get to pretend like you care who I date or what's going on in my life."

"I do care," he says, dropping the attitude. "I've never not cared, Bellamy."

"Sure, sure." I nod. "Are we done here?"

"No. Are you dating Montgomery?"

"That's none of your business."

"My players and my daughter are my business."

"I need to find Amanda. Thanks for the invite; we'll be leaving." I move to step past him, and he reaches out to gently grab my arm to stop me.

"Don't go."

"I can't be here right now."

"I'll drive you home. You're upset."

"Amanda's with me. Besides, we both know you can't leave. This job is your life. You chose it over me and Mom, so why would I ever think that you would choose me now?" I jerk my hand out of his. "Bye, Coach Warner," I say, before rushing off to find Amanda.

It's time to get the hell out of here.

CHAPTER 9

Reid

I'M LYING IN BED, LETTING TODAY REPLAY IN MY MIND. I CAN'T believe she's here. My dream girl lives in Nashville. Fuck me, she's my coach's daughter. He's pissed that I talked back, but at that moment, he wasn't my coach. He was my girl's dad, and although I don't know every detail, I know things aren't good between them—and his mistakes are being held against me. He can fuck right off for that.

It's his fault she's using their past against me, and it still pisses me off. Who leaves their wife and kid? I can't wrap my head around it. Of course, there could be pieces I'm missing. I'm certain there are. I'm sure there are pieces that Bellamy is missing, too, but that's for another day.

Scrolling through my phone, I find her number and change her contact to *Dream Girl*. I scrunch my nose. Backing out, I try again. *My Dream Girl* is much better. Once I have her name saved how I want it, I fire off a text.

> Me: Did you make it home okay?

I wait, staring at the screen. I can see that she's read the message, and as soon as the little bubbles start to bounce, my heart starts to race. I assumed she'd ghost me. But, to my surprise, she's not. Her reply pops up, and I grin, seeing her name.

> My Dream Girl: I'm home.

> Me: Good deal. How are you?

> My Dream Girl: You don't have to check up on me, Reid. I'm a big girl. I can handle some drama.

> Me: I don't want drama between us. I don't want anything that keeps me away from you.

Maybe our kids one day, if they climb in bed with us, but I have a feeling that if I tell her that's where my mind went, I'd just freak her out even more. Do I think we'll ever get there? I hope so, but we aren't there yet. We still have a lot to learn about each other, and we have this hurdle to jump where her fears regarding my career are concerned.

I can say that one night with her changed me, and that she's the only woman I see or think about. That has to be enough for now.

> My Dream Girl: Goodnight, Reid.

> Me: Night, Dream Girl.

Plugging my phone into the charger, I place it on the nightstand and turn off the light. Today changes nothing for me. I don't care who her father is. He can't bench me. He doesn't have a good enough reason. I'm one of the highest-ranked tight ends in the league. Sure, he can make my life hell at practice, but that's a small price to pay for her. It's going to take some time, but I'll show her that I'm not going to make the same mistakes her father did. I stare at the shadows on the ceiling for hours, thinking about her and what steps I'll take to prove to her that she's my priority, before sleep eventually claims me.

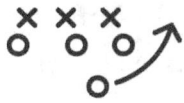

As soon as I step into my condo, I drop my gym bag to the floor and drag my ass to the couch. I hit the gym with the guys to get ready for training camp. Knox, our quarterback and team captain, keeps us all in line. Even Landry is doing better this year with diet and cutting out alcohol, but something tells me that has more to do with his wife than him. That man loves to eat, and he doesn't care if it's on the approved list of foods or not. Pulling my phone out of my pocket, I fire off a text to Bellamy.

Me: Are you free for dinner?

Her answer is going to be the same as it has been every day for the past five. Ever since seeing her at family day, I've texted her, asking her to have dinner with me. She always has an excuse.

My Dream Girl: I'm washing my hair.

A laugh bursts out of my chest. The past four days have been filled with plans or late nights at the office as her excuse, but this is an obvious blow-off, and it makes me smile.

Me: I can help with that. I have big hands, great for massaging the scalp.

My Dream Girl: Thanks, but I'm going to have to pass.

Me: You sure? I'm really good with my hands.

She knows this. She got to experience what my hands can do to her firsthand, but a little reminder never hurt anyone.

My Dream Girl: I'm sure.

Well, fuck. I toss my phone onto the cushion next to me. How am I going to be able to show her that I'm not her father if she doesn't let me see her? It's been five days since I laid eyes on her—five days since I've heard her voice. I went a month before, but then I didn't know where she lived. She's in my city, yet she still feels so far away.

Grabbing my phone, I'm about to order takeout, but instead, I end up hitting her contact and placing the phone to my ear. It rings, once, twice, three times before she picks up. I was starting to think she wasn't going to.

"Hello?"

"Hey, Dream Girl."

"Reid," she breathes my name, almost as if she's both relieved and annoyed that I'm calling her. Honestly, I don't think she knows which way she's feeling right now either.

"How was your day?"

"It was fine." She pauses. "How was yours?"

It's the polite thing to do to ask me back, but she hesitated. "Good. I hit the gym for a lift session with the guys. We try to meet every day during the week about a month before training camp to get back into shape, and now, I'm sitting here, trying to decide what to do for dinner. My girl is busy washing her hair."

She chuckles. "It's a thing."

"Oh, I have no doubt. She has beautiful, long, dark brown hair. I offered to help her, but she turned me down."

"Maybe she doesn't need a man to take care of her."

"She definitely doesn't need anyone to take care of her, but that doesn't mean I don't want to." She doesn't say anything, but I can hear her breathing change. "I miss you, Bell. When can I see you?"

"I—I don't think that's a good idea."

"How am I supposed to prove to you that I'm not him if you don't let me?"

Another heavy sigh from her. "We've been over this."

"We have, but we're still at an impasse. Let me bring you dinner. You don't even have to eat with me. Just let me drop off dinner so you don't have to cook."

"I shouldn't," she says, and I can hear it in her voice. She thinks she shouldn't, but she wants to.

Disappointment washes over me, but I'm not giving up. Shouldn't is better than no. She needs to see that I'm willing to work for her time, and I am. I'm willing to do whatever it takes to spend more time with her.

"Can you look at your schedule and let me know when we can make plans to have dinner? Or hell, lunch or breakfast, even all three. Whatever you want. Training camp starts soon. I was hoping to see you before that started."

There's a silence that hangs between us. I wait, giving her time to come up with another excuse, and when she doesn't, I speak again. Just one word. "Please." I try to remember a time when I ever begged a woman for anything, and I'm coming up empty. Only my dream girl could pull that type of need out of me. It's more than wanting to spend time with her. It's a need at this point. I know there's something more between us. I know that she's scared, and that's okay. I'll beg, I'll say please, I'll keep showing up, because at the end of the day, that's what she's most afraid of. Me not showing up like her father. I'm not him, and I don't care how long it takes; I'll prove that to her.

"I usually take a late lunch, and that's when you hit the gym with the guys," she says.

Elation washes over me. She's giving me an inch, and I'm taking every millimeter of that inch. She's testing me, and that's okay. I expect her to. "Tell me when and where, and I'll be there." More silence, because I'm certain that's not the answer she was expecting.

"Tomorrow. One o'clock." She rattles off the name of a small café that's not far from the stadium.

"I can't wait to see you," I tell her. I'm not just blowing smoke up her ass either. I wish I could see her every single day.

"Are you sure you can make the time?" she asks. Something that sounds an awful lot like hope laces her tone.

"Yes." No bullshit, no sweet lines, just the honest truth. I'll make the time for her.

"I should go," she says.

"Okay. I'll see you tomorrow, Dream Girl." I end the call, not giving her time to say her own goodbye or to back out of our lunch date. Part of me is fearful she's going to try anyway. The other part of me is wondering if she works that close to the stadium. There's so much I still don't know about her, but it doesn't change anything. She's still, without a doubt, my dream girl.

I know she has reservations, and I need to tread lightly, but I also need to be bold enough to let her know that she's who I want, and that if it's time she needs, it's time I'll give her. Time for me to show her that I'm not the man she thinks I am, just because I play football for a living. Time for her to adjust her beliefs in what she's always known, or what she's always assumed, that she's known. All I can do is keep trying. I'll keep asking, keeping showing up, and one day, my dream girl will see that she's everything I want, and more than that, she's everything I need. One day, I'll scale those walls around her heart and knock them down.

The guys and I always meet at the gym at noon, work out for a couple of hours, and get a run in on the treadmill. Today, I show up dressed in cargo shorts and a polo shirt, which has all four of them raising their brow.

"I'm not working out today."

"Sounds good to me. Let's go grab some lunch," Landry says.

"No can do, bro. I have a lunch date with Bellamy." I don't have to look in a mirror to know I'm smiling like a damn lovesick fool.

"Fuck yeah!" Landry offers me his fist, and we bump knuckles.

"She finally gave you a shot?" Knox asks.

"Yeah—and I'm not going to screw it up. She knows what time we meet every day to work out. I think her picking this time was a test to see if I would tell her I couldn't make it."

"Ah." Baker nods. "That makes sense."

"So, do you want us to move the time? We can all come back later," Foster offers.

"Nah, go ahead. I'll just hit my home gym when we get back. I don't know how long she has free to eat lunch, and no way am I rushing this." Missing a workout with the guys isn't the end of the world, but ending my lunch early with my dream girl just might be.

"Good plan." Landry nods.

"Yeah, so I'm off." I rock back on my heels as excitement courses through my veins. This is new for me. I've never been this excited to see someone.

"What time do you meet her?" Baker asks.

"Not until one, but I'm not going to be late and miss her. I'm not taking any chances." I'll be there, and I'll be ready. Missing her isn't an option, not when she finally took a leap of faith and offered me an olive branch.

"Let us know how it goes," Knox says.

With a nod and a wave, I head back out to my truck. At twenty minutes after twelve, I pull up outside the small café. I'm forty minutes early, but that's fine. Good things come to those who wait. Isn't that what they say? Either way, I'm going in there to get us a table, and I'm going to wait for my girl.

After ordering a bottle of water, I find a table and scroll through my phone. Then an idea hits me. I take a picture of the chair across from me and text it to her.

Me: I saved you a seat.

Me: I'm not sure how much time you get for lunch. Would you like me to order you something? You can tell me what you want, and I'll have it ready when you get here.

The three little bubbles bounce, and then her reply comes through.

My Dream Girl: You're thirty minutes early.

Me: I know. No way in hell was I risking getting caught in traffic or any other disturbance that could have delayed me. I'm not missing this time with you, Bellamy.

The bubbles bounce again, then go away. This happens three times before the bubbles disappear altogether. I don't know if I made her mad, but I don't think so. I think she doesn't know how to take me. I'm aware that I'm coming on strong, but I know what I want, and I'm already fighting a battle I didn't start because of my chosen career. Besides, I'm not into drama and games. I'm always going to be open and honest with her, no matter how over the top it may make me sound.

Not only that, but after everything I know about her relationship with her dad, and the reason she hates the game of football, I need to be strong-willed to a certain extent. I'd never force her, and if she truly said to never contact her again, I'd respect her wishes, but that's not what she's telling me. She's scared, and I know that if I'm too over the top, she'll get even more scared, but I also know I can't just walk away without showing her that I'm willing to put in the work. It's a delicate balance, and I pray that I'm handling this right, because I know that if it comes down to it, and I do have to walk away from her, it will gut me.

My leg bounces as I keep my eyes glued to the door. My bottle of water sits untouched on the table in front of me, and her seat remains empty. Finally, at ten minutes till one, our scheduled time to meet, I see her. She pulls open the door and scans the small café. Immediately, I push back from the table, on my feet, and head toward her.

When I reach her, I bend, wrapping my arms around her in a hug. "Fuck me, I missed you," I say, keeping my voice quiet, just for her.

I pull back, lace her fingers through mine, and lead her to the counter. She doesn't try to pull away, which makes my smile widen.

"Hi, what can I get for you?" The young woman behind the counter bats her long, fake lashes at me.

"Babe?" I ask Bellamy.

She turns to look at me, surprise evident. "You go ahead. I'm still deciding."

"We need a few minutes," I tell the girl. She nods and continues to watch us.

Finally, Bellamy speaks up. "I'll take a turkey club and an order of Saratoga chips, please."

"And you?"

"I'll have the chicken bacon ranch and Saratoga chips, as well."

"And to drink?"

I nod to Bellamy, and she rattles off her order of a sweet tea. "Make that two," I tell the server as I pull out my wallet to pay. Bellamy reaches for her purse, but I place my hand over hers to stop her. "No way, Bell. That table over by the window is ours. That's my bottle sitting there. Let me pay, and I'll be right there." Leaning down, I place a kiss on her temple before passing the server my credit card.

"Is she your girlfriend?" the girl asks, loud enough for the entire café to hear.

"One day. I'm working on it," I tell her honestly. I say it loud enough that I know Bellamy heard my answer, as well as everyone else who's hanging on to my every word. There's a very good chance one of them is a Rampage fan, and the news will spread like wildfire. Not that I care. I'd love to tell the entire world that the beautiful Bellamy Warner is all mine.

For the most part, the guys and I can walk around Nashville without issue. However, there are times we get noticed and asked for autographs, or intrusive questions like the one I just got. Usually, it's those questions that annoy me. It's a side effect of the job, one none of us like, unless it's from a kid. However, today, it served me well. Bellamy got to hear my answer, and so did everyone else. If I'm lucky, tabloids and social media will be raging with the fact that Reid Montgomery is off the market.

Taking my receipt and shoving my wallet back into my pocket, I work my way back to our table and wait for our number to be called. "How's your day been so far?" I ask her.

"Busy," she replies with a soft smile.

"What is it that you do?" I hate that I don't already know the answer to the question, but we've got all the time in the world to learn everything about one another.

"I'm the operations manager for Riggins Enterprises."

"Nice." I nod. "Do you enjoy it?"

"I do. It's always something new, and Grant and his brothers are great to work for."

"Good guys. I've met them a few times. They have a cabin in Gatlinburg, and the guys and I have stayed there before."

"Small world," she says, just as our number is called.

"I'll be right back," I tell her as I stand, making my way to the counter to grab our food and carrying it back to the table.

"What about you?" she asks, as we both dive into our lunch. "How's your day been?"

"Good. I did some laundry this morning, then met the guys at the gym to tell them I was skipping today. Then I came here."

She coughs, and I pause the bite I was ready to put into my mouth until I know she's okay. "You canceled on them?" Those big brown eyes are wide with shock.

"Of course, I did. I wanted to see you."

"Aren't you required to be there? I'm sure you missing a workout pisses off my dad." I can't get a read on her to see if she's happy or not, but either way, she's engaging in conversation. She's here, sitting across from me, sharing a meal, and that's more than I had hoped for with all the previous rejections she's given me.

"Nah, this is just something the guys and I do about a month before training camp starts to get back into shape from the off-season."

"Oh. So, you blew them off."

"I wouldn't say I blew them off. I told them I was meeting my girl for lunch."

"Are they mad?"

"Why would they be?"

"Because you're here with me."

I lean forward, resting my elbows on the table. "They know you're all I can think about. They know I'm fighting for time with you. They're my friends. They'd never be mad at me for putting my girl first. Knox and Landry would do the same for their wives, and Baker for his son. Foster would, too, if he had someone."

She nods but doesn't speak as she picks up her sandwich to take another bite.

"What are your plans this weekend? Do you have any free time for me?" I ask her.

"Reid, we can't do this. I don't date football players, especially not my father's football players. This won't go anywhere."

"Then that means I'm the only one risking the pain if that's true, right? So, have dinner with me. We're actually all getting together to have a cookout before training camp starts next week. I'd love for you to be there, to hang out with me and everyone. You can bring Amanda," I offer, hoping that will be more enticing for her, knowing that her best friend will be there with her.

"I don't think that's a good idea."

I nod, disappointed, and I don't hide that from her. "Okay," I say, feeling the heaviness of her rejection. "Training camp is tough, long days, but I'll have my phone, so I'll check in with you at night. They have a family day, too. It's not like the family day you just went to, but close. I know it's not your thing, but I'm going to add your name and Amanda's to the list. If you change your mind and want to come, I'd love to see you."

"You're making this harder than it needs to be," she says. Her tone tells me everything I need to know. She doesn't want to keep rejecting me, but she feels like she has to.

"You let me worry about that. I'm not afraid of putting in the work, Bell."

We both go back to eating, making small talk about the weather, and all too soon, she's glancing at her watch. "I need to get back."

"Can I drive you? Walk with you?"

"It's just around the block."

"Can I walk with you?" I ask again.

She shrugs, and I take that as a yes. Quickly, I clean up our trash and push the door open for her. Together, walking side by side, we make our way back to her work. She stops outside the Riggins Enterprises door and turns to face me.

"Thank you for lunch, Reid."

"You're welcome. Can I ask a small favor?"

"Depends." She eyes me skeptically. "Ask, and I'll tell you if I'm willing to help you."

Here goes nothing.

"Can I have a hug?" I keep my eyes trained on her, hoping like hell she can see how badly I need her in my arms again. I hugged her when she got to the restaurant, but this time, I want her to grant me permission. I want her to see that she holds all the control. I'm just a man ready and willing for any amount of her time she's willing to offer me. I wait patiently for her to answer me, and finally, she gives me a slight nod.

"Okay," she replies. If I'm not mistaken, there's a hint of longing in her tone. Her eyes lit up at my question. I know she has reservations, and while I respect her wishes, I also know that it's mostly fear. I'll keep showing up. I'll keep asking her to dinner and showing her that there's more to us than one incredible night. I'll show her that taking that leap and allowing me to be a part of her life won't hurt her. I'll never hurt her.

Fighting my grin, I say, "Come here." Sliding my arm around her waist, I pull her into a hug. I hold tightly, breathing her in. She wants this as badly as I do; she's just scared. I'll show her. I'll prove to her that there is nothing to be scared of. I'm all in with her.

"Let me know about this weekend," I tell her as I release her.

She smiles and waves before disappearing inside. The walk back to my truck is short, and although I'm stoked to have had lunch with her, it wasn't enough. I'm not sure any amount of time, not even forever, is long enough where Bellamy is concerned.

CHAPTER 10

Reid

SHE'S NOT HERE. I'VE ASKED HER EVERY DAY SINCE THE DAY we had lunch together if she would come, and every single time, she told me that it's not a good idea. It wasn't a no, so I kept asking. I'm trying hard not to be salty about it. I understand where she's coming from. I genuinely do, but how am I going to prove to her that I'm not her father if she doesn't let me?

And dammit, I wanted her here today. I wanted her to get to know my friends. I know the girls have been texting her, and they're planning on getting together while we're away at training camp. I'm glad she's going to be hanging out with them. I'm also man enough to admit that I'm jealous as hell that they get time with her.

"What's going on?" Foster asks. He takes the lounger next to mine, stretching out his legs.

"Just taking it all in," I tell him.

"You're sitting over here in the corner all by yourself, moping." He's not pulling any punches, calling me out on my shit.

"I tried to get her to come today, but she refused." There's no need for me to elaborate about who I'm talking about. They all know I could only be talking about my dream girl.

"Ah." Foster nods. "You're really into this girl, huh?" he asks.

I laugh. "Yeah, you could say that."

Foster doesn't speak for a long time. The silence between us isn't uncomfortable as we watch Knox, Corie, Rowan, and Landry play a game of chicken in the pool. Sloane is the self-appointed referee, while Baker has Camden in a floaty, tugging him around the shallow end. Camden's laugh has my lips tilting in a grin. I love that little dude something fierce.

"If you want her, you have to keep trying," Foster says, breaking the lull of silence. "You have to keep showing up."

"You sound like you know something about that?" I ask. There's something from his past, something he holds tightly to his chest. We don't pressure him about it. He knows that we're here for him when he's ready to talk about her. Because sometimes there's this pain in his eyes, and it could only be caused by a woman. Ironically, I'm placing some of that pressure on Bellamy. Not because I'm an asshole, but because I know my dream girl, and I want to help her over this fear of getting too close to an athlete. I'm not that man. I have my work cut out for me, and that's fine. Hard work got me where I am today, and what is it that they say? Nothing worth having comes easy?

"Maybe," he says, not really committing. "What I do know is that if you don't keep trying, if you don't know that you've exhausted every effort to fix whatever this is between you, then you'll live with that regret for the rest of your life."

"Who is she?" I ask him. It's a ballsy move on my part, but if he's going to offer his words of wisdom, I should know if he truly understands.

"She's in the past, but I have those regrets, Reid. I didn't fight hard enough, and that's something I have to live with. I don't want that for you."

"I'm not giving up on her. She's different, you know? She sees me, but this is a first: a woman refusing time with me because of my career.

She doesn't care about fame or my bank account. And I crave her company," I tell him. It's more than that. I crave the feeling of her soft skin against mine, the taste of her on my tongue, and the feeling of her wrapped tightly around my cock. I miss the conversation, the laughter. Fuck me, I just miss her. She's the entire package, and I'll be damned if I let her slip through my fingers.

"Maybe it's not too late for you," I tell him. "Maybe you didn't fight hard enough then, but you can now."

"Nah, my time has long since passed."

"But you want her?"

"With every breath I take," he says. He clears his throat and stands. He's said too much, gotten too close to his past, and he's running from it. "Don't stop fighting, Reid. Trust me on this one." He nods, as if his words are the final say in my life, and walks away. He settles on the edge of the pool and starts talking to Baker as he pushes a still-laughing Camden around in his floating baby innertube.

I watch everyone for a while, but the ache of her not being here is too much. I need to hear her voice. Grabbing my phone, I dial her number and place it to my ear.

"Hello?" she asks, sounding weak.

"What's wrong?" I'm immediately on alert.

"Nothing's wrong."

"Bellamy."

"Nothing's wrong. I just ate some bad food. I had leftover Chinese for lunch, and it's not agreeing with me. I think it might have been bad."

"Do we need to take you to the hospital to be checked out?"

"Reid, I'm fine. I'm just feeling blah, so I'm holding down the couch, watching trash TV."

"Do you need anything?"

"I'm good," she assures me.

"Now, I feel like a dick."

"What? Why?"

"Because I'm sitting here at Landry's place for the cookout, moping because I wanted you here with me today, and now I find out you're sick."

"Just a little blah. I'm fine, and you're not a dick. I kind of wish you were a dick. That would make my life easier," she says.

"How so?" I ask her, ignoring everything around me and focusing on our conversation.

"Contrary to what you might think, I don't hate you, Reid. I hate your job. I hate your connection to the game and my father. I hate that you're the first man to make me feel anything, and I can't have you."

"You can have me," I tell her. "I'm right here waiting for you."

"I can't have you. It was hell, the way he walked away. I can't risk that happening."

"That's him. Not the job," I remind her.

"It's the same to me. I know that might sound irrational, but I don't know any other way to feel about it. I'm sorry, Reid."

"Let me show you," I tell her. "I'll show you that you come first."

"We barely know each other. It's hard for me to believe that you're all in after one night."

"One incredible life-changing night, Bell."

"I should let you go. You're with your friends."

"I'm doing exactly what I want to be doing. No, that's not true. I'd rather be holding you while you're sick, but talking to you will have to do. Are you sure you're okay?"

"I'm sure," she replies, her tone soft.

"Will you call me if you need anything or if you start to feel worse?"

"Probably not," she admits. "You're busy, and I'm just going to lie here and watch mindless TV, then go to bed. I'm not going to bother you when you're busy."

"Please?" There it is again, me begging for more from her. There's a knot in my gut thinking about her sitting in her house all alone when she might need me.

"Fine," she concedes, but we both know she's lying. She's agreeing to humor me.

"I'll call you in a little while to check on you. Will you answer?" I ask her.

There's a long, silent pause. "Yeah," she finally says. "I'll answer."

"Get some rest."

"Okay." There's a slight pause, and it feels as if she wants to say more. "Thank you for wanting to check on me. Bye, Reid," she says, and the line goes dead. She ends the call, not giving me a chance to rejoice in the fact that I feel her thawing. She wants this, wants us, and slowly, I'm scaling those walls. It's a good thing, because this was starting to shape up to be one of those "you hang up, no, you hang up" teenage situations. I didn't want to end our call, but she's not feeling well, and hanging on the phone with me is the last thing she wants to do.

Standing, I shove my phone into my pocket and join my friends. Foster's right—I'm moping, and that's not me. I'm not that guy. I sit next to Sloane on the edge of the pool, and help her ref the game of chicken, which is more laughter and ribbing each other than actual game play.

"You doing okay?" Sloane asks.

"Yeah."

"She still avoiding you?"

"She had lunch with me earlier this week, but I pretty much begged her to come with me today, and she turned me down."

"She's scared, Reid. She wants you, but it goes against everything she ever claimed she would steer away from. It's going to take her some time to adjust to that."

"I know, and I'm going to be here when she figures it out. I wanted her here. I just talked to her, and she's not feeling well. So now, I feel like an ass."

"Then go to her."

"I don't know where she lives. I can't go there, and I can't ask her to meet me when she's not feeling well."

"Okay, watch them." She points to where Rowan and Corie are still going at it, trying to knock the other off their husbands' shoulders. Sloane pulls out her phone, taps at the screen before placing it to her ear. "Amanda, hey, it's Sloane, how are you?" she asks.

My head whips around to stare at her. Sloane rolls her eyes and points to our friends, telling me I'm not doing my job. Turning back, I stare at our friends, but all of my attention is on Sloane and the conversation she's having. Amanda, that has to be Bellamy's best friend, Amanda, right?

"Hey, so I need some advice," Sloane says. She pauses. "We're all at Landry and Rowan's place for a cookout before the guys have to live, eat, and breathe training camp. Anyway, Reid's bumming that Bellamy wouldn't come. He called her, and she's not feeling well. He wants to go check on her, but he doesn't know where she lives."

Another long pause. "He cares about her, and honestly, he's stressing out about training camp. He's not going to be able to pursue her like he would like, and he's worried about losing any momentum that he might be making," Sloane says, reading me like a damn book. She listens again, then nods. "Sure, hold on." She hands the phone to me. "She wants to talk to you."

"Hello?" I ask, my hands suddenly sweaty as I grip the phone.

"What are your intentions with my best friend?" Amanda asks.

"Everything," I answer.

"Explain that," Amanda says, her voice calm.

"The night we met, she didn't recognize me. She wasn't sitting next to me to try to rise on the social ladder or to latch on to a meal ticket. She was just Bellamy, and I was just Reid, and getting that time with her was the greatest gift. I want more of her time. I want to hear her talk and see her smile. I want her. All of her, whatever that looks like."

"You don't just have a hill to climb, Reid Montgomery, you have a damn mountain. She's got some deep-rooted anger at her father, and it's not just him she blames. It's football. It's irrational, but we were young when her parents split, and she needed something and someone to blame."

"I know." I'll scale the fucking mountain if that means when I get to the top, she's mine. I wish I could explain it. I don't have the right words. I can say she's different or that she's special and that we had a connection. All of that is true, but it's more than that. It's everything: the laughter, the conversation, the sex... It's her. I know with everything inside me that she's it for me. I can't explain it, but I've always trusted my gut, and my gut tells me that no matter how many mountains she makes me climb or how long I have to wait to prove to her that we'd be different, it will all be worth it. She's worth it.

"She's not feeling well, but you already know that."

"Yeah, I just talked to her."

"She's not sick, just ate something that didn't agree with her."

"I'd still like to check on her."

"I'm going to text Sloane her address. I'm also going to call my best friend and confess my sins. Don't make me regret this, Reid."

"I won't. I just want to take care of her." I didn't realize that was my intention until the words left my mouth. "She's sick, and I want to show up. I need her to see that she's important to me, and no matter what's going on in my life, she's a priority."

"Good answer," Amanda says, approval in her tone. "Be good to her, Reid. She deserves nothing but the best."

"I promise." My words are firm and a vow, if you will, to her best friend for tossing me this bone. "Thank you, Amanda."

"You're welcome. She might not open the door because I'm telling on myself. I can get you there, Reid, but you have to put in the work."

"I'm not afraid of a little hard work."

"I'm counting on that. I want to see her happy."

"That's what I want, too," I tell her.

"All right. Get my number from Sloane, just in case."

"Thank you. Thank you so much," I tell her, ending the call and handing the phone back to Sloane. "You, Sloane Peterson, are a genius." I pull her into a hug as she laughs at me.

"Just like that, our happy-go-lucky Reid is back," she teases. Her phone beeps, and she raises it to show me the message from Amanda. "I'll send this to you," she says, her fingers flying across the screen.

"Can you send me Amanda's number, too? Just in case. She told me I could get it from you."

"Sure, but just because she said to give it to you in the message that she sent me." My phone pings twice, and it makes my heart race. I stand and call out, "I'll be back."

"Where are you going?" Baker calls after me.

"Bellamy's not feeling well. I'm going to check on her."

"What can we do?" Corie asks, all attention now on me.

"Nothing. I'm just going to take her a few things and check on her. I'll be back." I wave over my shoulder and rush into the house. I grab my shirt, wallet, and keys before heading out the door.

Thirty minutes later, I'm pulling up outside her building. She lives in an apartment on the fifth floor. Reaching over, I grab the bags of essentials from the passenger seat and make my way inside.

Stopping outside her door, I pull in a deep breath and slowly exhale. I don't know if she's going to let me in. She knows I'm on my way, but will she open the door for me? I guess there's only one way to find out.

Raising my hand, I rap my knuckles against the door and start to count. I'm almost to one hundred when the door opens. Bellamy stands there, her hair a mess and no makeup on. She's wearing pajamas with stars and moons all over them, and she's never looked more beautiful. I can see in her big brown eyes that she's not feeling her best.

"I brought a few things," I say, holding up the bags.

She steps back, allowing me to come inside.

"I wasn't sure about food, so I stopped and got some chicken soup, and then there are a few other things that the internet told me to try for an upset stomach, and this." I hand her a paperback book. "The woman at the pharmacy said it was popular with the ladies. I know you read, and you might have read it, but yeah." I shrug.

"Thank you, Reid. I haven't read it, and this is very sweet of you, but unnecessary."

Closing the space between us, I rest my free hand that's not holding the goods against her cheek. "I was worried about you."

"So I've been told."

I smile. "Amanda gave me the third degree. She didn't hand over your address easily," I tell her. "I hope you're not mad."

Her shoulders drop. "I'm not mad."

"Are you hungry?"

She shakes her head, her face looking a little green at the thought of food. "Okay, I'll put that in the fridge for later. There's also crackers, ginger ale, Sprite, and peppermints," I say, moving toward her kitchen. I put what needs to be refrigerated away and leave the rest on the counter.

"What are you watching?" I ask her.

"*Gilmore Girls.*"

"Nice." I sit on the opposite end of the couch, pull her feet into my lap, and start to massage them.

"Reid?"

"Yeah?" I turn to look at her.

"What are you doing?"

"I'm taking care of you."

"You're supposed to be at a cookout with your friends."

"I was, but you needed me."

"I'm fine, just a little blah," she says, just as she did on the phone.

"Well, now, I'm here in case you need anything."

"You don't have to babysit me."

I chuckle. "I'm not. I'm sitting with my girl, hoping to help her feel a little better while she's under the weather. Now hush. I need to see what happens."

"You want to watch this?"

"Bell, baby, I'd watch paint dry if that meant I got to spend time with you."

She doesn't say anything, but her cheeks turn pink as she pushes her gaze back to the TV and presses *play*. I'm watching, but I'm not paying attention. My hands gently massage her feet, and when I glance over, her eyes are growing heavy.

"Bellamy?"

"Yeah?"

"Come here." I hold my arms open, waiting for her to come to me. Hoping that she will.

"We shouldn't."

"Just let me hold you." *Please, let me hold you.*

"This isn't—we're not together."

"Just for a little while."

She bites down on her bottom lip. I can see it in her eyes. She wants to come to me, but her heart and her head are at war with one another.

"We'll watch a few episodes. Then I'll go. Come here, Bell. You need rest, and you'll rest better in my arms."

"You don't know that."

"Fine, I'll feel better knowing that's where you are. Come on."

Slowly, she moves and settles next to me. I wrap my arm around her and pull her into my chest. She brings her legs up to the couch and tucks them under her. I help her adjust her blanket so she's nice and snuggled. Even though it's a million degrees outside, the air condition-ing is cool in here.

I press a kiss to the top of her head and try to focus on the TV, when really, all I want to do is watch her. This is huge. Not only did she open the door for me, but she also let me inside, and she's in my arms. This night couldn't have ended any better.

CHAPTER 11

Bellamy

I'M WEAK. NOT BECAUSE I'M FEELING SICK, BUT BECAUSE EVEN though I should tell him no and stay on my side of the couch, I cave. I want what he is offering. I want his arms around me. I tell myself that this is it. This is the last time I allow myself to indulge in what this man is offering. It's not fair to either of us to keep pretending this could be more.

My stomach rolls, and I bury my face in his shirt, breathing him in, hoping it will settle, and luckily, it does. It's going to be a long damn time before I eat Chinese food again.

"You all right?" he asks, rubbing his hand gently down my back.

"I'm okay," I whisper. His kindness brings tears to my eyes. Oh, how I wish that things could be different for us. Why does he have to be a damn football player?

"Can I get you anything?" he asks.

Just you. "I'm good," I assure him. As long as I don't move or think about food, the nausea stays calm. He continues to rub my back, and my eyes feel heavy. I try to fight sleep, but I can't seem to stop it. I'm too warm, too comfortable. I don't know how it's possible, but I've missed being close to him. One night was all it took for feelings to take root, feelings I refuse to allow myself to act on, so I push them aside and give myself tonight as I drift off to sleep.

A soft curse and a thump jolt me awake. "What's wrong?" I ask, my voice groggy with sleep.

"I dropped my phone. I'm sorry. I didn't mean to wake you," Reid replies softly.

"What time is it?" I ask, rubbing the sleep from my eyes.

"After two."

My mouth falls open. "In the morning?"

"Yeah, you needed the rest."

"You're still here?" Why is he still here? He stayed while I was sleeping? Why would he do that?

"Where else would I be, Bell?"

My belly flutters, and this time, it's not from the food poisoning; it's from the man. I secretly love the way he calls me Bell. To everyone else, I'm Bellamy or Bella, but Bell, that's just his, and it's something for me to hold on to when he's no longer around. "Home, or at your cookout with your friends."

Reaching over, his hand lands on my thigh, and he gives it a soft squeeze. "I'm where I want to be," he assures me.

"You should go. It's late, and you have to get ready for training camp." My words sound dismissive, and while they are, I don't mean them to be harsh. I'm falling for him. Who am I kidding? I've already fallen for him, but I can't act on those feelings. I *can't* let this happen. I refuse to set myself up for heartbreak.

"I'm ready," he assures me. "I'm packed, and the only thing I'm missing is time with you."

"It's late," I say again because my brain is still trying to comprehend that he's still here—wide awake, while I use him as my personal pillow.

He's here, and he's telling me that I'm all that he's missing. My heart wants to throw caution to the wind, but my mind tells me that I know better.

"Are you hungry?" He ignores my words, telling him that he should go. Instead, he tries to continue to take care of me. I feel my resolve softening, and I can't let that happen.

"No, I'm going to go to bed." Tossing off the cover I was wrapped up in, I stand. My words are abrupt, but I need some separation. My body is trying to betray me. "Thank you for coming to check on me." I soften my tone. I do appreciate him coming to check on me, and he stayed. He had other places he could be, but he chose to stay here, on my couch, letting me use him as a pillow. I'm trying to wrap my head around that.

"You don't have to thank me for coming to check on you when you're not feeling well, Bellamy." He tucks my flyaway hair behind my ear, and it's hard not to melt. "I wanted to take care of you," he says, his voice soft. His blue eyes, boring into mine, will me to trust him.

That's part of the issue. I do trust him, but I shouldn't. My mom trusted my dad, and look how that turned out. I can't fall into the same trap.

"Be safe driving home," I say, trying to keep my tears at bay. I don't know why I'm so emotional all of a sudden. That's a lie. I do know why. I don't want him to go. I want him to stay, but I can't do this. I can't fall for a football player. I won't be able to handle the heartbreak. My dad leaving me for his job was one thing, but choosing a man who could potentially do the same thing... I just can't do it.

I can't knowingly sign up for a broken heart. It hurts too much already, and he's not even mine.

Reid climbs to his feet. "Can I have a hug?" he asks, his voice sounding sad.

I nod, feeling the tears burn. I should say no, but I want his arms around me. "Yes," I reply softly, trying to mask the sound of tears clogging my throat.

"Come here," he says, sliding his arm around my waist and pulling me into his chest. He holds me tightly, and I'm about three seconds away from losing this battle with my tears. I can't let him see me cry. "Call me if you need me."

"Thank you," I whisper, because even though I don't want them to, his words mean everything to me.

He pulls back and presses his lips to my forehead. "Lock up behind me," he says, kissing my forehead one last time, before turning and walking away.

I stand frozen as I watch him walk out the door, and as soon as I hear the click telling me he's gone, my tears start to fall. Why does the universe hate me? Why did this man drop into my life? Why is he perfect for me? I drag myself toward the door, twist the lock, and turn off the lights before shuffling to my bedroom and crying myself to sleep.

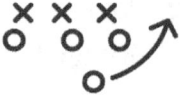

"We shouldn't be here," I tell Amanda, as I pull my car into Corie and Knox's driveway.

"What? Why not?" she asks.

"These are *his* people. I'm just making this harder for both of us." It's been a week since training camp started, and Reid has called me every night. He always sounds dead on his feet, but he calls me without fail before he goes to bed. Every night, I tell myself that I'm not going to answer, but I crave his gruff, exhausted voice in my ear each night before I go to bed. I keep telling myself I can't have him, but there are two sides to every coin. The other side is that I want him. His persistence is something no man before him has ever had. He knows my hangups with his career, and no matter how tired or how long a day he's had, he makes time for me, and that warms a part of my heart that's been cold and jaded for far too long.

"It's fine. We were invited. Besides, I'm pretty sure that Reid will be stoked to find out that you're hanging out with *his* people," she replies.

"I'm making this harder on myself," I grumble.

"Finally!" Amanda exclaims. "She finally gets it."

"What are you talking about?"

"I'm talking about you pushing that man away when it's obvious to anyone who's looking that he's head over heels for you."

"He's not." Even as I say the words, there's a tiny piece of me that says that's a lie. Reid has continued to show up, to keep his word, and he never stops asking to spend time with me. I don't know about head over heels, but our time together definitely affected him just as much as it did me. He's just allowing himself to act on it. I, on the other hand, am scared to death to let myself believe we could make this thing between us work.

"Okay, queen of denial. I love you, Bella, you're my bestie, my ride or die, but with this, when it comes to Reid, you're wrong. You're letting your parents' past keep you from what very well could be a fairy-tale future."

"Fairy tales don't exist in real life," I counter.

"Uh-uh," she says, reaching for the door handle and climbing out.

"I guess we're doing this," I mutter as I grab my keys, purse, and phone and quickly follow her to the front door. Corie said to bring nothing but ourselves, that we'd order in, so here we are, empty-handed, getting ready to knock on their door. I'm about to put myself further into his world willingly. I'm itching to run, to race back to my place and hide, but I know that Amanda would never let me. I just need to suck it up.

It's one night, right? What's the worst that could happen?

Amanda's hand is raised to knock when the door opens to three smiling faces. "You're here!" Sloane and Rowan reach for our hands and drag us inside, while Corie bounces Camden on her hip. Their excitement makes me smile.

"Thanks for having us," I tell Corie. Reaching out, I tickle Camden's feet, and he giggles. "Are you crashing girls' night, little man?" I ask him.

"He's always welcome," Corie coos, kissing his cheek. "It's not Baker's week to have him, but his mom had another photo shoot overseas or something." Corie rolls her eyes. "And the nanny is visiting family this weekend, so I offered to keep him."

"We fought her on it," Rowan says.

"She won," Sloane adds. "But that's okay, because now we're all here, and we can share him." She takes Camden from Corie and kisses all over his tiny little face, making him giggle.

"We need some more ladies around this place," Corie tells us. "Even the little men are taking over. Come sit. What can I get you to drink?" she asks.

"I'm okay for now," I tell her.

"Amanda?" she asks.

"Maybe in a little while." She smiles politely.

Neither one of us knows what we're getting ourselves into, but I admit their friendliness and excitement to see us helps lessen some of my anxiety.

"Okay, so we're going to give you a recap," Sloane says. She points at her chest. "I'm the bestie, hers first, and then this one came along." She points to Rowan. "I'm unattached. Rowan works for the Rampage and is married to Landry, Corie's brother. Corie is married to Knox and also works for the Rampage. And this little man belongs to Daddy Sin." She coos to Camden.

"How'd that go over? Marrying your brother's best friend?" Amanda asks.

"Better than you would expect. We hid it for a long time. But when Landry found out, he was more hurt that we didn't tell him than anything."

"And you both work with your husbands?" I ask.

"We do." Rowan smiles. "It's an adventure, to say the least."

"What about you?" I ask Sloane. "What do you do?"

"I'm a teacher." She grins. "I get to spend my days shaping little minds."

"What grade?" Amanda asks.

"Right now, I'm at the preschool level. I'm licensed through fifth, but I love my littles." She smiles, hugging Camden to her chest.

"What about the two of you?" Corie asks.

"I'm the operations manager for Riggins Enterprises. It's a logistics company based here in Nashville," I explain.

"She works with the hottie Riggins brothers all day," Amanda teases.

I can't help but laugh. "They are easy on the eyes, but they're all happily married, and no other women exist in the world but their wives." It's not an exaggeration. All five of those brothers are obsessed with their wives. Oftentimes, I wonder what having that kind of love would feel like. I ignore the voice in my head telling me that I might be missing out on my only chance to find out, and focus back on the conversation.

"So what you're telling us is that Reid doesn't have any competition where the brothers are concerned," Sloane teases.

"Nope," Amanda says, answering for me.

"What do you do?" Rowan asks her.

"I'm the talent coordinator for the Country Fiddle downtown. I book all the bands."

"You win," Sloane says, bouncing Camden on her knee. "Your job is the most fun."

"I don't know." Rowan smirks. "Sneaking away at work with your husband has its benefits." She wags her eyebrows, and we all crack up laughing.

We spend the next hour laughing and talking. We all have our turn loving on baby Camden, and I admit, hearing his laughter is enough to put anyone in a better mood. When Corie's stomach growls, we order pizza for delivery. Everyone offers to pitch in, but Corie insists that it's her treat, and we can all take a turn next time. My eyes find Amanda's, and she nods. These ladies, the people that Reid Montgomery surrounds himself with, are good. Not just because Corie is buying dinner, but they're just kindhearted, laid back, and easy to be around.

They're not at all what I expected.

Thirty minutes later, the doorbell is ringing, which has Corie jumping off the couch to go collect our food. Amanda goes to help her, and I follow Sloane and Rowan into the kitchen to set up. Rowan starts getting the high chair ready, and I smile because, despite this not being his home, the baby stuff scattered around makes you think Camden is here full-time. As soon as Corie sets the boxes on the counter, Sloane lifts the lid and groans. It takes a few seconds, but as soon as the smell hits me, my stomach rolls.

I swallow, trying to breathe through it, but that's not going to work this time. Slapping my hand over my mouth, I take off sprinting down the hall, dropping to my knees in front of the toilet, where I lose the minimal lunch that I ate earlier today.

I groan. Is there anything worse than throwing up? Yeah, there is. It's throwing up in your new friend's guest bathroom, who also happens to be married to the best friend of your one-night stand, who's trying to make one night be... more. That's worse, trust me.

"Are you all right?" Amanda asks, appearing next to me. Corie shows up with a wet cloth and a bottle of water, handing them to me.

"I'm sorry," I tell them after swishing the water and spitting it into the toilet. I stand, wiping my mouth. "I was sick with food poisoning last weekend. I guess it's still lingering a little," I tell both of them, who are standing and watching me with concerned expressions.

"Here." Corie bends down, opens the vanity drawer, and grabs a spare toothbrush and a travel-size toothpaste. "We get them from the dentist, and I hate to throw them away," she explains.

"Thank you. I'll be right out," I tell them, feeling my face heat with embarrassment. This experience was not on my bingo card for tonight. Quickly, I brush my teeth, wash my hands, and make sure I didn't leave a mess in the bathroom before turning out the light and making my way to the living room. I'm met with four pairs of eyes, peering at me with concern. Then there's Camden, who coos and holds up a tiny piece of pizza squished in his hands. Again, I smile because I can't seem to help myself, regardless of how shitty I feel.

"Is that good?" I ask Camden, and he just grins, shoving more pizza into his mouth.

"How are you feeling?" Rowan asks.

"Blah," I answer, because I don't know how to explain it. Food poisoning isn't supposed to last this long, right? What if there's something else wrong with me? Before I can panic about that, my best friend sets free a panic I hadn't considered.

"Bellamy?" I turn to face Amanda. "Is it possible that you're pregnant?"

"What?" I ask, shock racing through my veins. "No. No, I'm not. We—nope." I'm shaking my head because Reid is the only man I've been with in months, and I'm on the pill.

I'm not pregnant.

I can't be pregnant.

"Bella, you don't know for sure."

"We were careful," I say, well aware that Reid's friends, the ones he calls his family, are witnessing our conversation.

"I have tests," Corie speaks up. "If you want to take one."

"What?" Sloane asks. "Why do you have tests?"

Corie shrugs. "We're not trying, but we're not preventing either."

"So that means you're trying!" Sloane moves around the table and crushes her best friend in a hug. "I'm so happy for you," she mumbles.

"I'm not pregnant." Corie laughs. "Not yet." She's smiling when her eyes find mine. "You're welcome to use one. I have several. I just wanted to be ready if and when I ever needed one."

"You should," Amanda tells me. "Or we can take you to the doctor and have them check you over."

"I'm fine," I assure her.

"It won't hurt to take one. Just to see," Rowan suggests.

My heart is racing, and my hands are sweaty. I can't be pregnant. What will Reid say? He'll think I did this on purpose. He'll think I tried to trap him, right? Isn't that what women do when they're dating professional athletes? Not that we're dating, but—argh. As bad as I hate to admit it, I need to take that damn test.

"I'll take it," I say, my voice quivering.

"You got him?" Corie asks Rowan, who's sitting next to Camden in his high chair.

"We're good." Rowan nods.

Corie stands and nods for me to follow her. "Do you want me to come with you?" Amanda asks.

"No. I'll be okay," I tell her, turning back to follow Corie to their bedroom.

"You can use my bathroom. The entire bottom drawer is tests. Knox might have gone a little crazy when he found the three I bought, and bought more." She's grinning as she says it.

"He loves you."

She nods. "Do you want me to stay with you?" she asks.

"Do you mind waiting in the bedroom for me?"

"Of course." She steps closer and wraps me in a hug. "No matter what the outcome is, it's all going to be okay. Reid Montgomery is a good man. He's not one to not take care of his family."

There's so much conviction in her words, it's hard not to believe her. As she steps out of the bathroom and closes the door behind her, I send up a silent prayer that if this test is positive, that its daddy wants to be a part of its life, even though he's a football player.

It's too late to turn back now.

With shaking hands, I grab a test out of the bottom drawer and read the instructions. "Here goes nothing," I mutter as I take the test, place it on some toilet paper on the counter, and wash my hands. I glance down, not expecting to see a result yet, but it's already there. Glaring at me like a beacon in the night.

Pregnant.

I grip the counter and bow my head. It could be a false positive. I could take another one, but that would just be wasteful of Corie's generosity. I know the test is right. I've been feeling off and overly emotional for a couple of weeks now. The signs were all there. I just ignored them.

I can't ignore them anymore.

My hands rest on my belly, and I pull in a deep breath. Single and pregnant is not the plan I had for my life, but it's the one I've been given. Grabbing the test, I wrap it up in toilet paper and step out of the room. Corie sees my face and smiles widely.

"Congratulations," she says, hugging me tightly. "He's going to be thrilled, Bellamy."

"He's going to think I did this on purpose."

Corie tosses her head back in laughter. "That's going to be the furthest thing from his mind. I know there's something in your past with your dad that has you keeping him at arm's length, but Reid is his own man. He's not going to blame you, and he's not going to walk away. If you thought he was persistent before, watch out." She grins.

"He is persistent," I agree. He's never wavered, not since the first minute I met him. He's not my father. He's this baby's father, and I need to find a way to give him the chance he's been asking for. I owe it to our baby.

"So, how are we doing this? Keeping the news to ourselves? Telling the others? Tell me what you need."

"I don't want to lie to them. Can they keep quiet until I can tell Reid?"

"You can trust us," she says, linking her arm through mine and leading me back out to the living room.

"Well?" Amanda, Rowan, and Sloane ask as soon as they see us.

"I'm pregnant," I say, choking on the words, as I hold up the wad of tissue paper and plop down on the couch. I don't bother to check the tears as they race down my cheeks. I'm lost in my head, in my feelings, and they give me the time and the space I need to work through both.

CHAPTER 12

Reid

"**W**E SHOULD PROBABLY TELL THEM WE'RE COMING," Foster says.

"Why would we do that?" Landry glances at him in the rearview mirror. Foster, Baker, and I are in the back seat of his truck, while Landry and Knox are up front.

"You're crashing girls' night," Foster explains. "We're men."

"Camden's there," Landry argues.

"My son is not even a year old yet." Baker laughs.

"Still, they're doing women shit, and we're just going to barge in on them."

Knox turns to face us from his spot in the passenger seat. "I haven't seen my wife in five days. Five long fucking days. We're going."

"I'm not saying we should turn around, just that we should warn them. Besides, it was your choice to stay at camp and not come home every night."

"It's what we do," Landry speaks up. "We build camaraderie, but what he said." He tilts his head toward Knox, keeping his eyes on the road. "Five long fucking days."

"I miss my kid," Baker says. "I don't care if we call or don't, but I'm hoping my boy is awake."

"Of course, he's going to be awake. He's going to be surrounded by five beautiful women," Landry says. "He's my nephew. He's not going to want to miss a single second of their cuddling him."

Baker laughs. "True enough. He does love to soak up attention."

"I'm just saying," Foster continues. "When we walk into that house and find your wives half-dressed with shit all over their faces, don't gouge my eyes out when I look."

"Don't look," Knox says, his voice gruff.

"I mean, five beautiful ladies," Foster says, and I can hear the humor in his voice. He's teasing them, which is not something Foster does often. He's the serious one in our group. He leans over Baker to look at me. "What about you? Excited to see your girl?"

"Five long fucking days," I say, and we all laugh. I'm excited as hell to lay eyes on her. I've called her every single night, but we haven't seen each other since I left her place last weekend. I didn't know it was possible to miss someone like I miss her. She's not my wife. But fuck, she's my everything. One day, if I'm lucky, we'll be there. I understand Knox's and Landry's obsession to come home, even though our asses have to be up and watching film at six tomorrow. The visit will be worth it.

Landry parks his truck, and we scramble out and to the front door. Knox pushes the door open, and we follow along behind him. The house is too quiet, which is surprising for five ladies who are supposed to be having a fun night, and a baby.

Stepping into the living room, we find everyone gathered around the couch, hovering around— "Bellamy?" I rush toward her. The other ladies step back as I fall to my knees. "What's wrong? Why are you crying? Are you hurt?" My eyes rake over her, looking for injury. Did someone pass away? Coach is fine. He was at dinner earlier. Is it her mom? My hands rest against her cheeks as I wipe at her tears with my thumbs, but it's no use because they keep falling unchecked.

"Bell." My voice cracks. "Baby, tell me what's wrong? Please," I plead with her. Her tears are tearing my heart to shreds. She shakes her head, more tears falling, so I turn to ask the others what the fuck is going on, but we're alone. The room is clear of everyone but us.

Standing, I sit next to her on the couch and pull her onto my lap. She comes willingly, snuggling close as she rests her head against my shoulder. My arms band around her, holding her with all I've got.

"I don't know what's wrong, but whatever it is, we'll face it together," I tell her. "Can you at least tell me, are you hurt?" I scanned her for injuries and didn't see anything, but that doesn't mean I didn't miss it. Maybe it's a pain I can't see.

"No." Her voice cracks. "I'm not hurt."

"Fuck," I say, holding her tighter. "Whatever it is, you can tell me. I'm right here, and I've got you. We'll get you through this. Tell me what's causing these tears, Bell. You're breaking my heart, baby."

"I got some news earlier," she says, not lifting her head from my shoulder.

"Okay. What can I do? What do you need from me?" I don't know what I'm dealing with here. I want to tell her that whatever it is, I'll handle it. "Whatever it is, we'll handle it together. You and me," I assure her.

"You don't even know what it is," she says, her voice soft.

"I don't care. It involves you, and you're important to me. I'll do anything I can to help you through whatever this is. You have to talk to me, though. I can't help you if I don't know what I'm dealing with."

"What if it's something that will change both our lives?" she asks.

"Will you still be in my life?" I ask her.

"Yes."

"Then, let it change them. You're the only thing I won't change."

"What do you mean?" she asks, lifting her head to stare at me with those big brown eyes. They're misty with tears, and the sparkle is dulled. I hate it.

"I mean that you're the only thing in my life I'm not willing to walk away from," I tell her honestly. I keep one arm wrapped around her, while the other palms her cheek. "I mean, I don't want to lose you." Her eyes widen, but she doesn't speak, so I keep going. "I fell for you on an evening stroll on the beach. With each minute that passed, I fell harder. We talked, we laughed, and you saw me. I see you, too, baby," I tell her. "So, yeah, as long as whatever it is doesn't mean I'll lose you, then it's all going to be okay. Whatever it is that's causing these tears, we'll face it together."

"I didn't expect you, Reid Montgomery. You crashed into my life like a tornado without warning, and you're flipping the script for everything I thought I knew."

"I won't apologize for that. Meeting you is the best thing that's ever happened to me." More tears well in her eyes, and I curse myself for causing them.

"I believe you," she whispers. "It goes against everything I ever said I would do, but I trust you, and I believe you."

"Yeah?" I ask. My heart starts to race. "Does that mean you're going to stop fighting me? Are you going to let me show you that we're good for one another?"

"I have to tell you first. You might change your mind," she says, biting down on her bottom lip.

Gently, I tug her lip free as I lean forward and press a soft kiss to her lips. "Nothing you could say is going to make me change my mind. Nothing," I tell her, peering deep into her eyes, willing her to believe me.

"I'm scared to tell you. For the first time in my life, I want to break my own rules. For you."

"Fuck breaking the rules, Bell. Destroy them. I am not him," I say, referring to her father. "There will never be a time in our lives that I don't put you first. Not ever."

More tears spill. "I want to believe that."

"Give me a chance to prove it to you."

"How are you going to do that?" she asks.

"Move in with me." I blurt out the words, but I don't regret them.

"What?" Her mouth hangs open in shock.

"Move in with me. My schedule is insane, but you'll be there every night when I get home. And when I'm traveling, I'll know you're in our bed. I'll know that you're with me, even when you're not."

Her voice cracks, "You want me to move in with you?"

"Yes." No hesitation. The more I think about coming home to her, falling asleep next to her every single night, the idea sparks hope inside my chest. Is this fast? Yes, it is, but am I certain she's who I want? Also, yes. There's no timeline for this kind of thing, and I don't care if it's today or six years from now—it will still be here. My night with her changed me, and no matter what her answer is, that truth will remain the same.

"That's a big step."

"These are big feelings," I say, taking her hand and pressing it over my heart. "I've never been indecisive. I make a choice, and that's it. That's what I want."

"And I'm your choice?"

I smile at her. "Yeah, Bell, you're my choice. Do this with me. Give us a real chance at this."

"I have to tell you first. You might change your mind," she says again, her eyes closing briefly before they open again.

"Try me."

She takes a deep breath, slowly exhales, and her words, "I'm pregnant," change my world.

It takes about three seconds for her words to register, and I pull her into my chest, hugging her as tightly as I can. It's probably too tight, considering she's carrying precious cargo, but fuck me. We're having a baby.

Finally, I ease up, and she pulls back. She's sobbing again, and I swallow a lump of emotions in the back of my throat, because fuck, I'm going to be a dad. "We're having a baby," I say, my voice gruff.

She nods. "But you can take it all back," she says. "I don't expect anything or need anything from you. I can do this on my own—"

I place my hand over her mouth. "Don't. Don't insult me like that. This is my baby, Bell. *Our* baby. He or she needs me, and so do you. You won't do a single fucking thing on your own from now on. It's you and me. Together. We've got this," I say, then my mind goes another direction. "You—" I swallow hard because fuck, I can't even say the words. "You want this baby, right?"

"I do. But I didn't do this on purpose to trap you. I don't want you to feel obligated."

"I want it all, Bellamy. You, this baby, and the life we're going to build." Leaning in, I kiss her. "I." Kiss. "Want." Kiss. "You." Kiss. "And our baby." Kiss.

She accepts each kiss, which creates an intense spark of joy and hope for what our future could be together. She's no longer pushing me away. Fucking finally, she understands, we are meant to be. I just want to stay right here, with her wrapped in my arms. I've managed to do the impossible, and I tore down her walls.

"I want what you're saying. I want to build a life with you, but, Reid, I'm so scared. I know I can't keep letting my past guide my future, but I'm already too far gone. If we take this leap, and you decide I'm not what you want, I won't survive that. I've had one man who was supposed to love me unconditionally walk out on me. I can't do it again."

"You won't have to. You and this baby, you're my entire world." I move my hand to her flat belly. "Fuck, how do you love someone you've never met?"

"Promise me we won't end up like them. Tell me we won't end up like my parents."

"I promise you that will never be us, baby. Never," I say with conviction. Then I grin. "So, you're moving in, right? Wait, maybe we should buy a place. Our kid needs a yard to play in. I don't want to raise our kids in a condo."

"Kids?"

"What? You want to stop at one?" My brow furrows. I couldn't possibly imagine only having one child with her. The smile she gives me in answer to my question warms my heart.

"Can we maybe get this one here first?" she asks, grinning. I know that she's secretly elated at the prospect of a future with a family of our own beyond this baby. I can see us with a house full of kids, and the vision alone builds hope in my chest.

"Sure, sure." I nod, but I'm already seeing us sitting on the back porch, watching our kids play in the yard—our future flashes in my mind like a movie I want to watch on repeat.

"What about my dad?" she asks.

"What about him?"

"He's not going to take this well."

"I don't care what he thinks, Bellamy, or how he takes it. I'm one of the highest-ranked tight ends in the league. I show up and give everything I've got on the field. He can ride my ass in practice and in games. Hell, he can bench me. My contract is solid. Besides, it doesn't matter what he tosses at me. I can learn the play."

"What if you get traded?"

"Then we'll figure it out together."

"He's going to be hard on you."

"Fine." I nod. "Then I get to come home to you. So, like I said, he can push me as hard as he wants, because at the end of the day, you're mine. He didn't fight like he should have. He and I are not the same."

"Okay," she whispers.

With my index finger, I lift her chin, and she gives me a small smile, which brings back some of the sparkle in those big brown eyes. "Okay?"

She nods. "I'll move in with you."

In an instant, there's a weight lifted from my chest, and my heart soars. I exhale a heavy breath and wrap my arms around her, pulling her into my chest. She fits perfectly, like she always has.

"We've got this," I whisper into her hair.

She leans into me, her voice muffled against my shirt. "We've got this," she repeats softly.

"Can we tell them?" I nod toward the kitchen, where I notice the others standing around. They're far enough away that we've had privacy. Not that I care. I'll tell anyone who will listen about my girl and our baby.

"The girls know."

"Can I tell the guys?"

She tilts her head to the side. "They're your family, Reid. Of course, you can."

"I know some people wait, so I wanted to make sure you were okay with that."

"I'm pretty sure Knox and Landry will find out anyway." She laughs. "And the others, I want your friends to know if you want them to know."

"Baby, I want to yell it from the rooftops."

She giggles. "Can we maybe keep it to everyone here at least until I go to the doctor?"

"Are you okay?"

"Yes, I'm fine, but you know, let's let the professionals confirm and take a look before we start shouting from rooftops."

I laugh and pull her into a hug. "Anything you want, Dream Girl." She wiggles out of my hug, and I kiss her lips. "Yo! Family meeting!" I call out.

Slowly, feet shuffle, and everyone surrounds us. I wait for everyone to find a seat before glancing at Baker, who's holding Camden.

"Come here, buddy," I say, holding out my arms. Baker must sense something because he stands and brings Camden to me. He snuggles into my chest, and my heart melts. Soon, this will be me. I'll be holding my son or daughter. "Guess what?" I ask Camden. He lifts his head and places his hands on my cheeks. "You're going to be a big cousin."

"Fuck yeah!" Landry cheers.

I smile and glance at my friends, their wives, even Sloane and Amanda. "Bellamy's pregnant," I say, and I don't need a mirror to see the happiness on my face. I can feel it deep in my soul.

Everyone says congratulations. Camden claps and giggles, feeding off our energy. "This will be us soon," I whisper to Bellamy.

"It's scary and exciting all at the same time."

"I agree, but we've got this." I kiss her once more, before Camden wants down, so I place him on the floor, and he crawls to Foster, who lifts him into his arms.

"What time do you have to leave?" Corie asks.

"We have to be back at six in the morning," Knox tells his wife.

"I get you all night?" Corie grins.

"Come home with me?" I ask Bellamy, my lips next to her ear.

She turns to face me. "You have to be up early."

"I don't care. I need you there. I can come to your place if you want."

"Your condo is closer to where you need to be."

"Our place it is." I grin. "One more week of training camp, but I'm not staying overnight anymore. I'll give you a key when we get home, and I'm coming home to you and this little one every night," I say, placing my hand on her belly.

"No. Don't change your routine for me."

"I think you're on to something," Knox says. "We used to do it because we didn't have anything waiting for us at home. Now, we do."

My eyes automatically go to Foster, and he swallows hard. I'm sure no one else notices because they weren't looking.

"Well, Cam, how about we invite Uncle Foster to our place, and it'll be boys' night every night," Baker asks his son. He must have noticed Foster's reaction, as well, and hell, maybe he, too, is feeling lonely.

"Don't you two jokers be corrupting my nephew." Corie points a finger at Baker and then at Foster.

"I would never." Foster places his hand to his chest as if he's offended. The grin that's replacing his usually stoic expression gives him away.

"I'm down for sleeping in my own bed," Foster says.

"What? You're going to abandon us?" Baker asks.

"Camden can spend the night at my place," Foster replies, making us all laugh.

My arms wrap tightly around my girl, and it hits me that I'm holding my entire world in my lap. This incredible woman dropped into my life when I wasn't looking, but I'm so fucking glad I opened my eyes.

CHAPTER 13

Bellamy

I'M SITTING IN THE WAITING ROOM, SCROLLING THROUGH MY phone, minding my own business, when someone sits in the seat next to me. Never mind there are several other unoccupied options. This person decides they need to be all up in my space. On instinct, I glance over, and my mouth falls open. "Reid."

"Hey, Dream Girl." He leans in for a kiss, one hand resting on my cheek, while the other presses gently against my belly.

"What are you doing here? You're supposed to be at practice." Training camp has been over for a week. Just as he requested, I stayed at his place and haven't left since. I still have to move all of my things and handle my lease. I've been going and grabbing more clothes as I need them. Eventually, I'll have everything moved. There's a part of me that wants to hold on to my place just a little longer, but that's not fair to Reid or me. I told him I'd give this a shot, and I am. We've just been busy and haven't had the chance.

"You're here."

"You're supposed to be at practice." I raise my eyebrows because he's avoiding the question.

"Yeah, about that. I might have pissed your dad off so bad he decided I was done for the day."

"What did you do?" Dread washes over me. I don't want to come between the two of them. They had a good working relationship before I came into the picture.

"Told him I was leaving early."

"So he punished you by giving you what you wanted?"

Reid shrugs. "Yep."

"What are you not telling me?"

"This is your first appointment, and I wanted to be here. I told Coach I had to leave an hour early, and he wasn't impressed. He wanted to know why, and I told him it was personal. He didn't like that either. He ran me hard, and when it was time for me to leave, I started to walk off the field. He screamed and yelled, said he would fine me, and I kept walking. He then shouted after me to get out of his stadium."

"I'm sorry. It's my fault he's being hard on you." It makes me despise my father even more.

"It's not. That man makes his own decisions. I can see where he's coming from. They pay me nineteen million a year. I'm supposed to be there, but this was more important."

I choke on my spit. I knew he made good money, but damn. "I could have told you what the doctor had to say."

"You could have, but I'd rather be here to hear it on my own. It was an hour, and I gave him everything while I was there, just like I do every other day. I've never missed a practice for any reason. He can fine me. It's fine."

"In the future, I'll make my appointments later in the day." I should have done that with this one, but I thought we were good for me to come on my own and report back to him. I should have known better. If I know anything about my baby daddy, it's that he doesn't do anything halfway.

He kisses my temple. "I'll be here," he assures me. My heart squeezes in my chest. He's never hesitated. Not once. He's a solid foundation that I find myself leaning on. There's still a little voice in the back of my head, telling me that I can't trust this flutter in my chest when he's near or when I think about him, but I push it away.

Reid is not my father.

My gut tells me this is true. My head still stumbles from time to time, but that's okay. I know it will take some time, but I'm not fighting this. Heartbreak be dammed. At least I won't ever have to ask myself *what if*.

"Bellamy Warner." My name is called, and we stand. Reid grabs my hand, and together we make our way to the exam room. "I see you're here to confirm pregnancy?" the nurse asks.

"Yes," Reid and I reply at the same time, making her laugh.

She rattles off questions about how I'm feeling, the first day of my last period, and if I took a home test. She takes my temp, has me step on the scales, which are in the room instead of the hall, something I've never seen before, and takes my blood pressure before handing me a gown, telling me to strip down and cover up with the blanket. "We'll take a blood test after you see the doctor. She's running about fifteen minutes behind, but she'll be with you as soon as she can." The nurse smiles and leaves the room.

"You need some help?" Reid asks.

"I can manage."

"You sure? I think you need help." He stands from his chair and walks toward me. No, that's not right. He's not walking. It's more of a swagger.

When he steps in front of where I'm sitting on the exam table, I open my legs for him to step between them. He smiles softly as he cups my cheek and kisses me. That's all he's done is kiss me. Don't get me wrong, I love his kisses. There isn't a single part of this man that's not addictive.

125

He holds me every night, but never takes things further. Two weeks of sleeping next to the sexiest man I've ever seen, hormones from my pregnancy in overdrive, and I feel as though I might combust.

"I'm sure," I say, once he pulls his lips from mine.

"I don't know… I think you could use the help." His hands find the hem of my blouse that I wore to work today, and he lifts it over my head. I watch as he folds it neatly and walks it to one of the extra chairs before coming back to me. "What about this?" he asks, running his index finger under the strap of my bra.

"That can stay," I say, not recognizing my own voice.

"Bummer," he says, bending his head and placing a kiss on my bare shoulder. Stepping back, he removes my shoes one by one, before his hands grip my hips and he lifts me from the table.

I stand with my arms at my sides, my body aching for his touch as he unbuttons my dress pants, lowers the zipper, and pulls them over my thighs.

"Lift for me," he says, and I do, raising one leg, then the other to step out of my pants. He folds them neatly just as he did with my shirt, before he's back to me. This time, he stands before me, letting his eyes roam.

"Reid," I murmur, and his eyes find mine. They're filled with the same heat that I feel coursing through me. "We can't do this. Not here."

He nods and clears his throat. Reaching for the gown, he helps me into it before reaching beneath and tugging off my panties. He brings them to his nose, and I can feel the blush coat my cheeks as he inhales deeply before slipping them between my shirt and my pants on the chair. "I'll help you," he says when he sees me moving to get back on the table. His hands again find my hips, and he lifts me effortlessly.

"You're beautiful," he tells me, giving my hips a gentle squeeze before releasing me. He moves back to his chair and sits. I watch as he adjusts himself.

"You all right there, big guy?" I tease him.

"I'm used to it," he replies. "Any time I think about you, this is what happens."

It's on the tip of my tongue to ask him why he's not acting on it when there's a knock at the door, and the doctor walks in. I guess she's not running as far behind as they thought. My eyes find Reid's, and he winks.

"Hello, Bellamy, I'm Doctor Armstrong."

"Nice to meet you."

Doctor Armstrong turns toward Reid and offers him her hand. "Reid Montgomery, baby daddy." He grins, and she laughs.

"Well, all right, then. So, I see here you've taken a home test?" she asks.

"I did. It was instantly positive."

"Okay, well, we'll take a listen and see what we can find. If the dates of your last period you gave the nurse are correct, then that puts your due date on March third."

"After the season," Reid says, his smile growing. We'd already worked that out in our heads, with the help of the internet, but it's good to have it confirmed.

"Lie back, and we'll take a listen. It might be too early yet, but from the dates you provided, you're close enough that we'll give it a try." Doctor Armstrong smiles politely.

I do as she says and lie back. She arranges the blanket to cover my lower half before she squirts warm gel on my belly and places the Doppler there.

"What are we listening for?" Reid asks. The words are barely out of his mouth when a loud whooshing sound echoes around the room.

"That." Doctor Armstrong smiles at him. "Your baby's heartbeat."

"Wow." Reid moves next to me and reaches for my hand. His eyes are glued to my belly, and tears burn the back of my eyes as I watch him watching me. When he finally breaks his gaze and looks at me, his eyes are glassy, too. Bending, he kisses me softly before resting his forehead against mine. "Our baby," he whispers.

"Our baby," I repeat.

"We're going to do blood tests just to confirm, and should have the results in a couple of days. Usually it's the next day, but I like to warn that it could be longer if the lab runs behind." Doctor Armstrong wipes off my belly, and Reid helps me pull my gown back together. "I do need to check you. Is it okay if this one stays in the room?" she asks, pointing to Reid.

"It's fine," I assure her. I raise my hand, and Reid laces his fingers through mine.

"I'm here," he says, bending to kiss my temple.

I follow the doctor's instructions, who tells me to put my feet in the stirrups and scoot down. This is the worst part, but I knew from my online research that they'd do an exam today. Reid's grip on my hand tightens, but he doesn't say anything. The exam is over just as quickly as it started, but that doesn't make it any less humiliating.

"All set. Do you have any questions?"

I look up at Reid, and he shakes his head. "No, thank you." I smile at the doctor.

"You can get dressed. Take your time. When you're ready, stop at the counter. The receptionist will have a new mom packet for you. We'll see you back in four weeks."

"Thank you, Doctor," Reid tells her, and she closes the door, leaving us alone.

Letting go of Reid's hand, I move to stand, and he's there, helping me. Together, we discard my gown, and I get redressed. He takes his time, touching me reverently. So much so that his tenderness brings tears to my eyes. Once I'm fully dressed, we leave the room and stop at the reception. I schedule my next appointment for the end of the day and move it up three days, because there's an away game that week. Reid shared his calendar with me so I'll always know where he's going to be.

"I'll see you at home?" I say, as he walks me to my car.

"Yes." He nods. He gives me a sweet kiss before opening my door for me. "Be safe. I'll be right behind you."

"Okay." I buckle in, and he shuts the door and walks to his truck. I give him a couple of minutes before I pull out, and he eases out right behind me. All the way back home, he stays right there, as if he's afraid that if we get separated, it will be for life or something.

He was quiet after the ultrasound, and I get it. It's big and scary, but I can't help but wonder if he's having second thoughts. I hate to even ask him, but if we're not open with each other, this relationship will fail before we've ever really given it a fair shot.

Pulling into my spot in the parking garage, I barely have the car turned off, and he's there, opening my door and offering me his hand. Reid keeps his palm on the small of my back as he leads us to the elevator. We're both quiet as we watch the numbers rise. Once we reach our floor, we exit, still not speaking.

Inside the condo, he tosses his keys onto the entry table, takes my purse from me, dropping it to the table, as well, turns the lock, and leads me down the hall to our bedroom. Inside, he flips on the bedside lamp and turns toward me. His eyes rake over me. They're heated, and they have my body tingling, aching for his touch.

Reid doesn't speak as he finds the hem of my shirt and lifts. I raise my arms for him. He tosses it to the floor before reaching behind me and unclasping my bra. It, too, gets discarded, but neither one of us cares to see where it lands. Why would I when his mouth is on me? He sucks a hard, aching nipple into his mouth, causing me to moan and bury my hands in his hair. With an audible pop, he releases one only to latch on to the other.

The next thing I know, he's dropping to his knees, wrapping his arms around me, and resting his forehead against my belly. I run my fingers through his hair, giving him time to feel what he's feeling. He finally kisses my belly and tilts his head back to look at me.

"Our baby is in there, Bell. A piece of you and me," he rasps.

"It's surreal," I confess.

"I knew I wanted kids and a family, but I didn't understand what it would feel like when it happened. You've given me everything," he says.

"I had some help," I tell him with a smile.

His lips go back to my belly. "Hey, baby, I'm your daddy. I've never met you, but I already love you more than you'll ever know. I can't wait to meet you."

My eyes are leaking, something that seems to be happening to me a lot lately. Reid gets to work removing the rest of my clothes before standing and stripping out of his own. When we're both completely bare, he offers me his hand. "I need you."

Three words that pack a punch of meaning. Eight letters voicing so much with so little. "I need you, too." Need doesn't seem strong enough, but it's the best I've got. Releasing his hand, I climb onto the bed and wait for him. He reaches into the nightstand and pulls out a new box of condoms and tears them open.

"We don't need those. I mean, unless you want to." My hands move to my belly. "This little peanut helped out with that," I say, my voice quivering.

Reid tosses the box over his head and climbs onto the bed. "Only you. Only ever you," he says, before his lips find mine. He settles between my thighs, his hard cock pressing against my pussy. He's close, but not close enough. I need him inside me.

His kiss is gentle, reverent. It's as if he has all the time in the world while I'm burning for him. Reaching between us, I grip his length and guide him to where I want him to be.

"You ready, baby?" he asks.

"My body feels like a firework ready to blow," I admit.

"I read that pregnancy hormones are intense."

"You could say that, and sleeping next to you with nothing the past couple of weeks, that's just taking my need to a higher level."

"You should have told me you needed me."

"I didn't know if you'd changed your mind. And today, you were quiet after the appointment. Second thoughts?"

"No. Never. Just… taking it all in. I didn't want to rush you into anything you weren't ready for. We have forever," he says, making my heart melt for him.

"I don't need time, Reid. I just need you."

"I'm yours, Bellamy," he says as he takes over, pushing forward with his hips, finally giving me what I need. "I never want anything between us ever again," he whispers.

"That's how we got here."

He chuckles. "I guess that means we need to make sure we have a house with lots of bedrooms when we start looking."

I don't argue with him. He's convinced this is what we need, and if I'm being honest, the idea of a house with a big yard sounds perfect.

"Less talking, more thrusting," I tell him, making him laugh.

"Yes, ma'am," he says, still taking his time.

With each forward motion of his hips, there's a slow withdrawal. My eyes burn because it feels like he's making love to me. Reid Montgomery is more than I ever could have imagined, and as I find my release and call out his name, I realize he just knocked down another wall around my heart and stole a bigger piece for himself.

CHAPTER 14

Bellamy

"Is all of this for Camden?" I ask Reid. We're getting ready to go to Baker's for Camden's first birthday party, and there are a lot of gifts sitting next to the front door.

"Yeah."

"Reid, he's turning one." My tone is gentle, but it still says *you went overboard.* "When did you decide to buy all of this?"

"I know. One's a big deal, and I shopped online."

"What are you going to do when he turns sixteen?" I ask him.

"Buy him a truck?" He shrugs.

"You do know his parents will probably be the ones to do that, right?"

"Fine, I'll give him gas money."

"I know you love him, but this is—a lot." I chuckle.

"I know, but the little dude is just so cute, and his mom's a bitch, so I felt like I needed to get him more. Besides, I'm vying for the favorite uncle title. I can't let the others beat me."

"He's one, Reid. He's not going to remember who got him what, and to be honest, he's probably going to like the boxes, bags, and wrapping paper better than any of the gifts."

"What?" His mouth hangs open. "No, he won't."

"We'll see." I grin. My boss, Grant Riggins, and his wife, Aurora, often tell me that when the kids were little, they'd have preferred to have everything except the gifts. That's partly why they started doing experiences as a family instead of lots of gifts. It's something I hope that Reid and I can do for our baby as well.

"Are you ready?" he asks me.

"I am. I'll grab a handful of gifts on my way out," I tease.

"No, ma'am, you will not. No lifting for you."

"Reid, come on. They're gift bags with toys inside. It's not like I'm carrying around fifty pounds in each bag."

"Humor me, Dream Girl." He comes to stand next to me and wraps me in his arms. "I'll start packing these down to my truck."

"I can help you."

"Nope," he says, popping the *p*.

"Okay, well, have fun with that." I point to the mound of gifts.

"I was thinking ahead," he says, before darting down the hall. He comes back holding something I can't make out until he unfolds it. It's a wagon, and he grins as he loads up all the gifts.

"When did you get that?" I ask him.

"It was delivered the other day. I figured that when our little one arrives, we could use it too. Although there are really cool ones that have straps for the kids and everything."

"You've been looking at stuff for the baby?"

"Of course, I have. I have a lot to learn," he says, and tears burn the back of my eyes.

"You're my favorite," I tell him. I want to tell him that I fall harder for him every day. Or hell, every time he opens his mouth, but I can't seem to form the words.

"Ah, Dream Girl." He kisses my temple as he rolls the wagon past me to the front door. "You're my favorite, too," he says, holding the door open for me.

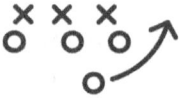

"Did you leave anything at the store?" Foster asks as I hold the door open for Reid, and he wheels in a wagon full of gifts.

"Unfortunately, I did." Reid grins. He parks the wagon next to the gift table that's overflowing and doesn't even bother to unload it. "Where's the birthday boy?" he calls out.

Baker comes walking out of the kitchen with Camden on his hip, wearing a T-shirt that reads *Birthday Boy*. "Bud, you want to go see Uncle Reid?" he asks Camden, who's already leaning toward Reid to take him from his daddy's arms.

I stand and watch as the man, who's the father of my unborn child, loves on one of his best friends' son, the one he refers to as his nephew. This is what our child will get—a loving, fun father who wants to be present.

He's definitely not my father.

"Hey," Rowan says, stopping next to me. "Do you want something to drink?"

"I'm good for now. Thanks, though." I look around the room. "Where's his mom?" I ask, keeping my voice low, just between us.

"She's on a shoot in Paris. She claims she'll celebrate with him when she gets home."

"She took a shoot, knowing it was his first birthday?" I ask. I don't know why I'm surprised. My dad used to do the same thing, and my birthday wasn't even during the season. He didn't care about what was going on in our world, but my mom was there for every moment.

"Yep," Rowan says.

"Damn, poor little guy. Now, I'm glad that Reid went all out with the gifts, even if he'll never remember." I chuckle.

"It wasn't just Reid. Did you see that gift table? All the guys went overboard. I asked Landry what he was thinking about getting him so I could pick it up, and he assured me it was handled. Then, today, he comes walking up the basement stairs with more bags than I was expecting."

"We brought a wagon," I tell her, laughing.

"Are you talking about how over the top they all are?" Corie asks as she and Sloane join us.

"We are." I nod.

"It's ridiculous and charming at the same time," Sloane says, smiling.

"Are those Baker's parents?" I ask.

"Yeah, they're in from out of town. They still live in Philadelphia," Corie explains.

Knox is now the one holding Camden, and he gives him up easily when his grandma comes to get him. Baker calls out that it's time to eat, and the kitchen is a flurry of activity as everyone makes their plates. Reid sits next to me, with his hand on my thigh, as we eat, talk, and laugh with everyone.

Camden handles the first few gifts well, but he quickly moves on and just wants to play with a bag and a bow. Baker and his mom help him with the rest, while we girls take lots of pictures to give to Baker. I make a mental note to tell him how great a job he's doing. These men are proving what Reid was trying so hard for me to understand when we first reconnected. Their jobs do not define them, and they should not be held accountable for someone else's decisions. Baker Sinclair is a single dad, and he's killing it. I know from experience that Camden will see that as he gets older. He's lucky to have his dad in his corner.

"I think it's time for a nap," Baker says, when Camden becomes fussier.

"I'll take him," his mom offers, but Camden only wants his daddy. Baker smiles softly as he turns to head down the hall to put his son down for a nap.

"You ready for all of this?" Reid asks, stepping up behind me and wrapping his arms around my waist.

Placing my hands over his, I reply, "Yeah, I think I am. You?"

"I can't fucking wait, Bell." He kisses my cheek, and again, he steals another piece of my heart. We stand together, wrapped up in one another, just enjoying the day. Our child will have this love and this giant support system, and I'm incredibly grateful for that. I'm truly ready to see where this next chapter leads us. I'm pushing my fears aside and living for the here and now.

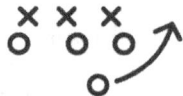

"This was a terrible idea," I say, as I race around the kitchen in the condo I'm now sharing with Reid, trying to make sure everything is perfect. We had food brought in. I wanted to cook, but Reid insisted that I be able to relax. There is no relaxing. I need it to be perfect because any minute now, my mom and his parents are going to be here. They're going to meet for the first time, and we're telling them together that we're pregnant. We went back and forth on inviting my dad, and decided not to. He's been an ass to Reid, and well, he and I are still estranged, so Reid came up with the idea that I could meet him one day after practice, and we'd tell him. I'm dreading that more than I am today. Not because I'm worried about what my father thinks, but I'm certain he's going to take his frustration with me and our relationship out on Reid.

"Bell, it's going to be fine. Come here." He snags me around the waist and pulls me into his chest. I wrap my arms around him and let the steady rhythm of his breathing ground me. "Today's just a formality. We need to tell our parents about the baby and make introductions. It doesn't change us. No matter what happens today, which will be nothing bad, but no matter what the result is, it's still the three of us. Our own little family. Everything looks perfect, because you've thought of every little detail."

"I want your parents to like me."

"They're going to love you. Trust me."

"Are you worried about my mom?" I ask, tilting my head back to peer up at him.

"No. I mean, sure, I'd love for her to approve of me, but nothing she can say, nothing any of them can say, will change what's going on right here." He taps his hand over his heart. "You and this baby are my family. Nothing is ever going to change that."

Resting my head back on his chest, I breathe him in. "Reid?"

"Yeah, Dream Girl?" he answers.

"I'm glad it was you that night. I'm glad I sat next to you at the hotel bar."

"It was always meant to be me, baby."

"You really believe that, don't you?" I pull back, smoothing out his shirt.

"I do. The universe knew I was ready for my dream girl, and this little one"—he places his hand on my belly—"was a nice little bonus."

I open my mouth to say the words, to tell him what he means to me, but I can't seem to form them, and then the doorbell rings, saving me from myself. Hand in hand, we make our way to the door, and Reid pulls it open. His parents greet us with warm smiles. They bypass Reid and head straight for me, first his mom, then his dad, as they hug me.

"It's so nice to meet you," I say, once they've moved on to hug their son.

"Honey, you have no idea. I've waited years for Reid to finally settle down with a good woman."

"Mom, you make it sound like I'm at retirement or something," Reid teases.

"Oh, hush." She waves her hand in the air as the doorbell rings again.

"Go make yourselves at home while we get the door." Reid takes his hand in mine again as we greet my mom.

"Hey, Mom." I smile at her. She still lives here in Nashville, so I see her more frequently than Reid sees his parents, who still live in Atlanta. However, Reid seems to think that once they find out about the baby, they're going to finally make the move to Nashville to be closer.

"Mom, this is Reid, my—" I freeze because what do I call him? My boyfriend? My baby daddy? My one-night stand turned live-in orgasm provider? I'm freaking out and being ridiculous.

"Boyfriend," Reid finishes, saving me as he leans in to kiss my mom's cheek. "It's nice to meet you, Candice. Come on in." He steps back, allowing Mom to enter.

I link my arm through my mom's and lead her into the living room.

"Mom, Dad, this is Candice, Bellamy's mom. Candice, these are my parents, Sam and Paula."

Our parents exchange pleasantries, and I take a deep breath. Everyone is smiling. Now, just to give them the rest of our news, and then we're on the home stretch.

"I hope you're hungry. We ordered from a local diner," Reid tells everyone. "Bell wanted to cook, but I told her to take a break and just enjoy the time with everyone."

"Aww," my mom and Paula both coo.

"Son, we raised you right," Sam tells him. "Always take care of her, and she'll take care of you."

Reid's eyes find mine, and he winks. We make our plates and settle in the dining room. I was careful to order food that hadn't yet set off my morning sickness, and thankfully, I'm able to eat and make it through the meal without an episode.

"Who wants dessert?" Reid asks.

"I couldn't eat another bite," my mom tells him.

"Why don't we catch up and then have dessert?" his mom, Paula, suggests.

In the living room, Reid and I take the loveseat, his parents are on the couch, and my mom is in one of the two recliners. Right away, they jump into chatting about everything, from football to Nashville to the weather.

"Son, how's the team looking this season?" his dad asks.

"Good. We're ready," Reid tells him. He glances at me, looking to see if I'm ready, and I give him a subtle nod. Reaching over, he takes my hand, laces our fingers together, and rests our joined hands on my thigh.

"How long have the two of you been seeing each other?" Sam asks.

"A few months," Reid answers.

"Months?" Paula says. "Reid Montgomery, why are we just now meeting her?" his mom asks, and I can't help the laugh that escapes me.

"She's my dream girl, Mom. I wanted to keep her all to myself."

"Well, tough. We taught you to share," she says, humor lacing her tone.

"Well, since you're so big on sharing, I have some news," Reid says. He pauses, and his mom huffs out a breath.

"Don't leave her hanging, son," Sam says.

Paula looks over at my mom. "They live to torture us, don't they?"

"They do," Mom agrees with an amused smile, because she and I had this conversation a few days ago. When we found out Reid's parents were coming to visit, Reid thought it would be a good idea to tell them all together. When I called Mom to invite her, that's when she found out about Reid and that we've been living together.

"Bellamy and I are having a baby." Reid blurts out the news, as if he's asking if they're finally ready for their dessert.

Our parents stare at us in shock. It's Sam who finally speaks. "Congratulations!" he says, his deep voice loud as he stands, and we do, as well. He pulls us into a hug at the same time before Mom and Paula take their turns.

They ask how I'm feeling, when I'm due, and what they can do, if anything. Instant acceptance and support bring tears to my eyes. These damn pregnancy hormones are going to be the death of me.

Reid's parents leave first, promising to catch up with us more before they leave. They're here for a few more days before heading back to Atlanta, where the first preseason game for the Rampage happens to be held.

"It was so nice to meet you, Reid," Mom says, hugging him.

He steps away and kisses my temple. "You too, Candice. I'm going to go start on clean-up," he says to me before walking away.

"He's very handsome," Mom says as we watch him leave.

"He is."

"He plays football?"

"He does. For Dad."

She nods. "I never thought I'd see the day, but I'm happy for you, Bellamy. You didn't let your fears keep you from something special."

"What if he turns out to be just like Dad?"

"Sweetheart, he won't. Your father isn't a bad man. He threw himself into his career, and he got lost. He was so lost that he couldn't find his way back to us, and we grew apart. He loves you. I know he wasn't around much, but you pushed him away after the divorce."

"I know, because I didn't know how to deal with the anger. I tried to push Reid away, too, but he kept fighting."

"That's the difference. Don't let the past control what you have here. He looks at you as if you're his entire world, Bellamy."

"He makes me feel like I am," I confess.

"Come here." Mom pulls me into a hug, and I return her embrace.

"I think I'm falling in love with him," I tell her, before pulling out of our hug.

Her eyes shimmer with tears. "Don't be afraid to fall. He's going to catch you."

"How do you know?"

She grins. "He's looked over here half a dozen times since he walked away. If I had my guess, I'd say he feels the same. You should discuss it together. Communication is everything."

"Not yet," I tell her. "I need more time."

"There's no rush. That man of yours isn't going anywhere." She hugs me again. "Take care of you and my grandbaby." Her eyes light up. "I can't believe I'm going to be a grandma."

"You still have some time to get used to the idea," I remind her.

"Call me," she says, after another quick hug.

Closing the door behind her, I make my way to the kitchen, where Reid has everything cleaned up. "That went well," I tell him.

"It did. How are you feeling?" he asks, gripping my hips and lifting me to the counter.

"Good. Relieved," I confess, wrapping my arms around his neck.

"The realtor sent me a few houses for us to look at. How about I grab my laptop, and we can have some of this cheesecake and look through them?"

"You make it hard for a girl to say no," I say, pecking his lips with a kiss.

"Good," he says, grinning. He lifts me off the counter and smacks my ass lightly. "Go settle in. I'll be right there."

"I can help," I offer.

"And you can let me take care of you. Off you go." He moves to swat at my ass again, but this time, I'm ready for him and jump out of the way, laughing as I move to the couch, pull the blanket into my lap, and settle in, just like he asked.

CHAPTER 15

Reid

"**I** THINK THAT'S IT," I TELL BELLAMY, GLANCING AROUND HER empty apartment. I paid out the rest of her lease, which took some convincing. Since we finally have a home game this week, every day after practice, and when she gets off work, we've been packing and deciding what to donate and what to keep.

"Yeah," she agrees, as she, too, spins to look at the now-empty apartment.

I just took the last box down to my truck. The guys offered to help, but I knew this was going to be hard for her—giving up her space to come to mine—so I wanted her to have the freedom to process her emotions without an audience. There's a teenage boy who lives in the apartment across the hall, and I paid him a couple of hundred bucks and an autograph to help me carry the furniture down to my truck.

I wish we were moving into a house, one that was ours alone, but that takes time. I couldn't wait. I needed her with me. I was too impatient to wait, and my dream girl wanted that, too. She's pushing back at her fears, choosing to trust me, to trust us, and that's something I'll never take for granted.

"You need me to give you a moment?" I ask, sliding my arm around her waist and pulling her close. She rests her head on my chest and sighs.

"No, I'm okay. This is just a big step, and it's so fast."

"Not fast enough," I grumble, and she laughs.

"I've slept in your bed every night since we found out," she reminds me.

"Our bed, Bell, you've slept in *our* bed. No other woman but you has ever slept there," I assure her. She peers up at me under long lashes. The sparkle in her brown eyes shines bright, telling me she's happy. I'll do everything I can to keep that sparkle there.

"Let's go home," she says. Her voice is strong, resolute, and it takes everything I have not to toss her over my shoulder and race us down to the truck.

After leading her to the door with my arm around her waist, we step out into the hall and lock up the apartment for the final time. When we reach my truck, I open the door for her and help her inside. "What do we do with the keys?" I ask.

"I need to drop them off at the main office up town."

"Do you want to do that now?"

"Do you mind?"

"Not at all." I kiss her softly before closing the door. As I walk around the truck to take my seat behind the wheel, I glance up at her place and grin. She's coming home where she belongs. If she notices my excitement, she doesn't comment as I drive us across town.

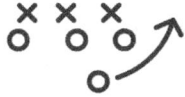

Sunday. Game day. And I'm ready. I've never been this amped up to play a game, and I know why. She's going to be here. My dream girl is going to be up in the suite with Corie and Sloane, while Rowan will be down on the field with us. Corie will have to step away to work some, but she's assured me it won't be much, and that's okay, because Sloane will be there to keep her company.

I know that convincing her to come to the game was hard, and I'm so damn proud of her for being here. Not just for me, but for her, too. In her eyes, the game I love ruined her life. Now, it's going to be a huge part of hers, and she's facing her fears. I wish I had the words to tell her what that means to me.

More than her just being here, we've agreed that tonight, after the game, we're going to try to get Coach alone and tell him about the baby. Not because she wants her father to know that he's going to be a grandpa, but because I may need to take time off to be with her. Maybe? I know for sure I will when the baby is born, but thankfully, our little peanut is due at the beginning of our off-season. I'll have several months to help her heal and for us to bond as a family. I'm fucking stoked.

"What's that shit-eating grin for?" Baker asks.

"Bellamy's here."

"Yeah?" He smiles. "That's great, man."

"He know yet?" Knox asks, nodding toward Coach's office.

"Nah, but we're going to try to catch him to tell him tonight."

"We'll stick around," Landry tells me.

"You don't have to do that," I tell him.

"We're going to anyway. Besides, I know my wife will want to check on Bellamy."

"Mine, too," Knox agrees.

"I can stay," Baker says.

"Nah, you go home to see my nephew. None of you has to stay."

"What else have I got to do?" Foster says, with a shrug.

Baker looks torn.

"I'm a big boy," I assure him. "I don't need his blessing, but my nephew needs his daddy."

"I'll call the nanny. If he's sleeping, which he should be, I'll stay."

Not gonna lie. Their support means the world to me. I meant what I said. I don't need Coach's approval. He has no say over her life or mine. He can make mine hell all he wants, and he has been. He rides my ass at practice like he's fucking me, but that's okay, because that's a handful of hours at best, and then I get to go home to her. That makes it all worth it.

My eyes glance up at the suite, and I see her standing there with Sloane. They're laughing, and when she catches me staring, she waves. I can't see it from here, but I bet her cheeks are a gorgeous light shade of pink. Turning back to the field, I get my head in the game. We're up by four, and there are only three minutes left on the play clock. Defense is on the field, and I watch as one of our linemen sacks the quarterback from Washington.

"Fuck yeah!" someone roars. I don't know who, but I'm agreeing with him as I slip my helmet back on and jog out onto the field. We need to score again and bring this win home.

In the huddle, Knox calls the play. "Rampage on three!" he shouts.

We all place our hands out, stacking them on top of each other, and shout, "One, two, three, Rampage!" before we break into our positions. I line up next to the right tackle, getting into position. I'm balanced, focused, and ready. Knox calls out the play, taking the snap from our center, Thomas Keen, and I explode off the line, brushing past the linebacker and pumping my fist, cutting left to the center of the field. Knox pulls his arm back and tosses a Hail Mary to Landry, just as he's tackled to the ground.

We made it to the red zone.

Twenty more yards to move the ball to the endzone.

Blood rushes in my ears. It doesn't matter that this is a preseason game. I'm an athlete and a competitive asshole. I want to bring home the win. For me, for my team, for my dream girl, who faced her fears to watch me play the only thing I've ever loved, until I met her.

Fuck.

I'm in love with her.

I knew I felt strongly for her, but it's standing here on the field, doing the job that almost made me lose her, when I realize that I love her more than the game—more than anything. My eyes glance up at the suite, and I grin before getting back into position, keeping my head in the game. I'm bringing this fucking win home.

Keen snaps the ball when Knox calls the play. Space is tight as the defense closes in quickly. They know they have to stop us, but what they don't know is that my girl is here watching, and how big a deal that is. My eyes scan the field, and I fight for a spot, right between the safeties, to slip through. I turn in time to catch Knox's gaze as he launches the ball in my direction. Hands extended in the air, I snatch the ball, stepping just out of reach of a defenseman, and over another as my legs sprint the final eight yards to the endzone.

Touchdown Rampage!

My teammates jump on me, and then Landry appears, shaking his ass for the crowd, and I can't leave my boy hanging. We do a little jig, and I glance up at the suite, pointing to my girl. *This one's for you, Bell.*

Back on the sidelines, I pull off my helmet and suck down some water. I watch as Washington tries to score, but our defense holds them. On their final drive, the clock counts down to zero. Mark that as a win for the Rampage. Media swarms us, but I manage to skip past them all. With my helmet in my hands, I jog off to the locker room. Landry loves that shit, and Knox, well, he's the face of the team, and I have no doubt his wife is on her way to him, if she's not already there, to take pictures for social media. We have a team photographer, but I can't blame the girl for using that as an excuse to get to her husband.

By the time they make it to the locker room, I'm climbing out of the mandatory ice bath and rushing to take the world's fastest shower. I'm zipping up my bag, anxious to meet Bellamy in the hallway. I showed her where to go, and Sloane, who knows the drill by now, is with her. I'm not worried about Bell. I just want to see her. Wrap my arms around her, kiss her, maybe even tell her that I'm in love with her. I can't stop my grin from forming at the thought.

"Montgomery!" Coach Warner bellows.

I fight the urge not to roll my eyes. "Yes, Coach?" I ask, keeping things professional.

"Ice bath."

"Already done." He narrows his eyes at me, and I hold his stare. "Gotta go see my girl," I tell him. He needs to know that I'm hers, and she's mine, and no amount of riding my ass is going to change that. His face is red, and he knows he has nothing else to bitch at me about, because I give him all of me when I'm on that field, and at every practice. I wonder if that vein in his forehead will pop out when he finds out his daughter is living with me and having my baby.

I wave to the guys and push out the doors with my bag slung over my shoulder. I spot Bellamy and Sloane instantly. They're standing against the wall, at the end of the hallway, almost as if they're trying to stay hidden. I'm sure Bellamy didn't want to run into her dad.

"There's my dream girl," I say, dropping my bag, snaking an arm around her waist, and pulling her into a hug. "How are you doing?" I ask, keeping my lips next to her ear. She nods as she pulls back. "Okay?"

"Yeah." She smiles. "It was nice to see you play."

"Say the word, baby, and I'll get you a flight and tickets to every damn game."

"You know that's not feasible," she says, her hands resting over her belly.

"No, but I want you there. As long as you know that, then we're good. Now, I'm gonna need you to turn for me," I tell her.

"What?" She furrows her brow.

"Oh, that's an easy one," Sloane tells her. "He's going to go all caveman on you once he reads his name on your back." She picks at the jersey she's wearing, which just so happens to be Knox's. "It's a thing," she says, as if she's experienced it first-hand. "I've watched Knox and Landry both go through this stage. It's fun." Sloane grins. "More fun for you, I'm sure." She winks, and Bellamy's cheeks flame red.

"Turn for me, baby," I tell her.

She shakes her head but does as I ask, and I groan when I see my name on her back. Fuck, I didn't get it when Knox, Landry, and even Landon would talk about seeing their girl in their jersey, but I now understand the appeal.

Speaking of Landon, I need to call him and tell him I met my dream girl at his wedding. I haven't mentioned Bellamy to him yet. He asked me where I had disappeared to, and I told him I'd gotten a drink, taken a walk on the beach, and gone to bed. It's not a complete lie. Those things happened, but a whole hell of a lot happened in between.

Stepping up behind Bellamy, I align my front to her back before placing my lips next to her ear. "You know what would make this better? Well, two things, actually," I tell her.

"What's that?" she asks, turning to look at me over her shoulder.

I peck a kiss on her lips. "If our little one were here, and if that name you're wearing was yours."

She sucks in a breath, her body sagging against mine. I hold her tighter as we chat with Sloane, waiting for the others. Corie joins us, and then Knox, Landry, Foster, and Baker come out. Finally, Rowan appears, having to stay back and work on any of my teammates who need it.

"Anyone left in there?" I ask Rowan.

"Just the staff," she says.

I nod. "Ready?" I ask Bellamy.

"If I have to," she says, stepping out of my hold.

I take her hand in mine and address my friends, our friends, "You guys don't have to stay."

"Oh, we're staying," Corie tells me. "Bellamy's family now." She crosses her arms over her chest as if I'm going to fight her. I won't. My girl needs all the love she can get, especially where my team is concerned. They're showing her that it's not the game, but the choices of the person.

They're choosing her, just as I did.

"Baker, go home to Cam," I tell him.

"The nanny said he's sound asleep. I'll hang for a little while," he says, leaning back against the wall.

There's a lump in my throat. "Thanks," I tell them. "Your support means everything."

"We'll be here," Rowan says, reaching out to squeeze Bellamy's arm gently.

"Thank you," she murmurs.

With her hand in mine, I lead her into the locker room. It's pretty much cleared out, just as Rowan said, except for the staff. When we reach Coach's door, I knock, and he calls out to enter.

"Hey, Coach," I say, pulling Bellamy inside the room behind me. She's suddenly stiff, and I wrap my arm around her, keeping her close, letting her know I'm here, and I'm not him. I'll always put her and our baby first.

"Montgomery," he greets coldly. "Bellamy," he says, his tone softer. "What can I do for you?" He glares at where my arm is around her waist, and that glare only intensifies when Bellamy places her hand on my chest, connecting us even further.

"We wanted to let you know that Bellamy's moved in with me." And there it is, the vein on his forehead has officially popped. "And," I add, because we might as well rip off the Band-Aid of truth, "you're going to be a grandpa," I tell him.

"What?" he explodes. He stands from his desk, his chair sliding back and hitting the wall as he slaps his hands down on the wood of the desk so hard I'm surprised it doesn't buckle. "Get your hands off of my daughter, Montgomery," he says through gritted teeth.

Bellamy curls into me at his demand. "No can do, Coach. You see, she's my dream girl, and we're having a baby. I choose her," I tell him, my voice clear. "Nothing you say will have me walking away from her."

He's fuming mad, and if it were possible, I think we'd be able to see smoke coming out of his ears. "Bellamy, you don't want this," he says, his tone softer, but the edge of his anger is still there, simmering at the surface.

"You don't know what I want."

"You don't have to live with him. You can come and live with me, or with your mother."

"I don't need Reid to take care of me, William," she says, using his first name instead of Dad. I wince at the same time he does. My girl is out for vengeance. "I'm living with him because we care about each other. We're going to raise this baby together. I know that's a concept you aren't able to comprehend, but trust me when I tell you, I'm where I want to be."

Fuck me, my heart races at her words. My arms pull her closer, holding her a little tighter.

"You don't want this life. How many times have you told me that? You hate football. You hate what it does to families."

"Yeah," she agrees. "Until I met a man who puts me first despite his busy work schedule. He calls me before and after every game. He calls me every night to tell me goodnight when he's away, and if I don't get a call, I have a text every morning telling me to have a good day. When he's home, he's home with me. We talk, we plan, we laugh, and we do all the things you were never willing to do."

"I was building something great to take care of you and your mother," he says, sounding almost defeated.

"Maybe," she says, shrugging. "But you sacrificed us in the process. If Reid's taught me anything, it's that you have to want to find the time. I understand the desire to have a career, support your family, and grow in your career, but you lost your way. You claim you were building a better life for us, but you didn't fight for us either. You let us go."

"It was the right thing to do," he says, his voice raspy.

"Let's agree to disagree on this one, *Dad*," she sasses.

"I want to know my grandchild."

"Well, insulting his or her father and treating him as if he's less than when he's one of the top-ranked tight ends in the league isn't the right way to earn that right."

They stare at one another until finally, Coach Warner nods. He clears his throat. "How are you feeling?" he asks softly, the anger suddenly drained out of him.

"Fine. We're due in March," she says, tossing him a bone.

"So, after the season." He nods before he turns his gaze to me. "I'm watching you, Montgomery."

I open my mouth to tell him he can watch all he wants, but my girl talks first, beating me to it.

"Good, then you can see how a man can have a successful career and a family that he enjoys being around at the same time. You might learn something, William."

Ouch. Her words hit as his shoulders droop, and he casts his gaze toward the floor. I kinda feel bad for him, because I know what it would do to me if she shut me out, but there are years of hurt between them, which he's not going to be able to repair overnight.

Bellamy peers up at me under long dark lashes. "You ready?"

"Yeah, baby, I'm ready." We turn toward the door as Coach calls out for us to wait.

Bellamy freezes before turning to glance over her shoulder, and I do the same. "What?" Her tone isn't unkind, but it's laced with pain and years of hurt.

"Can we do dinner, or maybe lunch?"

She glances at me, and I shrug. "Your decision, Bell. I'm behind you no matter what," I tell her.

"I'll think about it."

Coach is dejected, but he nods. "Anytime, anywhere," he says with conviction in his tone.

Bellamy doesn't say anything. She doesn't even nod as she turns back and steps out of his office, with me hot on her heels. We reach the door to the locker room, and I stop her. "You okay?"

"He's about fifteen years too late," she says, wiping at her eyes.

"I know, baby. I know he hurt you, and you owe him nothing, but maybe keep an open mind? People can change."

"He's not getting close to our baby until he's proven that," she says, her voice strong.

"That's fine by me, but if you're considering that, you have to give him a chance."

"Ugh," she groans, resting her forehead against my chest. "Can we go now?"

I know she's reached her limit. "Yeah, Dream Girl, we can go." When I push open the door, we're greeted by our friends, our family by choice. The ladies swarm Bellamy and take turns hugging her.

"We're going to dinner, catch up," Corie calls over her shoulder.

"I'm going to head home. You good?" Baker asks.

"We're good," I assure him. "Thanks for sticking around."

"I want to hear all about it," he tells me, picking his bag up off the floor.

"I'll call you tomorrow," I assure him.

"I'm following my wife and the food," Landry says, walking away in the same direction as the girls.

"Yep," Knox says, trailing behind him.

"What about you?" I ask Foster.

"Everything good?" he asks.

"Yeah, he was pissed, but my girl put him in his place. Lots of anger there," I confess.

"You stand beside her. She's what's important now." There's something in his eyes, as if he's trying to tell me without saying the words.

"I know, my man." I clamp a hand down on his shoulder. "I don't know who she is, or what happened, but it's not too late to make it right."

Foster doesn't acknowledge my words. Instead, he says, "Let's eat. I'm starving."

My friend has something he's holding close to his chest, and one day, he's going to let us help him through whatever it is. I want him to get his girl, the one who makes him as happy as my dream girl makes me.

Foster walks away, and I pull my phone from my pocket to text Landon.

> Me: Thinking about scaling a wall.

Landon will know what that means. He scaled that wall at the stadium during a game to get to his now-wife, Tessa.

> Landon: My man! I can't wait to meet her.

> Me: We're having a baby.

Ladon: Damn, bro, are you trying to make me look bad?
Looks like my wife and I have some catching up to do.

Me: Talk soon.

Landon: Take care of her.

Me: I plan to, my man.

There is nothing I want more than to take care of my family.

CHAPTER 16

Bellamy

PULLING MY SWEATER TIGHTER AROUND ME, I MAKE MY WAY up the front porch of my mom's house. It was warm enough today that wearing this sweater over my T-shirt was sufficient, but now that the sun's gone down and the wind's picked up, it's become cold. That's October weather in Tennessee.

Mom insisted on making dinner and that Amanda and I join her. When I told her I was going to watch the game, she made it a point to invite me to her place to watch it. I know this has to be weird for her, but she was insistent, and I couldn't tell her no. So, here I am, walking into my mother's house to watch my dad's team on TV. Not just my dad, but my man, too. Dad was coaching college when they divorced, and as far as I know, my mom doesn't follow his career or the team, but she has been this season because of Reid.

It's weird, and makes my belly twist with unease, but I'm here, and I'm thankful my best friend beat me here—she can be our buffer. I've never needed a buffer with my mom. Before meeting Reid, I told her pretty much everything about my life. Now, I feel guilty telling her how happy my football-playing baby daddy makes me, when her husband didn't do the same.

"There she is," Mom says as I walk into the kitchen, where she and Amanda are sitting. "Let's eat."

"Did you make your cheesy chicken, broccoli, and rice?" I ask, even though I'd recognize the smell anywhere.

"Yep." Mom grins.

We all busy ourselves filling our plates and carrying them to the dining room.

"Reid and his team are having a good season so far," Mom says.

"You've been watching?" I mean, I know she told me that she has, but I'm still shocked.

"Of course. Week five and undefeated. That's impressive," Mom boasts.

"They're doing well."

"Your father must be proud."

"I wouldn't know," I admit.

"How is he with Reid?" Mom asks. I've been waiting for this question.

"Honestly, in the beginning, he was riding him pretty hard at practice, always calling him out, but since the day we told him about the baby, Reid says he's been more dismissive than an asshole, so I guess that's better." I shrug.

"Bellamy, your father's a good man," Mom says gently.

"He left us."

"Sweetheart, relationships are tough, and it's just as much my fault as it was his. I wanted more of his time, and he was building a career to support us. He still supported us. He bought this house, paid for everything you might ever need, and then some. He might not have been here, but even after the divorce, he supported us."

"He left us." Thankfully, I've finished eating, or this conversation would have made me lose my appetite.

"He tried so many times to see you, and you refused. I wanted to make you, but your dad said not to. He didn't want to force you, but he missed you."

"That's not how I remember it," I tell her.

"Bellamy, you were so young. He sent cards and letters, and you told me to get rid of them. No matter how I encouraged you to read them, you wouldn't."

"Because he didn't choose us. He didn't choose me," I tell her, feeling tears prick my eyes.

"We fell apart, Bellamy. Sure, his job had a lot to do with that, but it was just as much me as it was him. I didn't fight hard enough to make it work. I wanted things to be simple, like a fairy tale. That's not life."

"Why are you telling me this? Why now, after all of these years?"

Mom smiles softly. "Because, my darling daughter, you're finally in a place in your life that you're willing to listen. You've carried this hate for so long, but since meeting Reid, you've changed. I can see the anger starting to fade away, and you're willing to listen. One day, you'll understand a parent's love for their child."

I place my hand on my small bump. At seventeen weeks along, there's no hiding that I'm pregnant. I love this baby fiercely, more than I ever could have imagined possible. "He should have tried harder."

"I'll be right back." Mom stands and walks out of the room.

"You doing okay?" Amanda asks me.

"Yeah, I just don't understand why she defends him. She's never once talked ill of him, and he left us."

"Bella, I love you, but your mom is right. You were young, and relationships are hard. There are things you didn't know or see, things you wouldn't have understood at ten years old."

"I can agree to that, but why now?"

Amanda shrugs. "You've had so much anger for so long. You've had a vise grip on those hurt feelings, and nothing anyone said could change that. How many times have I told you that maybe it was time to leave the past there and start fresh with your dad?"

"A lot," I mumble.

She grins. "Reid's changed you in so many ways," she tells me.

I think about her words as my phone rings, and an image of the man himself smiles back at me. I accept his video call because I miss him like crazy, and I need to hear the sound of his voice.

"There's my dream girl," he says, and instantly, a smile tugs at my lips.

"Don't you have a game to play?" I ask him.

"Yeah, we're in the locker room, about to take the field. If your dad catches me on the phone, he'll ream my ass, but I need to check on my girls before the game."

"You know, if we're having a son, he's going to be offended you assumed he was a girl all this time," I tease.

"I feel it in my gut, Bell. We're having a baby girl."

I don't question him because he's never wavered in that prediction, not once, and I don't care what we have as long as he or she is loved, happy, and healthy. "You ready for the game?"

He tilts his head to the side. "What's wrong?"

"Nothing," I answer too quickly.

"Come on, baby. It's me you're talking to. Are you okay? The baby?" he asks.

"We're both fine. I'm at Mom's with her and Amanda. She made us dinner, and we're going to watch the game."

His eyes widen. "Your mom is watching?"

"Apparently, she's watched them all this season to support you."

"Really? Give her a hug from me, yeah?"

Mom comes up behind me and wraps her arm around my shoulders.

"How about I give our girl one from you, too?" Mom asks, waving at the phone with her free hand.

"I like the way you think, Candice." He winks. "Amanda, tell them you want one, too. Can't have my girl's best friend being left out."

"I'll be collecting from both of them," Amanda calls out. "Don't you worry."

Reid laughs, and the sound sinks into my soul like a warm embrace.

"Go kick some ass," I tell him.

"You sure you're all right?"

"I'm fine. I promise." I smile, hoping to ease his concerns.

"I'll call you after the game."

"You don't have to. I know you'll be tired, and it'll be late."

"I'm not going to bed without telling you goodnight," he grumbles, and my heart soars.

"Good game."

"Thanks, Dream Girl." He blows me a kiss, and the screen goes black.

"He's a good one," Mom tells me.

"Did Dad ever do things like that?" I ask her. "Call before a game?"

"He did. When I was pregnant with you, as his career advanced, and as I settled into my role as your mom with my own career, we just kind of drifted. Bellamy, it wasn't all on your father. I didn't make the effort either. He was gone a lot, and I just stopped including him in our lives. I'm just as much to blame for our marriage falling apart as he is."

"All these years," I whisper, "you never said anything."

"You got upset anytime I tried. You couldn't see or feel anything but your anger, but I think your football player has helped you see that it's not the game, but the situation, and it's not all on the man, either. I was just as guilty for the demise of our marriage."

"I feel like the last fifteen years have been a lie," I confess.

"Oh, honey, I'm sorry. I should have insisted that you sit down and have this conversation. Your dad never wanted me to. He said you'd come around in your own time. With each year that passed, I tried less and less, which again, is on me. I failed you there. I was with you every day. I could see your anger, but I didn't sit you down to make you understand."

I glance at Amanda, and she smiles. "He loves you, Bella. I can see it when he looks at you. He was proud as a peacock that day at the stadium, during family day. He was introducing you to everyone, including Reid." She snickers.

"I like to think life has a way of working out. I think the universe knew you needed a man to show you. That's the only way you were ever going to work past the anger and resentment."

My head is spinning. All this time, it wasn't just him. Why have I never considered that? I know why: I was angry and needed someone to blame. He wasn't there, so he got all of it. The weight of all the years I've lost with my dad because I was too stubborn to see the forest through the trees sits heavily on my chest.

"What's in the box?" I ask my mom.

She gives me a sad smile and hands it to me. Pulling off the lid, I see lots of envelopes. "What's this?"

"They're all from your dad. You refused the first several, so after that, I just put them in this box. I thought maybe one day, you might want to see them."

Tears burn my eyes, and I try to blink them away, but it's no use. They fall unchecked, coating my cheeks. Lifting the first envelope, I flip it over. It's sealed, so I slide my finger underneath and pull out the contents. It's a birthday card—my thirteenth. A check falls out, for thirteen hundred dollars. "*I can't believe my baby girl is a teenager. I love you so much, my Bella. I hope you have the best birthday. I'd love to see you when you're ready. Love, Dad,*" I read his note inside the card.

"He loves you so much, Bellamy. After the first birthday, when the check wasn't cashed, he started wiring me the money, in addition to sending you a check."

"That's how we took those trips every year for my birthday?" I ask her.

She nods. "I mean, I make good money as a paralegal, but not that kind of money. You never asked, and I never told you, because anytime I mentioned his name, you got upset and even angrier. That's on me. I should have made you listen. As your mother, that was my job, and I'm sorry I let you down."

I want to be mad at her, but honestly, I'm so tired of being angry. I'm in such a good place in my life. I've met a man who makes me smile every day. We're living together and starting a family. I want to swim in happiness and push the sadness away. "I'm so tired of being angry," I say, choking on my tears.

"Oh, Bellamy." Mom pulls me into a hug.

"Damn you, Warner women!" Amanda scolds as she sniffs, and we all laugh.

"Leave them here, or take them. Either way, they're yours."

"I think… I think I'll take them with me."

Mom smiles. "Okay." She wipes at her eyes. "Now, we have to watch my ex-husband and my future son-in-law bring home a win." She winks and turns to head toward the living room.

"Did that just happen?" I ask Amanda.

"It did. You doing okay?"

I think about her question and nod. "Yeah, I think I am."

"Damn, Reid Montgomery must have some skills." She smirks, and we both chuckle.

She's not wrong, but it's not his skills that have changed me. It's him and his constant presence, whether we're at home together or he's on the road. There's never a doubt in my mind that he's not thinking about me. He makes certain never to let me forget. Reid is putting in the work, and I vow to do better.

This life we're building is what I want. He's what I want, and I'm not sure if I've done the best job at telling him or showing him. I've pushed past my fears, but no matter how hard I try, I've allowed them to linger. But no more. I meant what I said. I'm so tired of being angry. I just want to relish the happiness that's my life and enjoy every second of it.

Placing the box on the table, I link arms with my best friend, and we join my mom on the couch, cheering the Rampage on for a win.

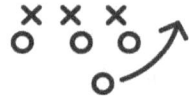

I'm sitting on the bed with the contents of the box spread out around me. I've opened every single envelope in the box. I've read every word my dad wrote to me, in addition to the cards he picked. There's a box of tissues that's half empty and a used pile of said tissues sitting next to it.

Basically, I'm an emotional mess, but when my phone rings with a video call, I don't hesitate to answer. "Hi." I smile through the tears.

"What's wrong?" Reid stands and starts walking. "Are you hurt? Is it the baby? Where are you?" he says, panic taking over.

"I'm at home. In our bed," I tell him. "I'm fine. The baby's fine. I'm just a little emotional."

"Call Amanda, or I'll call Sloane, and have her come stay with you. What can I do? I'll grab a flight out tonight," he says, rambling.

"Reid?"

"Yeah?" he asks, his chest heaving. Concern and worry shine in his eyes.

"I'm okay."

"What is it?" I hear my dad's voice. "Is it Bellamy? Is she okay? The baby?" Dad fires off questions.

"I'm okay," I say again, feeling warm all over at having both of them so concerned for me and the baby.

"Bellamy?" Dad grabs Reid's hand and moves to the phone to face him. "You're okay?"

"I am," I assure him. "Pregnancy hormones."

"Good. Good. Okay." He nods. "I'll uh, just go," he says, dropping Reid's hand.

Reid's eyes follow him as he walks away before focusing back on me. "Sorry, babe. We're getting dinner in a private dining room of the hotel. He was there and saw me freak out."

"It's okay." I smile because that's what this man does to me. He has me smiling all the time.

"Tell me why you're crying."

I pan the phone to the mess around me. "This," I tell him.

"What's all of that?"

"Letters, cards, invitations," I rattle on. "They're from my dad. Mom kept them all these years."

"She was keeping them from you?" he asks.

"No, not really." I go on to explain everything that happened tonight. "I was so angry for so long," I tell him. "And now, it's hard to hold on to all of that when all I feel is happy." This time, it's my words making him smile.

"Yeah?"

I nod. "I love the life we're building, Reid. I love this baby, and I don't want to be angry anymore—these cards, the letters, the invitations to work and social events. I was young and blinded by what I thought I knew, and too damn stubborn to listen to reason, and my dad, he didn't want my mom to push me," I explain. "So many years I've lost with him."

"That's a lot to take in. I'm sorry I'm not there."

"You are here, Reid. I'm in our bed. In the home we share." I want to tell him that I've fallen in love with him, but I can't do that over the phone. Besides, I'm wrung out emotionally. I need some more time to process all of this.

"What do you need?" he asks.

Just like that, instant support. This man, he's never stopped showing up for me. Even when he's thousands of miles away, he proves that he's in this with me.

"Just time," I tell him. "It's a lot to take in, but I feel lighter in a way I haven't in years. A lot of that is because of you."

"Me?"

"You never gave up on us. You knew what you wanted, and you showed me how it feels to be the first choice. Despite your hectic career."

"You and the baby are first always, Bell." His eyes soften. "Are you okay there on your own? Want me to hop on a flight tonight?"

"I'm fine. Just working through my emotions."

"I wish I were there to hold you."

"Tomorrow."

"You know it, Dream Girl. Try to get some rest. Call me if you need me. I don't care what time it is."

"I'm okay," I promise. "Congrats on the win, number twenty." I smile.

"Thanks, babe. Please try to get some rest."

"I will. Safe flight."

"Always, beautiful." He blows me a kiss as he always does, and when the line goes dead, I miss him.

CHAPTER 17

Reid

MY PALMS ARE SLICK WITH SWEAT, AND MY CHEST ACHES from the rapid thud of my heart. Today's the day. We're mere minutes away from the ultrasound tech walking through the door, and we'll see our baby on the screen for the very first time—tiny limbs, fluttering heartbeat, the soft curve of life just beginning. We also hope to be able to find out the gender. Are we having a little boy or a little girl to love, to raise, to build our world around?

It feels like we're standing on the edge of something vast and irreversible. A single moment, quietly enormous, is about to change everything. Up until today, I've seen our baby growing, the proof in Bellamy's rounding belly. I know he or she is in there, but seeing them, knowing we're only halfway there, that we still have months until we get to hold our sweet baby in our arms, is a delicious torture.

"How are you doing, Momma?" I ask Bellamy, pulling myself out of my thoughts. I wipe my hands on my sweats and offer one to her. She takes it without hesitation. She sits in a gown on the exam table. We've already seen the doctor, and everything is measuring great. Now, we wait for the ultrasound tech to come and show us our baby.

"I'm excited." Bellamy smiles up at me. "You?"

"Same. A little nervous," I admit.

"Me, too." She nods. "You sure you want to know the gender?" she asks.

"Yeah, I mean, unless you changed your mind?"

"No. I want to know. We can pick out a name and a nursery."

"In our new house." I grin. We've looked at several houses, and finally, one close to Knox and Landry came on the market, and it's everything we both wanted. We put in an offer for the full asking price and closed a couple of weeks ago. We get the keys this weekend to start moving in, which works out great, since we have a Thursday night game this week. It's away, but I'll be home Friday, and the guys are coming to help me start moving things over. Life is moving at a rapid pace, but I wouldn't change it.

"Yes," she says, her smile bright, and those big brown eyes of hers, so full of excitement, could bring a man to his knees.

"Knock, knock," a female voice says as she enters the room. "Hi, I'm Tina. I'm going to be performing your ultrasound today."

"Thank you," Bellamy says.

"Is this your first?" Tina asks as she gets busy setting up the machine.

"Baby, and an ultrasound," Bellamy replies.

"Perfect. Now, we do offer the 3D option, but that's an additional charge. I can do the regular, and if you want the 3D, we'll do it after."

"What's the 3D?" I ask.

"Oh, it's amazing." Tina picks up a book and shows us some sample images.

"Wow," Bellamy breathes.

"We want that, too," I tell her.

"It's not normally covered by insurance," Tina says.

"That's fine. We don't care about the cost. We want that." I nod to the book still in her hands.

"Great. Let's get started." She beams at us. She gets to work, pulling up Bellamy's gown and tugging down her pants so that her baby bump is exposed. She then squirts gel on my dream girl's belly and starts moving a wand around while clicking on the computer screen that we can't see. "I'm just getting some images and measurements for the doctor," Tina explains, before asking. "Are we going to find out the gender?"

"Yes," we reply at the same time.

"Today," Bellamy tells her. "No huge gender reveal, just mom and dad and baby."

"I love that." Tina smiles kindly. She clicks a few more times and then turns the screen to face us. "Mom and Dad, meet your little one. This is the heartbeat." She points to the screen, pointing out limbs and facial features. "And look at that, your baby girl is waving at you." She grins.

My heart stops.

I knew it. I fucking knew it. I blink hard, fighting against my emotions, but when my eyes find Bellamy's and I see that she, too, has tears in her eyes, I don't bother fighting them. This is us. This is real and raw and life-changing. I squeeze her hand gently before bending and pressing a kiss to her lips. "My girls," I murmur, and she laughs through her tears.

"You were right, Daddy," she says, smiling, her eyes once again glued to the screen where we watch our daughter.

"Now, let me print some of these, and then we'll do the 3D," Tina says.

Throughout the entire experience, I don't let go of Bellamy's hand for a single second. When Tina finally sends us on our way with a video and lots of pictures from both ultrasounds, I feel as if I'm floating down the stairs as we make our way to my truck. I lift Bellamy into the passenger seat, slide my hand behind her neck, and pull her into a kiss. I try to tell her everything I'm feeling. Everything I can't seem to find the words to say.

You're everything.

Thank you for this life.

I love you both more than anything.

There are so many things I want to say. There are things I need to say, because above all else, I need her to hear me say the words. I try to show her every day, but I also need to tell her. But not here. Not in the parking lot of the doctor's office.

When I pull back from this kiss, her eyes are once again misty with tears. She places one hand on my cheek, and the other rests over mine that's cradling her belly, while my other hand still grips the back of her neck.

"A little girl." She smiles.

I kiss her one more time, because I need to, like I need air to breathe, then make sure she's buckled up and race to my side of the truck.

"Who do we call first?" she asks as I start the truck to get the heater going.

"Our parents."

"Okay, let's call yours first," she suggests.

Not needing to be told twice. I hit my mom's contact, and the phone rings out in the cab of the truck.

"Hello?" Mom answers.

"Mom." My voice cracks.

"Reid? What's wrong? Is it Bellamy? The baby?"

I clear my throat. "We're all fine. We just had our ultrasound," I tell her.

"Oh!" I can hear the excitement in her voice. "Sam! Come here, Reid and Bellamy are on the phone," she calls out. "We both just got home," Mom explains. "Okay, he's here, and you're on speaker."

I glance over at Bellamy and nod. "Hi, Paula. Hi, Sam," she says.

"Hello, sweetheart," they say at the same time.

"We wanted to call to let you know that you're getting a granddaughter," I tell them, feeling emotion well in the back of my throat. My parents congratulate us, and we talk for a few more minutes. "Thank you," I tell them. "We're excited, but we have a few more calls to make."

"Of course," Mom says. "I'm so happy for both of you," she says. "Talk soon. We love you." She barely has the words out before the line goes silent.

"Your mom next?" I ask.

She smiles and nods as she grabs her phone out of her purse, dials her mom, and places the call on speaker.

"Hello, daughter of mine. How are you?" Candice greets.

"It's a girl!" Bellamy blurts.

"What?" Candice asks, voice cracking. "A granddaughter," she says lovingly.

"Yes!" Bellamy exclaims.

"I'm so happy for you. Tell Reid I said congratulations."

"I'm here, Candice," I speak up.

"You ready to be a girl dad?" she teases.

"You know I'm gonna rock that," I tell her, laughing.

"No doubt in my mind," Candice replies.

"You let me know if you need help with the nursery or anything else," she tells us.

"We will, Mom. Love you."

"Love you, too," she says, and ends the call.

"What about your dad?" I ask her.

"I don't know." She bites down on her bottom lip.

"We don't have to tell him."

"I should, though, right? I mean, that's the right thing to do?"

"Baby, we can do whatever we want."

"I guess I'll call him." She huffs out a breath of air and dials his number, placing the call on speaker.

"Bellamy? Is everything okay?" Coach Warner answers.

"Yeah. Um, yeah, everything's fine. I thought you might want to know that we're having a girl."

I reach over and place my hand on her thigh, letting her know I'm right here. Supporting her in the only way I know how.

"A girl?" he asks. I can hear the emotion in his voice. "That's great, Bellamy. You're feeling okay?" he asks.

"Yeah, I'm doing great." She glances over at me. "Reid takes great care of me."

"Good. That's good." He clears his throat.

"So, that's all I wanted to tell you."

"Thank you for telling me. Can we—" he starts, but she cuts him off.

"Sorry, bad service, I gotta go," she says, ending the call. "I'm going to hell, aren't I?" she asks.

"No, you're not going to hell. It's going to take time to build that relationship," I remind her.

"Yeah," she agrees. "How are we going to tell everyone else?"

I shrug. "Text message?"

My girl smiles. "Sounds good to me. Do you mind if we add Amanda to that?"

"Of course, we're adding Amanda. She's your best friend." Grabbing my phone, I pull up a new message and add the guys, their wives, plus Sloane, Amanda, and Bellamy to the message.

Me: It's a GIRL!!

Instantly, the replies start rolling in.

Landry: Uncle Landry will buy her a pony. Congrats, my man.

Baker: Congrats, brother.

Knox: Hell, yeah.

Foster: She's going to have you wrapped around her tiny finger.

Sloane: Congrats, and we all know she's going to have ALL OF US wrapped around her finger. Just like Camden does now.

Corie: I'm so happy for both of you.

Amanda: I'm glad I didn't bet Reid it was a boy. Congrats, I'm so excited for both of you.

Rowan: Our family is growing. Congratulations.

Me: Thank you. We've got pictures. We'll show you soon.

Bellamy: Thank you.

I glance over at my girl. She's smiling down at her phone, and my heart expands in my chest. I was right. Today, we're definitely on the edge of something irreversible. It's my love for my girls. Nothing will ever change that. I open my mouth to say the words, but her phone rings.

"It's Amanda."

"Answer it." Leaning over the console, I kiss her temple before putting the truck in Drive and pointing us toward home.

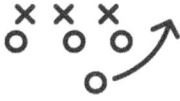

Dropping to the mattress in my hotel room, I sling my arm over my eyes to block out the light and groan. Tonight's game was brutal, and we walked away with a loss, losing by one point. One single missed field goal, but that's football. You win some. You lose some. I've been lucky enough to be part of a team that wins more than it loses, but those losses hit hard.

Grabbing my phone, I make a video call to Bellamy. I know she's probably in bed, waiting for me to call, and I don't want her to wait up any longer than she needs to for me to say goodnight. I don't know what it is, but I won't sleep when I'm away from home if I don't get to talk to her. My dream girl has become my addiction.

"Hey, babe," she greets. "Tough one," she says.

"Yeah. But we can't win them all, right?"

She nods. "Right."

"How's our baby girl?" I ask.

Bellamy's smile could light up all of Nashville. "She's perfect. She's been active today. We might have a kicker on our hands."

I chuckle. "You feeling okay?"

"I am. I miss you. I wish I were there to cheer you up."

"Yeah? What would you do to cheer me up?" I ask, already feeling better just seeing her smiling face and hearing her voice.

"Hmm, kisses. Lots of kisses."

"You know I love your kisses, Dream Girl."

She giggles. "I could run my fingers through your hair to relax you." She pauses. "I could get you off," she says, her voice small.

"How?" I ask gruffly.

"My mouth? My hand? Whatever you want."

"Your pussy?" I ask, and her face heats.

"That, too."

"What are you wearing?" I ask, reaching down and gripping my cock through my sweats.

"Just one of your T-shirts and panties."

"Show me."

She pans the phone so that I can see her. "Nothing special," she says, bringing the phone back to her face.

"Everything special," I counter. "Take it off."

"What?"

"Strip for me, baby."

"If I'm getting naked, so are you," she sasses.

"Done." I put the phone down, strip my T-shirt over my head, then, in one motion, my sweats and boxer briefs go, as well. When I pick the phone back up, my girl is sitting naked on our bed. "Fuck, you're a vision."

"Are we really doing this?" she asks.

"We don't do anything you don't want, Bell."

"I want. I miss you so much, Reid."

"I know, baby. I miss you, too."

"Show me."

"You wanna see my cock, Bell?"

"Yep," she says, popping the *p*.

"Show me your belly."

She pans the phone across her belly, and I drink her in. Never in my wildest dreams did I ever imagine thinking a pregnant woman was sexy, but here I am, drooling over her curves, and the swell of where our baby girl is growing inside her.

"So sexy," I say, gripping my cock, and giving it a rough tug.

"I don't know how to do this," she says, laughing. "I'm killing the mood, aren't I?"

"Never," I assure her. "If I were there, where would you want my hands?"

"My breasts. They're so sensitive," she says.

"Touch them for me. Show me what you would want me to do."

"I wanna see, too," she pants and tweaks a pert nipple. Her back arches off the bed.

"Fuck, knowing you're watching me makes me hard."

"Looks like you were already," she teases.

"Are you wet for me, Dream Girl?"

"Mm-hmm," she moans.

"Show me."

"That's going to be challenging," she says, before moving the camera to show me. She shuffles around and props the phone up on a pillow between her legs. My girl is a genius.

My cock aches, and I can already feel my release building. "Touch it. Rub your clit." My words are clipped.

"Like this?" she asks, taking my direction and gently rubbing circles over her clit, while pinching her nipples.

"Just like that, baby."

"Reid." She moans my name.

"I'm right here. I can almost imagine your pussy milking my cock and not my hand."

"Oh, damn," she mutters, sliding a single digit inside, and pumping slowly. I can't see her eyes, but I imagine them filled with desire, the way they do every time I'm inside her.

Fuck. I miss home. I miss my girl. Traveling this season without her has been torture. I miss her before we even leave Nashville. A few more years, as long as my body holds out, and then I'll retire. I'll never have to leave her or our kids again. If they can't be there, I just won't go, because not sleeping next to her every night is not an option. I've never thought about a time when I would be looking forward to hanging up my cleats, but knowing I'll have Bellamy and our kids—because yes, I want more— the fear of losing the game I love doesn't quite hit like it used to.

"Reid." She calls out my name, and I can see her pussy gush all over her hand.

"Bell!" I call out with a groan as I release all over my stomach.

"Wow," she says breathily, and brings the phone back to her face.

"There's my girl." I smile at her.

"I was supposed to be making you feel better," she says.

"Together," I tell her. "That's how we do it, baby. There is no me without you." It's not *I love you*, but it's damn close. I need to tell her. I just want the moment to be perfect.

"Together," she repeats.

"How was your day?"

She tosses her head back in laughter, and all I can do is sit here and smile. Before I called her, I was exhausted and over the day, and now, I just want to keep listening to her laugh.

"My day was good. Nothing eventful happened. I came home, heated up some leftover lasagna from last night, and watched the game."

"You're feeling okay?"

"I'm fine. We both are," she says, rubbing her belly. She's still naked, and so am I, but neither of us makes a move to change that, even though I should. I'm definitely going to need another shower, but no way will I cut this call short before she's ready.

"Did you order anything for the new house?" I left her a card in her name for my account and told her to go crazy.

"Not yet."

"Bell, baby, we need things. All the things," I tell her, and she laughs.

"I want to do it together."

"And we can, but we need stuff. That's a big-ass house we're moving into." Six bedrooms and eight bathrooms, with a full finished basement. We need a lot more furniture.

"I'll buy a few things."

"And I know we need stuff for baby girl. If you see something you love, buy it. I have no idea what we need, just that babies take a lot."

"They do." She smiles. "I want to pick the furniture out together."

"Okay. We'll do that when I get home. Right after we move into the new place."

"You think we can do that in one weekend?"

"Yep. I have everyone lined up. My parents and your mom are even coming to help."

"Really?"

"Yeah, the only person I didn't invite was your dad."

"Good call. How's he been?" she asks.

"Dirty looks, but he's not been as much of an asshole as he was in the beginning. It's a side of him I've never seen before, but that's all right. I'm following your lead, baby."

"I think it's best that he sits this one out."

"Maybe once we're settled, we can have him over for dinner or something?" I suggest.

"Maybe," she replies, covering her yawn.

"Get some rest. I'll see you tomorrow, Dream Girl."

"Good night, Reid."

"Night." Tossing my phone onto the bed, I rush to take a quick shower and climb back into bed. We roll out first thing in the morning, and I can't wait to get home to my girls.

CHAPTER 18

Bellamy

I LOVE OUR NEW HOUSE. IT'S HUGE—WAY TOO BIG FOR JUST THE three of us—but Reid said he wants to make this our home, and to be sure we have plenty of bedrooms for all of our kids and family when they come to visit.

It's the first week of December, and there's a light dusting of snow on the ground, making it feel more like the holidays. We have a massive Christmas tree in the foyer, and another in the living room, which isn't quite as tall. I love the holidays, and Reid has humored me in all the seasonal decorations I've been buying.

"I love bye weeks," Reid says. We're sitting on the couch, just having finished dinner. We're both in sweats and sweatshirts, and just lounging. I took the day off from work to spend some time with him.

"What? Don't let your coach hear you say that," I tease.

"He's not that scary," Reid jokes.

My phone rings, and I reach for it, seeing Rowan's name on the screen. "Hey, Rowan," I greet her.

"Hey, it's bye week!" She cheers, and I laugh.

"That it is."

"We're having everyone over tomorrow night. Low-key, comfy clothes, just the gang getting together."

"What time?"

"Anytime, but probably around six-ish."

"What do you need us to bring?"

"Just you—well, and that man of yours, too." She laughs. "We'll order in some food."

"I have a new dip I've been wanting to try. I'll make that."

"Not necessary, but we're not going to say no. You know my husband will eat anything." She chuckles.

"Yeah, Reid's not picky either."

"Great. See you tomorrow."

"Bye," I say, dropping my phone to my lap. "That was Rowan. They invited us to their place tomorrow. I guess everyone's going to be there."

"I'm glad they didn't say tonight," he says.

"Why's that?"

"It's my night with you." He pulls my legs onto his lap. "This is our day."

"We've been hanging around the house all day."

"I know, and it's perfect. We're in our new home, we're settled, it's the holidays, and I've had my girl all to myself all day long."

"It's been nice," I admit.

"We need to look at furniture for our baby girl's nursery. You feel like browsing online?" he asks.

"I've been looking. I have some to show you," I say, reaching for my phone. We both adjust our position so that we're sitting side by side so we can both see my phone, but then Reid decides that's not good enough and lifts me onto his lap.

"Better," he says, nuzzling my neck.

"I'm too heavy."

"Woman, please. I don't want to hear that come out of your mouth ever again. You're a fucking goddess, and you're growing our daughter." He gives me a stern look, letting me know that he means business. "Show me."

Pulling up the pictures I have saved on my phone, I hand it to him so that he can scroll through them. "I was thinking light pink and light gray walls, with white furniture."

"It's perfect. What about having an artist come in and do a mural of some sort on one of the walls?"

"Really?" I love this idea. "That's not too much?"

"Bell, this is our daughter. Nothing will ever be too much."

"She's not going to be a spoiled brat," I warn him.

"You're right." He nods. "She's going to be a spoiled princess."

"I'm in so much trouble, aren't I?"

He laughs, cupping my cheek and turning my head to kiss me. "You know our family. You saw Camden's birthday."

"I guess at least we have a big-ass house for all the things," I say, making him laugh.

"Let's order this. I'll call the painter and start looking for mural ideas."

"She's going to be here soon," I say, resting my hands over my belly. I'm twenty-five weeks, so over halfway there. It feels close, yet so far away at the same time. Our little girl kicks my hand where it rests on my belly, and I wince. "Ouch."

"What?"

"She kicked me."

Reid immediately moves my hand and rests his exactly where mine was, trying to feel her. He's never felt her move before. She lets out another hard kick, and his eyes light up. "Holy shit."

"Told you. We have the next Rampage kicker on our hands, or a soccer player."

"Come on, baby girl. Kick again for Daddy," he says, talking to my belly. She does, and he laughs. It's gleeful, and it melts my heart. "Thank you. Now take it easy on your momma," he tells our unborn daughter. "That's incredible, Bell."

"It is," I agree, as tears form in my eyes. "I'm glad you finally got to feel her."

"She's always sleeping, and I've been away so much I didn't think I'd ever get to feel her moving." She kicks again, and he grins. "Best night ever," he says, snuggling me closer. "Want to watch a movie?"

"Sure, I also need to shower and shave my legs," I groan. He goes to lift the leg of my sweats, and I swat his hand away. "No," I scold. "It's bad, trust me."

"Babe, I don't care if your legs aren't shaved."

"Well, I do, and it's getting harder and harder to make that happen with this belly."

"Change of plans," he says, lifting me into his arms and starting down the hall.

"Where are we going?" I ask, looping my arms around his neck to hold on.

"To shave your legs."

"What? No. That's not why I said that. I just meant that I wanted to do it sometime tonight before bed."

"It's tonight, and before bed."

"I thought we were going to watch a movie?"

"We were, and we still can. After I take care of you."

My heart melts. "Reid." I sigh softly because I don't know what to do with him sometimes. He's so damn sweet, and not at all what I expected after I found out what he did for a living. I was such a bitch to push him away like I did.

"I'm gone all the time. I feel like I'm not supporting you as much as I should. Let me have this. Let me help you."

"You've made every appointment. You call me multiple times a day when you're on the road. You're supporting me by thinking of me and our daughter. You might not be here, but I know that you want to be, Reid, and that makes all the difference. And I'm capable. It's just harder these days," I add.

"Then let me take that burden from you."

"You're going to shave my legs?"

"Bell, baby, don't you know by now, there isn't anything I wouldn't do for you or our girl?"

There's a huge part of me that wants to tell him that this is ridiculous, that I can manage—that I was just whining. But there's an even bigger part that wants to lean on him, because I know that I can. I know in my soul that Reid will catch me if I fall. And I have fallen. I'm irrevocably in love with him. He just doesn't know it yet.

He carries me to the bathroom, sets me on the vanity, and then re-arranges the space to make room. It's a double with lots of space in between. I sit silently as I watch him turn the water on and let it run before coming back to me.

He grabs one of the decorative pillows from the bed and brings it to me, placing it beside me to lean against. "Comfortable?" he asks.

"As much as a six-month pregnant woman sitting on a bathroom vanity can be," I tease.

He grins as he slides his hand under my sweatshirt to rest it on my baby bump. He waits for our little girl to kick. When she does, his grin grows wider, and his eyes glow with happiness. Moving his hands to the waistband of my sweats, he says, "Let's get you out of these," he says softly, tugging on my sweatpants.

I lift, allowing him to pull them down, off, and toss them to the floor. He runs his hands up my calves to my thighs and hums his approval. "So sexy," he says, his lips finding mine. His kiss is slow as his tongue lazily slides against mine. By the time he pulls back, there's steam coming from the sink, my panties are ruined, and from the bulge he's sporting, he's just as turned on as I am.

He plugs the sink, lets it fill with hot water, and reaches into a drawer, grabbing a new razor and a can of shaving gel. "Trust me?" he asks. There's a glint of playfulness in his eyes, but there's also concern, as if he's worried I might say no.

"Yes." I could say more, but I'm too turned on right now. And more words aren't necessary. My simple yes is all he needs to hear.

Turning off the water, he squirts a dollop of gel into his palm. He rubs his hands together before lathering my left leg. Razor in hand, he places it against my skin and makes a long, slow swipe. He's laser-focused on his task, dipping the razor into the sink to rinse it off, before taking another pass.

With each stroke of the razor against my skin, my body grows hotter for him. My heart thunders inside my chest. It's so loud, I'm sure he can hear it. He stays focused while I sit here in drenched panties, watching him care for me.

I never allowed myself to think about falling in love. I never wanted to go through what my mom did. I didn't think about the man I would marry, or even about having kids. That was something I'd pushed to the back of my mind and locked away, clouded by my anger.

Now, I can't imagine my life without Reid Montgomery. He's easy-going, attentive, hot as hell, responsible, hardworking, and a million other things; there are too many to list. Every single day, he shows up for me, cares for me, and proves that I'm important to him.

I'm starting to see things more clearly—specifically, my past. My mom was right. I was young, angry, and wanted to blame someone, so since Dad was the one who left, he became the easy target. As I grew older, the anger persisted, and I became stubborn, unwilling to listen to what she had to say. When I think about the cards and letters from my dad, I can't help but soften toward him. Maybe, just maybe, one day, we can get back what we lost.

"What's on your mind, Dream Girl?" Reid asks, as he wets a cloth and wipes off my left leg, before helping me turn and get adjusted so he can start on the right.

"Meeting you changed my life."

His gaze softens as he leans in for a kiss. "Mine too, baby."

"I think—I think I need to reach out to my dad."

He nods. "If and when you're ready, I'll be here for whatever you need."

"I can't do it without you."

"Yes, you can, but you don't have to." Another kiss, and then he gets to work shaving my right leg. When he's finished, he runs his hands over my now-smooth skin. "What about here?" he asks, as his hand slides between my thighs. He gently traces over the crotch of my soaked panties.

"I've been neglecting that area since this belly popped." Not that he needs me to tell him that. He has intimate knowledge that doesn't require an explanation.

"Do you want me to trim? Shave you bare? Buy a wax kit and wax you?"

"You don't have to."

"Bell, baby, trust me when I tell you that my hands on any part of your body is a have-to situation."

"You decide."

"It's your body, your choice. You're perfect just the way you are. I was just offering my services."

"Maybe—trim?" I ask, feeling my face heat.

"Trim it is." He starts digging around in the drawer until he comes up with an electric razor that I use when I can see what's going on down there. "Let's move the pillow behind your back, and then you can face me, but first, we need to get rid of these." He reaches for my panties, and I lift my hips, helping him as he removes them from my body.

I settle my back against the mirror and the pillow he propped up, and spread my legs for him. His heated gaze takes me in, and I know he can see how turned on I am, not that he needed further evidence with how wet my panties were.

"Let's scoot you down a little," he says, and I move my hips further to the edge of the counter.

"Like this?" I ask, pulling my sweatshirt up over my bump and out of the way.

"Yes. Hold on." He reaches over and grabs the vanity seat that's pushed under the counter, and sits, which puts him eye level with the goods. "Now, let's give my girl a trim," he says, moving one leg then the other to rest over his shoulders.

He grabs the trimmers and gets to work. "This is embarrassing," I mutter. However, my words are all breathy, because yes, it is embarrassing, but it's also hot as hell.

"Why?" he asks, stopping to peer up at me.

"You're doing that." I nod toward where he's working.

"Because we did this," he says, smoothing his hand over my belly. "There will never not be a moment that I won't want to take care of you or our kids, Bellamy. It's not embarrassing to lean on someone. It's trust. It's… everything."

It's on the tip of my tongue: *I love you.* It sits pretty, waiting for me to let those three little words free, but he starts the trimmer back up and gets back to work. A few minutes later, he's gently lowering my legs, making sure I'm steady, before stepping away and turning the water on in the bathtub.

"Now what?" I ask, as I watch him strip out of his clothing.

"We're taking a bath."

"Really?" I ask. We've not been able to take one together since we moved in, but we've both talked about how the tub is big enough for both of us.

"Yes, really. Let's get rid of this," he says, lifting the hem of my sweatshirt. I raise my arms, allowing him to remove it. "Come here, you." He lifts me into his arms, bridal-style, and carries me to the massive tub. He places me inside, keeping hold of me until I'm settled beneath the warm water, before climbing in behind me. He wraps his arms around me, and I settle back against his chest.

"This is as heavenly as I imagined it would be."

He cups some water and drops it over my breasts. "I agree. We should make this a nightly thing."

"Maybe, but once baby girl gets here, we'll be too tired for long, hot baths."

"Never," he says fiercely, his hands cradling my belly. "I can't wait to meet her," he says softly. "We should pick a name."

"Me, too, and there are so many that I love. I have a list," I tell him. "What about you?"

"I have one in mind."

"Yeah?" I turn to look at him over my shoulder, and he presses his lips to mine.

"Uh-huh," he says, kissing me deeper. His hand moves over my bump down to my pussy where he gently traces my clit with his thumb.

"Th—That's good," I breathe, and he chuckles.

"I want you to come for me, Bell."

I close my eyes because he's about to get his wish.

"Eyes on me, baby."

My eyes immediately pop open as I continue to stare at him over my shoulder.

"I want to watch you. Your eyes, they sparkle like diamonds, and I want to see that sparkle when you lose control for me."

It's all too much. His words, his touch, this entire night, and I shoot off like a rocket. My hands grip his arm that's wrapped around me. My body relaxes even further into his. I didn't know life could be like this. I didn't know that I could feel this strongly for someone. I didn't understand what it truly meant to open your heart and soul to someone else, inviting them in.

Reid is that person for me.

Once I've regulated my breathing, I carefully stand.

"Whoa, where are you going, baby?"

"Shower. I need to wash my hair."

"That's my job," he says, standing with me, stepping out of the tub, lifting me into his arms, and carrying me into the shower.

"I can walk, you know," I tease.

"Why, when you fit perfectly in my arms?"

Stepping into the shower, he moves me toward the controls, and I turn on the water before he quickly steps back so I don't get jolted with the cold spray. I smile up at him. "Always looking out for me," I say, pressing my hand against his cheek, keeping the other wrapped tightly around his neck as I lean in for a kiss.

When we step into the shower, Reid places me gently on my feet, and I turn to face him. "Have a seat, sir." I nod toward the bench in the shower.

He smirks but does as I ask. "Now what?" he says, gripping the backs of my thighs and pressing a kiss to my baby bump.

"Now this." I turn so that my back is to him. Reaching behind me, I grip his cock, and guide him inside until I'm sitting on his thighs.

"I fucking love bye week," he rumbles, gripping my thighs.

Laughter bubbles out of my chest as I rock my hips, making him groan. I don't stop until his body stills, and he releases inside me. My legs are like jelly as I stand and move into the spray.

Reid aligns his body with mine as he promised and washes my hair, then my body. He takes his time, making sure to leave no part of me untouched. By the time he's finished, I'm ready to go again, but exhaustion is weighing heavily on me.

"I'm going to finish up," he says, kissing my temple. "I'll be right out."

I nod and step out of the shower, wrapping a towel around my waist. I dry off, slip into one of his T-shirts, brush out my hair before pulling it up in a damp, messy knot, and slide under the covers. A few minutes later, Reid's turning out the light and snuggling up next to me.

We definitely love bye week.

CHAPTER 19

Reid

"**A**RE WE LATE?" BELLAMY ASKS AS WE PARK IN LANDRY and Rowan's driveway.

I bite down on my cheek to keep from smiling. "Rowan said six-ish, right?" I nod toward the dashboard that displays that it's fifteen minutes after six.

"There are so many cars here," she muses. "You know I hate to be late."

"It's a night with friends. *Ish* means there's no set time, so that means we're not late. We're right on time." I wink, climb out of the truck, and make my way to her door. I help her down and reach into the back seat to grab the dip she insisted on making. I tried to talk her out of it, but here we are, carrying in a covered dish to a party, of which she is the guest of honor, but I couldn't tell her that. It would ruin the surprise.

I offer her my free hand, and she takes it, allowing me to lead her to the front door. I don't bother knocking. They know we're here because I texted the guys in our group chat before we left the house. Now that we also live in the neighborhood, they knew we were just minutes away. As soon as we step into the house, everyone yells, "Surprise!"

Bellamy stops, her mouth falls open, and tears well in her eyes. "What is this?" she asks, as her mom comes rushing toward her, hugging her tightly.

"It's your baby shower, silly. Co-ed, of course," Landry calls out.

"Really?" Bellamy's voice cracks.

"Come on, Bell. Let's go say hi to everyone." Sliding my arm around her waist, I hand the dip off to Rowan as we make our way around the room. The guys, Corie, Rowan, Sloane, Candice, and Amanda are all here. Rowan wanted to invite her friends from work, but after a quick phone call to Grant, he told me they planned to have her an office baby shower, and by "they," he meant his wife and his sister-in-law, so it's just us—close friends and family. There's only one person who's not here, and I need to ask her about that now.

"Hey," I say, pulling her off to the side once we've hugged everyone to say hello. "We didn't invite your dad. I wasn't sure if you'd want him here."

She bites down on her bottom lip. "I mean, I guess I would have been okay with it."

"You want me to call him?" I ask her.

"Will that be weird? The coach being here?"

"Nope. What about your mom?"

She peers over her shoulder, catching her mom's eye, and waves. "Wait, who's that with my mom?" she asks, as they both start walking toward us.

"Bellamy, I'd like for you to meet Cliff. My boyfriend," Candice adds. She's smiling, but I can see the apprehension in her eyes. "I realize this might not be the best time to introduce the two of you, but he makes me happy, and I wanted you to meet him."

I'm holding my breath, waiting to see how she handles this meeting. When a bright smile curves her lips, I exhale. "It's so nice to meet you, Cliff. I've heard nothing about you." She laughs. "But I know that if you're here, you're important to my mom." She turns her gaze to her mom. "How long have the two of you been seeing each other?" There's no anger in her tone, just pure curiosity.

"A few months," Candice replies. "I didn't want to tell you in case it fizzled out, but he's still hanging around," she says, smiling at Cliff, before turning back to Bellamy. "Amanda convinced me you'd be okay with him being here."

"I can go if it makes you uncomfortable," Cliff adds. "We drove separately just in case."

"What? No, of course not. Stay, please," Bellamy tells him. Cliff slides his arm around Candice's waist, and she leans into him, which only makes my girl smile wider.

"Did you want something when you called me over here?" Candice asks her daughter.

"Oh, um—Reid asked if I wanted Dad to be here. I was going to ask you how you felt about that, but we don't have to."

"Bellamy, he's your father. He gave me the greatest gift in this life: you. Of course, you should invite him."

"Are you sure? I mean, it's last-minute, so I'm sure he's got work to do, or something."

"You won't know unless you try." Candice gives her a pointed look.

"Like he did," Bellamy whispers, and Candice nods. Taking a deep breath and squaring her shoulders, she looks up at me. "Will you call him?"

"Sure, Dream Girl. Anything you want." I kiss her temple and drop my arm from around her waist. "I'll be right back." Stepping into the hallway just off the living room, I hit Coach's number and wait for him to answer.

"Montgomery."

"Hey, Will," I greet him, and he growls. I'm not talking to my coach right now. I'm talking to my girl's dad. "What are you doing right now?"

"Going over plays."

I nod, even though he can't see me. "Well, I know it's short notice, but the girls are throwing Bellamy a surprise baby shower. We just got here, so the fun hasn't started, but she said I could call you and pass on the invitation."

He's quiet for a very long time. "She said that?" he asks.

"She did. No gifts are necessary, but this is your chance. This is her olive branch. Are you going to take it?"

"Where are you?"

"Landry's place. I'll text you the address."

"I have a gift," he tells me, which shocks me.

"Not necessary," I tell him again.

"I'll be there. I'm leaving now."

"Sounds good," I say, ending the call and slipping my phone back into my pocket. When I step back into the living room, I find all the ladies gathered around Bellamy. Corie has her hand resting on her belly, and they're all smiling.

A hand lands on my shoulder, and I look over to see Knox. "A lot has changed for us recently," he says, nodding to the group of women.

"Yeah," I agree.

"Gotta admit, I'm a little jealous," he tells me.

I turn to look at him. "Of what?"

"I'm ready for us to start our family."

"You trying?"

"We're not *not* trying, if that makes sense." He laughs.

"Give it time. Not everyone's swimmers are as strong as mine," I joke.

"Mine are," Baker says, joining us.

He's not wrong. We both had one-night stands that resulted in pregnancy. The only difference is that I'm in love with my baby momma, even though I haven't told her that yet, and Baker, well, he's miserable dealing with his, but he loves his son.

"I didn't think you had Cam this week?" Knox asks him.

"Natasha had another shoot. This time in Australia." Baker rolls his eyes. "Not that I'm complaining. I'll take more time with my son whenever I can get it."

"Fellas," Landry says as he and Foster join us in our little corner of the living room. He pops the last bite of cookie into his mouth. "I can get behind this having babies thing," he says. "The snacks are on point."

"Maybe you and your wife should work on that," Foster says.

"We'll get there. See, I need all of you to do it first so that I can learn from your mistakes. Besides, I'm already the favorite uncle."

"Keep telling yourself that," Foster jokes. "We all know, I'm the favorite."

"I don't know," Baker muses. "My son looks mighty happy sitting on Amanda's hip."

"Of course, he's happy," Landry replies. "He's surrounded by beautiful women who are giving him all of their attention."

Before we can reply, there's a knock at the door. "That's Coach," I say, moving to answer it. I hear the guys ask about why he's here as I make my way to the door. Pulling it open, I don't invite him in. Instead, I step forward, forcing him to take a step back, and close the door behind me.

"Glad you could make it," I say, crossing my arms over my chest.

"Do I get to go in and see my daughter? I'm not here for you," he says.

I know he's angry, but he doesn't need to be. I'm all in with his daughter. "You can go in, but remember, you're not here today as the coach of the Rampage. Today, you're just my girl's dad. She's happy and smiling, and that's how it's going to stay."

"What are you saying, Montgomery?" he asks.

"I'm saying that no matter how you feel about Bellamy and me, you keep that shit to yourself today. You will not ruin this day for her."

"I don't want to ruin anything for her."

"Candice is here," I tell him. "She brought her boyfriend." I watch as his face falls, and his shoulders drop. "Please be cordial. I don't care if it's fake. This is Bell's day, and she's extending you an olive branch. If you want more, you'll keep yourself in line."

"You're not my keeper."

"No, but she's mine, and that means I defend her and stand beside her always. That means that she's my entire fucking world, her and our baby. I don't give a fuck who you are. You won't upset her."

The door opens behind us, and Bellamy steps out. She wraps her arms around her waist to ward off the chill, and I immediately pull her close to keep her warm.

"Hi," she says, as I place my lips against the crown of her head.

"You're glowing," William says with a sad smile. "How are you feeling? The baby?" he asks.

She moves the hand that was resting against my chest to her belly. "Good. Really good. She's healthy, and so am I."

"That's great," he says, with a crack in his voice.

"Yeah, she's healthy."

"A granddaughter," he breathes, as if he's in awe of the fact that he's going to be a grandpa.

"Are you coming inside? What are the two of you doing out here?"

"I wanted to warn him that your mom was here with Cliff," I tell her. I don't mention that I also told him to keep his ass in line, but it's okay. It's not a lie if it's an omission, right?

"It's been a long time," William says. "I'm happy for her."

"Me, too."

He hands her a light pink gift bag. "This is for you and the baby."

"You have a gift?" she asks, surprised.

"Yeah, I was gonna wait until the baby was born, but when Reid called, I grabbed it on my way out the door. I'll just have to buy another one when she's here."

"That's not necessary. Thank you for this," she says, as a shiver races through her.

"Come on, babe, let's get you inside." She steps out of my hold and opens the door. I motion for William to follow her, and I trail them.

All eyes turn toward us. "So, uh, I know you all know who he is to you." Bellamy giggles nervously. "But he's also my dad." She looks up at William, and he smiles at her reassuringly. We were all there for family day as Coach introduced us to his daughter. Today, and her words, is a big step for them, for healing, and I hope it only progresses from here.

"Well, now that everyone's here, let's eat!" Landry calls out. Everyone laughs as we move to the kitchen to fill our plates. He's right, the food is incredible.

After everyone is stuffed, Rowan leads Bellamy and me to two chairs in the living room that are set up next to a table full of gifts.

"Have at it." Rowan grins.

"I've got pictures handled," Amanda calls out, showing us the camera in her hands. I wasn't sure anyone still used cameras other than photographers these days.

"And I'm making a list," Corie says, holding up the pen and notebook in her hands.

"All you two have to do is open all the new things for your baby girl." Rowan smiles.

"Thank you all so much for this. It's too much," Bellamy says.

"Like you wouldn't do the same for us," Sloane tells her. "Open mine first." She winks. "It's the pink bag with bears on it." She points out the bag. I grab it from the table and hand it to Bellamy.

"You open. I'll handle the trash and passing gifts," I tell her.

That's what we do. We're opening gift after gift, receiving so many tiny clothes and things our little girl will need. I feel myself getting choked up at the love of my friends for doing this for us.

"Last one," I tell Bellamy, as I hand her the gift bag from her dad.

She carefully removes the tissue paper and reaches inside. She pulls out a book. "Mommy and me," she reads and shows us the two small bears on the front cover. Reaching into the bag, she pulls out a soft, light pink blanket.

Next, she pulls out a small onesie. She reads what it says and drops it to her lap with tears in her eyes. Her lip quivers, and I glare at her father, but he doesn't see me. He only has eyes for Bellamy.

"What's it say?" Candice asks.

Bellamy shakes her head and hands it to me. Lifting the onesie, I read. "If you think I'm cute, you should see my mommy." I turn it so everyone can see, and the ladies coo. Reaching over, I lace her hand with mine, showing her my support.

Candice stands and moves to where William is sitting on the other side of the room. They said brief hellos in the kitchen as we all filled our plates, but that's been their only interaction that I'm aware of.

"You did good, Grandpa," she says, placing her hand on his shoulder. Coach smiles up at her, and that's when I see it.

He still loves her. It's written plain as day all over his face. He nods and pulls his gaze back to his daughter.

Slowly, Bellamy stands, as do I, in case she needs me. She walks until she's in front of her dad, who rises from his chair. "Thanks, Dad," she says, her voice cracking with emotion, and she shocks us all when she steps into him, wrapping her arms around his waist.

Coach stands frozen for maybe two seconds before he wraps his arms around her, closing his eyes, and relishing the moment.

"Damn allergies," Landry grumbles, wiping at his eyes, and everyone laughs—even Bellamy and Coach.

In a few long strides, I'm standing next to them. I slide my arm around Bellamy's waist, and Coach glares at me. "Thanks for coming," I tell him, ignoring his glare.

"You too," I tell Candice, leaning over to hug her with my free arm.

"Do you all need help getting all this carried out to your truck?" Cliff asks, joining us. He places his hand on the small of Candice's back, and she peers up at him with adoration. A glance at Coach reveals him clenching his jaw.

"That would be great. Babe, we're going to start loading all this up," I say.

"Thank goodness the bed of your truck has a cover." Bellamy smiles.

"Whatever won't fit, we'll put in mine," Cliff assures her.

"Thank you."

Bending, I press a quick kiss to Bellamy's lips. "Get off your feet. I'll be done in no time."

"Bossy," she says, chuckling.

"If being bossy means I'm taking care of my girls, then I'll own that." I kiss her again, smile at her parents, and leave the three of them to chat as Cliff and I load up all the gifts.

By the time we're finished, Candice has her coat in her hands and is ready to go. She hugs us both, wishing us well, and we both shake hands with Cliff, and they're out the door.

"I should go, too. Let you be with your friends," Coach tells Bellamy.

She glances around the room, then over to me. She slides her arm around my waist and rests her hand on my chest. I return her embrace, my hand going to her bump. "They're my family." She says it with such conviction that it squeezes my heart inside my chest.

"I can see that." He nods. "Congratulations, Bellamy."

"Thanks." She nods.

"Thanks for coming." I offer him my hand. He stares at it before eventually taking it into his. He squeezes hard, which only makes me grin wider and return with my own force. We release hands, and with one final look at his daughter, he grabs his coat and walks out the door.

"What about your parents?" Bellamy asks.

"They couldn't get away in time. My mom will have you for her own little shower, I'm sure of it. I told her we'd send lots of pictures."

"All right, time for some Name that Tune!" Landry calls out as Bellamy yawns.

"You want to go?" I ask her.

"No. I'm tired, but today has been wonderful. I'm not ready for it to end just yet."

So it doesn't. I pull her down onto my lap, just as Knox and Landry do with their wives. Amanda has Camden, and he's sleeping on her chest. Baker offers to take him, but she waves him away. Baker, Foster, and Sloane take up the couch, and we start to play. Corie kicks our ass, just as she always does, but it feels right. The moment, the day, the woman in my arms, and the baby in her belly. This is right. This is my future, and I can't wait to live it.

CHAPTER 20

Bellamy

BEING IN MY THIRD TRIMESTER OF THIS PREGNANCY IS exhausting. The last couple of weeks, I've been dragging. It's hard to get comfortable at night with my growing belly. I have a pregnancy pillow, and Reid has been incredible. He holds me, rubs my back and my feet, and waits on me hand and foot when he's home. He's even gone as far as having meals catered so I don't have to cook, and when he's home, he does the cooking. My man spoils me for sure.

It's not just that I'm tired and struggling to find a comfortable sleeping position. I've been dizzy today, and I'm sure it's my balance with this baby bump. Oh, and nothing fits. Nothing. Well, not nothing, but my Reid Montgomery jersey no longer fits. It won't go over my belly, and today is the third round of the playoffs. I have to wear his name and number. Plopping down on the bed, I sigh because my only other option is one of his old jerseys hanging in the closet, and they're way too big for me. I guess I'm going to look like a pregnant slob today because I refuse to show up at the stadium not supporting my man.

My phone rings, and I grab it off the nightstand to see Sloane's name.

"Hey," I answer with a sigh. She's on her way to pick me up, and I'm still not dressed.

"What's going on?" she asks.

"I have nothing to wear," I whine. I know I sound like a petulant teenager throwing a tantrum, but it's important that I represent Reid today. I have to. He's been so good to me, takes care of me, and this is the only way I know to return that favor.

Sloane laughs. "I'm pulling in now to pick you up. Come let me in. I'll help you figure it out."

"Okay. Give me time to waddle downstairs," I tell her, making her laugh.

"I'll be waiting," she assures me.

Tossing my phone onto the bed, I slip into my robe to cover myself and start the trek down the stairs to answer the door. Sloane has been my buddy at games, and I'm so grateful for her, especially on days when Amanda can't make it, which is today. Today, my best friend has a cold, which she blames on her career, so she's staying snuggled in bed, watching television. I offered to join her, but she exiled me for fear of my getting sick. I hate that she's not feeling well, but I'm grateful that I have Sloane to be there with me. Corie will pop in here and there, and Rowan will be down on the field like always.

By the time I open the door, Sloane is standing there smiling with a bag in her hands. "Hey." I step back, allowing her to enter, before closing the door.

"This is for you." She hands me the bag.

"What is it?"

"Just open it, silly girl. Come on, time's a-wasting." She claps her hands as if I were one of her pre-k students, but it works because I dig into the bag, pulling out the tissue paper and then an article of clothing. Sloane takes the bag from my hands as I hold up the item, and tears spring to my eyes.

"How did you know?" I ask, my voice cracking. These damn pregnancy hormones are going to be the death of me.

"You mentioned last week, when we were all watching the game, that your jersey was getting tight and that you were worried it wouldn't fit for the last few games of the season. So I thought I'd help you out."

I'm holding a Nashville Rampage crew neck sweatshirt with the team's logo on the front, centered on the chest. There's an embroidered arrow pointing toward my belly with the embroidered words *Number Twenty Did This*.

"Where did you find this?" I ask, laughing. Reid is going to flip when he sees this.

"I bought the sweatshirt, but I added the rest. Look at the back."

On the backside, she's added Reid's last name, Montgomery, in block letters just like on his jersey, the number twenty, and at the very bottom, just to the left of the zero, is small script that reads, *Baby Momma*. I can't hide my grin.

"Sloane, this is incredible. Thank you so much. I'll pay you," I tell her, feeling the stress of not knowing what to wear fall from my shoulders.

"You will do no such thing. It's a gift. I'm glad you like it."

"I love it, and Reid is going to flip when he sees it."

"Oh, I'm certain he will. Now, go finish getting ready. We need to watch your baby daddy and the rest of the guys bring home a win. We're going all the way again this year," she says confidently.

I pull her into a tight hug, as tight as my baby belly will allow. "Thank you so much." Tears well in my eyes. I keep thinking about how if I'd continued to be stubborn and let the past and my anger rule my future, I would have missed out on so much more than my love for Reid. He's brought an entire group of incredible humans into my life, and I'll forever be grateful.

There's a little more pep in my step as I make my way back upstairs to change into the sweatshirt and finish getting ready. Twenty minutes later, we're on our way to the stadium.

"Thank you again," I tell Sloane. "I love it."

"You're welcome. How are you feeling, Momma?" she asks.

"Good." I place my hands on my bump. "A little wobbly at times, tired all the time, but it's hard to find a comfortable position when sleeping these days, unless I'm in the recliner, but I like being in our bed, especially when Reid is home."

"Oh, I bet you do." She giggles. "All my friends are wifed up, and I'm still dating losers."

"How was the date you went on a couple of weeks ago?"

"Great. He was a nice guy, paid for dinner, which is nice, but he lives in his mom's basement and apparently talks to dead people." She shudders.

"Yikes."

"Yeah, I'd rather be single." She laughs.

"Amanda went through the same thing before she met Ethan. That's why I didn't date much before. It was too hard for me to trust." I also harbored a lot of anger in my heart. I blamed all men for the most part. Until one man broke past the walls of anger I'd built.

"I hear that," she agrees, pulling into the stadium.

Thankfully, we have a private VIP entrance, so we don't have to shuffle in with the rest of the crowd. Not that I mind going through the main entrance, but with my baby bump, it's a little harder to maneuver these days.

When we reach our suite, I'm surprised to see Corie there with Camden and his nanny, Mrs. Ward. "Hey," Sloane and I say at the same time.

We wave to Mrs. Ward, who's already sitting and bouncing a happy Camden on her knee. "I thought he was with his mom this week?" Sloane asks Corie, her voice quiet.

Corie rolls her eyes. "She's on vacation, apparently."

"Without her kid she rarely sees?" I ask, not bothering to hide my disdain.

"Yep," Corie replies.

"Damn," Sloane mutters. "That poor baby. She has no idea what she's missing out on. He's going to resent her for this once he gets older."

Corie shrugs. "I don't think she cares, to be honest."

"I figured you'd be down there getting some pregame footage," Sloane tells Corie.

"I did. Now it's all in the hands of the photographers. I'm done for the night. The photographers will send me everything, and I can use that for my content. Besides, I don't need to be down there bothering them when the guys are trying to get their heads in the game."

Speaking of, my phone rings. Digging it out of my purse, I show them the screen with Reid's face and step off to the side to answer the call. "Hello."

"Hey, baby. Are you here?" Reid asks.

"I'm here. We're in the suite. Corie's with us, and Mrs. Ward is here with Camden."

"Good. Yeah, Baker mentioned that Natasha was on vacation or something like that. Said she needed a break," he says, and I can hear the disapproval in his tone. "How're my girls?"

I smile. "Tired and happy," I tell him honestly.

"Won't be much longer," he whispers. "I think tired and happy is about to be our life for a while."

"You're right, but it will be worth it." I can't believe this is where life has taken me, but the universe knew what it was doing when it dropped Reid into my life. He's healed me in ways I never knew I needed.

"Do you need anything?"

"We have a suite all to ourselves. It's just me, Corie, Sloane, and

Mrs. Ward with Camden. There are tons of food and snacks. We're all set," I assure him.

"All right, Dream Girl. I'll see you after the game."

"I'll be right here waiting."

Someone yells, and he groans.

"Go. I'll see you after."

"Bye, babe," he says, ending the call.

"Everything okay?" Corie asks when I rejoin them.

"Perfect," I tell her, placing my hand on my belly. "Reid was just checking to make sure we made it here okay."

Corie nods. "I rode with Knox, or I would have gotten the same kind of call."

"Dada!" Camden calls out, pointing to the field, and we all turn our attention to him.

"Let me take him," Corie offers to Mrs. Ward. "Have a break, and grab a snack."

"Oh, he's just fine," she assures her.

"No, I insist. I need baby Cam snuggles." She holds out her arms, and Camden reaches for her, too, as she settles him on her hip.

We all take our seats as the opening ceremonies begin. We're playing the New York Tigers, and they get the ball first. On the first drive, Cody Martin, a defenseman, catches an interception and takes off down the field. He's tackled at the thirty, but everyone in Rampage Stadium goes crazy. This team has fought hard all year, and they want this. They want another league championship with their name on it. If this is how this entire game is going to go, it's going to be a nailbiter.

The game is back and forth. We're holding strong, up by a touchdown, and we've all been on the edge of our seats the entire game. Well, not technically. I've been shifting this way and that, trying to find a comfortable position, and my head feels a little fuzzy. I'm sure it's all the excitement and lack of sleep I'm getting these days.

Reid was right, though: tired and happy is about to be our new normal, and it'll all be worth it when we get to hold our baby girl in our arms.

"Go!" Rowan cheers as she holds Camden's arm in the air. His baby giggles fill the suite around us, and I grin. Next year, that will be me. Our daughter will be here with us, and Camden will have a friend to play with. It's not lost on me that I ran, scared of this life, and now, I've fully embraced it. I have Reid to thank for that. He's shown me time and time again that our daughter and I are first with him.

It's nearing the end of the second quarter, and the Rampage are still up by seven. It's been an intense game so far. I've already made what feels like fifteen million trips to the restroom. Thankfully, our suite has its own. I was trying to hold out until the end of the quarter, but baby girl is right on my bladder, and I have to go. Defense is on the field, so I won't miss Reid play.

"It's that time again," I tell the girls, and they smile and nod. When I stand, I do so quickly, and I feel a little lightheaded. That's happened a lot in the past couple of days. I slow my steps as I make my way to the small restroom that's just ours.

After handling my business, I wash my hands and pull open the bathroom door, and another wave of dizziness hits me. Suddenly, I feel more lightheaded than before, and my legs feel weak. I think I'm going to need some help to get back to my seat. I open my mouth to call for one of them to help me, but before I can, everything goes black.

CHAPTER 21

Reid

"HELL YEAH!" LANDRY CHEERS AS WE MAKE OUR WAY TO THE locker room at halftime. He hops onto my back, and I carry him a few feet before he jumps off and races ahead.

We're up by two touchdowns. Landry caught a perfect spiral from Knox with twenty seconds to go, strengthening our lead. If we win today, we'll play again next week for the championship in our conference. If we win that, we'll move on to the league championship. If we make it, this will be our third year in a row, and we're all salivating for this chance. We're breaking records, and I get to do it with my best friends, my family, and this year, my girl is here, and soon, our daughter.

As we make our way down the tunnel, everyone is in good spirits until we all spot Corie, pacing in front of the locker room doors. Knox rushes to his wife, with Landry hot on his heels. Baker, Foster, and I stand behind them, building a wall.

"Corie girl, what's wrong?" Knox asks, pulling her into his arms. She immediately pulls away, ignoring her husband and her brother to come and stand before me.

My heart drops to my cleats.

"What?" I ask, my voice breaking.

"Bellamy collapsed. She was coming out of the restroom in the suite, and she just fell to the floor. We called the paramedics, and they took her to the hospital. Sloane is with her," Corie rushes to tell me with tears in her eyes.

"When?" I grit out. My body is numb. My heart feels like it could pound right outside my chest.

Please let them be okay. I can't lose them.

"There were about four minutes to go in the quarter. They were taking her out when I raced down here to tell you."

Shoving my helmet at Baker, I strip off my pads, drop them to the floor, and take off running into the locker room to grab my keys.

"Montgomery!" Coach bellows. "What the hell are you doing? Why are you not dressed for game play?"

"I gotta go," I tell him. I'm not even sure he can hear my reply. Blood is rushing in my ears, and I feel like I'm in a tunnel.

"The fuck you are. We still have two quarters of a game to play," he rages.

"Fucking fine me. Fire me. I don't give a fuck. My family needs me, and that's where I'm going to be." Swiping my phone and my keys, I rush out of the locker room to him calling after me. Fuck him. I understand that I'm under contract, and I also understand that I'll get fined for this, but I'll be damned if I'm going to let the love of my life and our unborn child be in danger and not be there. I won't make his mistakes. If it costs me my career, then so be it. I've invested well, so we'll be just fine, but I won't be. Not if I lose them.

In the hallway, Corie's there. She takes my hand and leads me away, with the guys calling back to keep them updated. I don't bother to reply; I just let Corie lead me out to her car. She insists on driving.

"You'd better have a lead foot," I warn her.

"Trust me, I'm just as worried as you are." She nods to the police car that's in front of us. "I called ahead. They're going to escort us there. There are perks to being a Rampage," she says, trying to make light, but I can't even crack a smile.

"They have to be okay, Core. They have to be. I can't lose them. She doesn't even know that I love her. I didn't tell her. Why the fuck didn't I tell her? Fuck, what if I never have the chance to tell her?" I'm spiraling as I rest my elbows on my knees and bury my hands in my hair.

Please, please, let them be okay.

"Her mom. Amanda. I need to call them. Fuck, I didn't even tell Coach why I was leaving."

"Knox is going to talk to Coach and tell Rowan. I called Amanda while I was waiting, and she's going to call her mom."

"Thanks," I mutter.

Corie reaches over and takes her hand in mine. "She's going to be okay. They both are. She was starting to come to as they were loading her on the stretcher."

"The baby. Bell had a checkup last week. Everything was fine. Was she feeling bad? Did she say anything?" I'm racking my brain to see if I missed something. Was I not paying close enough attention?

"We're almost there," she says, as she follows the cop car into the hospital parking lot. He drives us straight to the ER entrance, and before the vehicle is even stopped, I'm reaching for the door handle.

"I'll meet you in there. I'm going to thank our escort and park," Corie tells me, as I jump out of the still-moving car and rush inside.

"Bellamy Warner," I say, slapping my hands down on the desk. "She was just brought in by ambulance."

"Are you family?"

"Yes."

"Your relationship?" the lady asks, but she has yet to lift her eyes to greet me.

"She's my everything," I tell her, my voice gritty with emotion.

She finally glances up, and her eyes widen. "You're Reid Montgomery. You're supposed to be playing today." She glances down at me, still in uniform.

"Bellamy Warner," I say, ignoring her.

"Can I have your autograph?" she blurts.

Taking a deep breath, I try to keep my anger and my fear in check. With gritted teeth, I reply, "I'll sign any fucking thing you want, if you take me to my girls," I say, barely holding on to my anger. I'll definitely be letting administration know how she's handling this.

"Oh, it's immediate family only."

"Listen," I grit out, ready to go off on her, when a male voice stops me.

"Mr. Montgomery?" I turn to face a man in a white coat and blue scrubs. "I'm Dr. Jones. I'm on call. Dr. Armstrong filled me in on Bellamy's history. Come on. I'll take you to her."

"Thank fuck," I mutter, and hurry along behind him. "How are they?"

"They're getting her settled in a private bay. I'm preparing to perform an ultrasound on the baby," Dr. Jones explains.

My hands tremble as we reach the end of the hall, and he grips the curtain tightly pulling it open before stepping back and motioning for me to go in. My heart stops when I see Bellamy lying in bed, hooked up to IVs and monitors on her belly for the baby. Her eyes are closed. She's pale. She's never been more beautiful. Rushing to her side, I pull a chair next to her bed and gently take her hand in mine, pressing a kiss to her palm.

My eyes find Sloane on the other side of the bed. She offers me a weak smile. "I'll give you some time," she says, standing to leave.

"Sloane," I call after her.

She stops and turns to look at me.

"Thank you for being with her until I got here," I say, with a lump growing in my throat.

"That's what family does," she says, before spinning and walking out the door.

Turning my attention back to Bellamy, I rest one hand on her belly, careful of the monitors, and the other gently pushes her hair back out of her eyes.

Slowly, her eyes flutter open, and she offers me a weak smile. "Hey, did you win?" she asks.

"I don't know," I reply, as I stand and lean over her, careful of all the wires. "Hey, beautiful," I say, pressing my lips to her forehead. "You took about fifty years off my life. How are you feeling?"

"Tired, but I'm okay. They said the baby's vitals look good, too," she tells me. "Wait, how do you not know if you won?" Her nose scrunches and her brow furrows as if she's trying to figure out why.

"I left."

She gasps. "What? What do you mean you left?"

"I left at halftime. Corie told me what happened, and I left." No way was I going to be able to concentrate on the game, knowing my family needed me.

"Reid!" she scolds. She tries to sit up, so I help her, propping pillows behind her back. "You're going to get fined, or worse, benched."

I shrug. "Don't care. This is where I needed to be." I drop another kiss to her forehead, before sitting my ass back in the chair. I feel as though I've run the length of the field a thousand times—my legs are weak, and my heart is still thundering from worry and fear for my girls.

"You can't do that. You have to go back."

"Not a chance in hell," I tell her fiercely. "I'm not leaving this hospital until you do."

Dr. Jones knocks and steps into the room. "How about we take a look at your baby?" he asks, stepping over to the ultrasound machine that's been rolled in. I help Bellamy raise her gown and keep her bottom half covered with the blanket before Dr. Jones adds the gel to her belly. Within seconds, the sound of our baby girl's heartbeat fills the room, and tears well in my eyes. Bellamy squeezes my hand, and I hold onto her tightly.

I was so damn scared of losing them. "H-How is she?" I ask as my voice wobbles, not hiding my fear.

"Everything looks great." He turns the screen so that we can see her. "No distress. She's doing just fine," he assures us.

"Do you know why she passed out?" I ask him.

"We're running some tests. The bloodwork should be back soon. I put a rush on the results. Right now, Mom and baby are both doing well. Vitals for both are excellent."

"Thank you, Doctor." I nod, and he hands me some towels to help wipe off Bellamy's bump. When I'm done, I pull her gown back into place and tug the covers up over her.

"The best thing you can do right now is let the fluids do their thing and rest. I'll be back as soon as the results are in," he explains before leaving us alone.

"Go back to the game, Reid," she tells me, her voice soft.

"Baby, I'm not leaving you. I don't give a single fuck about the game. You and our daughter are what's important. This is where I want to be. Where I need to be." I hold her gaze, willing her to believe me. I lean in close, pressing her palm against my cheek. "When Corie told me you collapsed, I couldn't get here fast enough."

She's quiet as she studies me, and I don't look away. I need her to see how sincere I am. This is where I am meant to be. Her eyes well with tears. I know she's scared. Hell, I was scared out of my mind. I open my mouth to ask what I can do. What she needs. What can I do to help her, but her softly spoken words stop me.

"I love you, Reid Montgomery."

My heart feels too big for my chest. She loves me.

"I love you so fucking much, Bell. I was so damn mad at myself on the way here. I was afraid I'd never get to tell you what you mean to me. I'd never get to see those beautiful brown eyes sparkle when I told you that you own my heart and soul, and that I'm not me without you and our daughter. I'll love you every day of forever," I vow to her, as a single tear slides down her cheek. I wipe it away with my thumb, and she smiles.

"You've changed my life, Reid. You've never given up on me. Fighting for me, for us, and our baby. I'm sorry I projected my fears on you at the start of us. I was scared of what you made me feel. Then, when we found out about the baby, again, you were there, ready to jump in with me headfirst. You've shown me true love and what it means to put those you hold dear first. I'm so grateful for you, and I'll love you every day of forever," she repeats my earlier vow.

"Did we just recite our wedding vows?" I ask, giving her a cheeky smile. My heart feels lighter at our confession, and I know that's where we're headed—to our happily ever after, with lots of babies, and a lifetime of love.

I can tell she's tired and needs to sleep. "Rest, baby, I'll be right here," I assure her.

"Okay." She nods and closes her eyes.

I watch her closely, and when her breathing changes to deep and even, I finally exhale.

They're going to be okay. I'm still worried about what caused her to faint, and hope the doctors can get to the bottom of it, but they're okay. My girls are safe, and that's what matters.

I keep her hand in mine as I watch her sleep. I don't know how long I've been sitting here when a soft knock comes to the door. I lift my head to find Corie standing there.

"How is she?" she whispers.

"Better. They're running tests, but they're both perfect," I whisper back.

"Oh, thank God." Corie's shoulders relax. "Her mom is on her way, and Amanda's sick, so I told her to stay home, but I'd update her," Corie explains, as she types a message out on her phone.

"Rowan and I have been texting. She and the guys will be here as soon as the game's over."

"Sloane?"

"She's out in the waiting room. Only two at a time are allowed back here, and she wanted to give me a turn."

I nod. "Thank you… both of you, for everything."

"I'm glad we were there. I'll send her mom back when she gets here," Corie tells me.

"Coach?" I ask.

"Knox handled him. I'm sure he'll be here, as well."

"Thanks," I whisper, and turn my attention back to Bellamy.

Corie leaves quietly, and I rest my head on the edge of the bed, letting the adrenaline of my fear flow away. I've never been that scared before in my entire life. How am I going to leave her ever again without worrying about her?

"How is she?" I hear someone ask. Lifting my head, I see Candice standing at the foot of the bed.

"They're both perfect. Vitals are strong for both. Doctors are running some bloodwork to see if they can figure out why she fainted."

"Has she been awake?"

"She has. She was awake for the ultrasound, and baby girl is looking great," I assure her.

"Thank goodness," Candice says, placing her hand over her chest. "How about you? How are you holding up?"

"I'm perfect as long as they're okay," I tell her.

"You look like you came straight from the game?"

"Ran out of the locker room at halftime," I tell her. Her eyes widen. "There's nothing in my life that's more important to me than my girls." Even I can hear the conviction in my tone.

"Oh, Reid, I'm so happy she found you. Thank you for fighting for her, for never giving up."

"She's easy to love."

Candice laughs. "I know my daughter, and I know the anger she carries around."

"That makes her more lovable. I asked her to give me a chance to show her, and she did. That's all I wanted, and now, I can't imagine my life without her. Without them."

"You're a good man, Reid Montgomery."

"She makes me better."

We sit in silence, just watching as Bellamy sleeps, getting the rest she so desperately needs. I don't know how much time has passed when Candice stands and stretches. "I'm going to go update Cliff. He insisted on coming with me."

"Good man." I nod. "I'll be here."

She smiles softly. "I know you will be, and so does she." She nods toward the bed. "Do you need anything?"

"Everything I need is in this room." Her hand again rests over her heart, and a smile tugs at her lips as she quietly steps out of the room.

The next knock is Rowan. She asks how my girls are doing and tells me there's a waiting room full of people who want to come and say hi before she slips out of the room. Knox, Landry, Foster, and Baker all take turns coming back to see us, and through it all, Bellamy sleeps peacefully. Just as I promised her, I never leave her side. I meant what I said. I'll leave this hospital when she does.

The door opens once more, and when I look up, I see Coach standing there. He's wearing a scowl that only softens a little when he sees Bellamy sleeping. "How is she?" he asks, his voice raspy.

"She's good. They're both good. They're running some tests. We should know something soon, but the doctor has assured me they're both going to be okay." I repeat the same message I've given each visitor who's stopped in to see us.

"You know you're going to get fined for today." His tone is neutral, not menacing as it was when I walked out of the locker room earlier.

"Yep. Don't care," I say, holding his gaze. "There's nothing on this earth that would keep me from them when they need me like this. I'll take the fine, the suspension, break my contract.... Whatever the outcome may be, I'll take it without a fight." I turn my eyes back to Bellamy. "The only fighting I'll do is for my family. For my girls."

We're both quiet after that. He takes the chair on the opposite side of the bed and just watches her sleep. Her breathing is deep and even, and the baby's heartbeat on the screen is strong. It's my constant reminder that they're really okay.

"I didn't fight for them," Coach says, his voice a gruff whisper. "I wanted to, but I didn't, and there's not a day that goes by that I don't regret it." He pauses, and I remain quiet, letting him process his thoughts. "I wanted to make something for myself, but for them, too. I wanted to give them everything, and in turn, I lost my way. Candice and I tried, but in the end, we both formed a life without the other, and we couldn't find our way back. Bellamy got caught in the middle, and I took the coward's way out. When she refused to see me, I told Candice not to force her. I didn't want to cause her any more pain, because her pain sliced through me like a knife."

Reaching out, he tugs up her blanket, even though it doesn't need it. "One weekend bled into two, into weeks, months, and then years. I missed so much because I didn't want to fight, worried it would hurt her even more, but I was wrong." His voice cracks. "I was so fucking wrong. I should have made her come to her scheduled visits. I could have shown her that she was my world, even if I struggled with how to communicate that. Instead, I let her run, and I lost my little girl."

"She's still that same little girl at heart," I remind him. "Show her now. It's never too late to fight for what you want."

"Like you? You fought for her, and here you are, knowing your career could be in jeopardy. Your team needs you, but you're here."

"I love the Rampage. I love the guys—they're family—but these two"—I nod toward the bed—"they're my heart. My entire world. Nothing compares to that."

"I want to get to know her. I want to be a part of her life, of my grandchild's life."

"You think you can learn the play, Coach?" I tease. I can see it in his eyes and hear it in his voice. He's going to fight now, just as he should have then.

He chuckles, and another lull of silence passes between us. "Thank you for loving her. For showing her what that looks like when I never did," he says quietly.

"I'm going to marry her," I tell him. I'm not asking for permission because I don't need it. The only permission I need is hers. "Loving her is easier than breathing," I admit, just as her eyes flutter open. Her gaze lands on me, and she smiles.

"I love you," she murmurs. "Thank you for coming to me when I needed you."

"Never thank me for loving you, Bell," I say, standing. Not giving a single fuck that her dad's in the room, I place a soft kiss against her lips. "I love you, too, Bell. You have a visitor. In fact, you've had several, but this one, he's special," I tell her. It's more for Coach than my girl. He's a broken man who thought he was doing the right thing. I get that, and I hope that the two of them can form the relationship they were always supposed to have.

Turning her head, she sees her dad and gasps. "Dad?"

"Hey, Bella. How are you feeling?" His voice is soft and gentle.

"I'm okay. We're okay," she says, her hands moving to her belly. "What are you doing here?"

"As soon as the whistle blew, I think half the team ran for the hospital."

"Did you win?" she asks him, but looks at me.

"I don't know, baby, I didn't ask."

"Reid! You need to know if you're going to play for the league championship. This is huge. How could you not ask?"

I laugh because when I first met her, she wouldn't have given a single thought to my career or the game of football. Now that she's invested, she watches all my games and supports me without a thought.

"We won," Coach tells her.

"Really?" Her eyes light up.

Coach nods, swallowing hard at her honest, elated reaction. "Can I get you anything?" he asks. There's a knock at the door, and Dr. Jones steps in.

"Bellamy, I have your bloodwork results. Is it okay to speak freely, or would you like for your guests to step out of the room?"

"This is my boyfriend, Reid, and that's my dad. You can tell us."

Coach's eyes widen, but he doesn't say a word.

"Right, well, your bloodwork shows that you're severely anemic. All of your symptoms check out, and that's what caused you to faint."

"How do we treat that? Are she and our daughter in danger?" I ask.

"Anemia can be very serious, but I'm certain that with a few days' rest and an iron supplement, you'll be back on your feet. Iron can often be hard to absorb. I'm going to order an iron infusion while you're here. Then you can start oral medication once released. We'll recheck your numbers in two weeks to see if the supplement is working or if we need to discontinue and proceed with regular infusions. Just as a precaution, I'd like to admit you for tonight. Let the iron infusion run its course, and we'll recheck your numbers tomorrow. If everything looks as I expect it to, we'll discharge you."

"Thank you, Doctor," I say.

"Hang tight. We'll get you moved up to a room." He leaves, and all three of us heave a sigh of relief.

I press my lips to my girl's forehead as I feel the worry ease from my shoulders. "I love you," I whisper. I'll never go another day without telling this incredible woman what she means to me.

She peers up at me, those big brown eyes twinkling, even in the dim light of the room. "I love you, too."

"I'll let you have some time," Coach says, standing.

"Dad?"

He freezes and gives Bellamy his full attention.

"There's something that you can do for me."

"Anything," he replies with conviction.

Her lip quivers. "Can I have a hug?" she asks, her voice sounding small.

"Oh, Bella," he says, stepping back toward the bed and bending to pull her into a hug. "I'm so sorry for so many things," he tells her.

Emotion fills his voice, and I smile. This moment tells me that they're both going to be okay. They're going to find their way back to one another.

"I'm sorry, too," she says as he pulls back. "I need to take some of the blame, as well."

"You were a child."

"I was. But even as an adult, I refused to listen, not until I met Reid."

Coach glances at me. "I never thought I'd see the day my little girl would be involved with one of my players."

"Well, get used to it," I tell him. "Pretty soon, she's going to have my last name." I wink at Bellamy, and she rewards me with a beaming smile.

That's not my proposal, but it's coming. The woman is my heart. It's only fitting I get to call her my wife.

EPILOGUE

Bellamy

The League Championship Game

THE STADIUM IS ELECTRIC AS FANS CHEER ON THEIR FAVORITE team. I can understand how they're feeling. It was a fight for Reid to finally concede to letting me travel. Dr. Armstrong said it was fine, as long as I was feeling okay. The iron has helped so much, and while I'm still tired, it's only as much as someone who's thirty-four weeks pregnant should be.

It's not that I needed his permission. I was coming to the game regardless, and he wanted me here. He was just worried about me and the baby. I get it. The last game I attended, I collapsed, and he was fined twenty thousand dollars for leaving. There was no way I wasn't going to be here to support him.

Making it to the league championships three years in a row is a damn big deal. Not to mention, if they win, that would be three in a row. That's huge, and I'm so proud of my man and his team—our family—for all they've accomplished and how hard they've worked to get here.

I'm currently in a suite with Corie, Amanda, Sloane, my mom, Cliff, Reid's parents, Knox's parents, baby Camden, as well as Baker's and Foster's parents. It's a family affair as we cheer on our boys to bring Nashville home another win.

"You doing okay?" Amanda asks me.

I smile at my best friend. "I'm doing great," I assure her.

"There you go!" Ridge, Knox's dad, yells.

I look back at the field in time to see the ball soar what seems like at least half the length of the field and land in Landry's hands. He spins and takes off running toward the endzone. We're all on our feet, me a little slower than the rest, but we're all cheering on Landry to sprout wheels on his cleats and slide into the endzone. He's tackled at the ten-yard line. I glance at the clock. There's just under a minute of playing time. We can do this. We're down by six. If we can make this touchdown and the field goal, we win. Worst case, we might go into overtime.

The guys line up again. Knox calls the play, and I see it. The moment Reid breaks loose, he launches into the air and catches the throw, then dives into the endzone.

"Touchdown Rampage!" the announcer calls out.

Our suite erupts with cheers, and my heart is fuller than it's ever been as I watch my man doing what he loves. Not to mention he's damn good at it, too.

Hank Martin, our kicker, lines up. We're all holding our breath as the ball is hiked, and Hank gives it all he's got. It goes soaring through the air, right through the uprights.

"The Rampage wins! For the third year in a row, the Nashville Rampage takes home the league championship!" the announcer bellows.

I don't realize that I'm crying until my mom pulls me into a hug and steps back, wiping at my tears. Her eyes are also glassy, as are every other eye in this suite.

Sam, Reid's dad, comes over to me and wraps his arm around my shoulders. "Let's get you down to see your man."

"Oh, I'm okay," I assure him.

"Yeah, well, my son made me promise to be your protection as you make your way down to the field. Something about precious cargo." He winks.

"Funny, me too," Cliff says, stepping to my other side.

"Um, I think he got to all of us." Ridge, Knox's dad, laughs.

"I feel like I have my own personal army of bodyguards. I'm pregnant, not in danger." I chuckle.

"He's just worried about you and the baby," Corie defends him.

"Let the man fuss," Paula, Reid's mom, tells me.

"Thank you all for being here for us. For him," I say, getting choked up. It's still sometimes hard for me to believe that this is my life.

"That's what families are for." Sam winks as we make our way out of the suite.

It's evident why Reid wanted them next to me. The crowd is thick, and having an army of men around me, pushing through the crowd, definitely helps. The ladies are in the center, while all the men surround us.

"There's Daddy," I hear Jared, Baker's dad, tell his grandson behind us.

My eyes scan the crowd for Reid, but I'm too short. Finally, I see him at the same time he spots us. He moves with purpose, heading our way, and he doesn't bother to stop and talk to anyone. When he reaches me, he hugs me tightly before dropping to his knees and kissing my belly. I run my fingers through his sweaty hair, not having a single care. He glances up at me with wet eyes and so much love.

I watch as he holds his hand out for his dad, who places a small box into it. We're starting to gain attention, but I ignore everyone but the man kneeling before me.

My man.

"Bellamy Warner, I love you." His voice is loud, even with the crowd, or maybe it's just that we're so in tune it feels that way to me. It's hard to tell.

"I love you," I tell him.

He grins. "When I met you, I didn't know that my entire world would be flipped upside down. I was out of bounds, trying to find my route, but I knew that for you, I would learn the play. This little one, she's our audible, and I want a lifetime of audibles with you. Bell, baby, will you do me the incredible honor of being my wife? Will you marry me?"

I'm nodding as my vision blurs. "Yes. Yes, I'll marry you."

Reid climbs to his feet and kisses me like no one's watching. This man, he's my heart and soul, and I can't wait to see what the future holds for us.

EPILOGUE

Reid

Six Weeks Later

MY EYES WON'T STOP LEAKING. SERIOUSLY, IT'S AN ISSUE because my wife and our newborn baby girl are blurry, and they should only be seen with vibrancy. I guess that's what happens when you become a dad.

Holy shit, I'm a dad.

I've had months for the concept to sink in. However, now that she's here, it's life-changing and indescribable. I thought I loved her before she was born, but now, my entire fucking world sits on this hospital bed next to me.

"She's perfect." Bellamy coos down at our daughter, who's resting peacefully after her momma endured twelve hours of labor to bring her into the world.

"Just like her momma," I reply.

"We need a name," Bellamy says. "I know we've tossed around a lot of ideas, but we can't wait any longer. We have to decide."

"Coral," I blurt. It's a name I've been thinking about for months, but I've kept it to myself. I hinted once that I had a name in mind, but we got sidetracked.

"Coral Montgomery." Bellamy tries it out.

"Yeah, I don't have a middle name idea. But Coral is fitting because it's the color of the dress you were wearing the night we met. The same dress that ended up on your hotel room floor, and how this little miracle came about."

"Reid," Bellamy breathes. "It's perfect.

"Did you know that our moms share a middle name?"

"No way! Really?"

She nods. "Coral Renee Montgomery. It has a nice ring to it, don't you think?"

"I do." I stand and move to sit on the edge of the bed. I need to be closer to them.

"Daddy loves you, Coral Renee." I kiss the pad of my thumb and gently press it to my daughter's forehead. "I love you, too, Bell. Thank you for doing all the heavy lifting. You were incredible."

"You were there every step of the way. Not just for the delivery. Every moment since I found out we were pregnant, you've been there. You're the backbone of our little family, and I love you." She glances down at our baby girl. "We love you."

"I think I need to see a doctor," I tell her. "My eyes won't stop leaking."

She giggles, and it's the most beautiful sound.

"I'm not a crier, but damn, watching you give birth to our daughter, that gets me all up in my feels. When can we do it again?" I ask her.

More laughter, and I'm rewarded with the sparkle that I love so much in those big brown eyes of hers. "How about we get this one home first, and let me get past my six weeks at least," she says, shaking her head.

"You tell me when you're ready. Coral needs a little brother or sister, or maybe a couple of each," I suggest.

"Slow your roll, Number Twenty. We're in the off-season," she jokes.

"All right, all right. Coral, tell your mommy that Daddy's just a man in love with his family."

Bellamy leans in and kisses my cheek. "Speaking of family, I think we should start letting them in now. You know there's a room full out there waiting."

"Fine, if I have to share you." I text my mom, telling her to send in the parents. "Our parents and Cliff first, if that's okay with you?"

"Perfect. Wait, can we have that many back here?"

"Meh, it's easier to ask for forgiveness than permission." The words are barely out of my mouth when the door opens, and in walk my parents, Cliff, Candice, and Coach. I guess I need to start calling him Will, but that feels weird to me. I'm sure it's equally as odd to see me married to his daughter. Which will be happening very soon.

"Oh my goodness," our moms say at the same time.

"Guys," Bellamy speaks up. "Meet your granddaughter. Coral Renee Montgomery."

"After me," they both say, then turn to look at one another.

"It's rather convenient that the two of you share a middle name." Bellamy laughs. She turns to her dad. "Would you like to hold her?" she asks him. I can hear the uncertainty in her voice.

"Yes. Of course, I want to hold her." He stands and rubs his hands on his pants before bending down and taking Coral from her arms. He stares down at her in wonder, and I see the moment something changes in him. "I'll do better," he tells her, his voice low, but we all still hear him. "I promise you, I'll do better," he tells my daughter.

Bellamy bursts into tears, and her dad looks panicked.

"It's okay," I assure him. "They're happy tears."

He looks at Bellamy. "Yeah?"

She nods before burying her face in my chest.

Coach holds on to Coral for the longest time, until Candice steps up and tells him to stop hogging her. He laughs and hands her over. Each of our parents, and even Cliff, gets a turn to snuggle our baby girl before they step out and send in everyone else.

The room is packed, just like my chest. It's full of love and a giddiness I've never felt before. I'm certain the guys would give me a hard time if they could hear my thoughts. Well, maybe not Daddy Sin. He's been in this very moment. Although his looked different, the outcome was still the same. He's a dad, just like me, and it's life-changing.

"I love you, Mrs. Montgomery," I whisper to Bellamy, and Landry and Knox argue over who gets to hold Coral next.

Bellamy peers up at me. "We're not married yet," she reminds me.

"That's one play I can't wait to learn," I tease, and I bend to press my lips to hers. One day soon, when we get into the groove of being parents, she's going to be my wife. In my heart, she already is. But one day soon, she'll be Bellamy Montgomery, and I have a very sneaky suspicion my eyes will be leaking then, too.

Thank you so much for reading *Learn the Play*!

Want more from Reid & Bellamy?
Read a bonus scene by scanning the QR code below.

Are you ready for more from the Nashville Rampage?
Follow the Play releases December 16th! Reserve your copy today.

Never miss a new release: Newsletter Sign-up Be the first to hear about free content, new releases, cover reveals, sales, and more.

Discover more about Kaylee's books at www.kayleeryan.com

Start the Riggins Brothers Series for FREE.
Download *Play by Play* now.

Start the Kincaid Brothers Series for FREE.
Download *Stay Always* now.

Contact Kaylee Ryan:

Website: www.kayleeryan.com

Facebook: www.facebook.com/KayleeRyanAuthor

Instagram: www.instagram.com/kaylee_ryan_author

Reader Group: www.facebook.com/groups/kayleeryanfans

Goodreads: www.goodreads.com/author/show/7060310.
Kaylee_Ryan

BookBub: www.bookbub.com/profile/kaylee-ryan

TikTok: www.tiktok.com/@kayleeryanauthor

OTHER BOOKS

With You Series:
Anywhere with You | More with You
Everything with You

Soul Serenade Series:
Emphatic | Assured
Definite | Insistent

Southern Heart Series:
Southern Pleasure | Southern Desire
Southern Attraction | Southern Devotion

Unexpected Arrivals Series
Unexpected Reality |Unexpected Fight
Unexpected Fall | Unexpected Bond
Unexpected Odds

Riggins Brothers Series:
Play by Play / Layer by Layer
Piece by Piece / Kiss by Kiss
Touch by Touch | Beat by Beat

Standalone Titles:
Tempting Tatum | Unwrapping Tatum | Levitate
Just Say When | I Just Want You
Reminding Avery
Hey, Whiskey
Pull You Through
Remedy | The Difference
Trust the Push | Forever After All
Misconception | Never with Me
Merry with Me

Entangled Hearts Duet:
Agony | Bliss

Cocky Hero Club:
Lucky Bastard

Mason Creek Series:
Perfect Embrace

The Kissing Games Series:
Kissing the Rival

The Everlasting Ink Series:
Does He Know? / Is This Love?
Are You Ready? / What About Now?
Can We Try?

ACKNOWLEDGMENTS

There are so many people who are involved in the publishing process. I write the words, but I rely on my team of editors, proofreaders, and beta readers to help me make each book the best it can be.

Those mentioned above are not the only members of my team. I have photographers, models, cover designers, formatters, bloggers, graphic designers, author friends, my PA, and so many more. I could not do this without these people.

And then there are my readers. If you're reading this, thank you. Your support means everything. Thank you for spending your hard-earned money on my words and taking the time to read them. I appreciate you more than you know.

Special Thanks: Becky Johnson, Hot Tree Editing.
Julie Deaton, Jo Thompson, Jaime Ryter, and Jess Hodge, Proofreading
Lori Jackson Designs – Cover Design (Guy Cover)
Mary, Books N Moods – Special Edition Cover
Michelle Lancaster – Photographer (Main Guy Cover)
Chasidy Renee – Personal Assistant
Leanne Trn - Content Team
Jamie, Stacy, Lauren, Franci, and Erica
Bloggers, Bookstagrammers, and TikTokers
Lacey Black & Kelly Elliott
Designs by Stacy and Ms. Betty - Graphics
The entire Give Me Books Team
The entire Grey's Promotion Team
My fellow authors
My amazing readers